Checking Out of the Hotel Euthanasia

GERARD GRAHAM

RINGWOOD PUBLISHING

GLASGOW

First published in Great Britain in 2017

by

Ringwood Publishing
24 Duncan Avenue, Glasgow, G14 9HN

www.ringwoodpublishing.com

e-mail mail@ringwoodpublishing.com

ISBN 978-0-692-04735-4

British Library Cataloguing-in Publication Data

A catalogue record for this book is available from the British
Library

Printed in the US

by

IngramSpark

ABOUT THE AUTHOR

Gerard Graham was born and raised in Glasgow, Scotland, living and working as a social work manager and independent consultant. He and his wife Barbara moved to Portugal for eight years and are now resident in Charleston, South Carolina, USA, to be closer to their two sons and four grandchildren. Gerard has written and illustrated a number of children's books as well as creating artwork for other authors. *Checking Out of the Hotel Euthanasia* is his first adult novel.

ACKNOWLEDGEMENTS

Thank you to Barbara, my wife, for initial encouragement with the concept of writing a humorous book about assisted dying as we sat in a bar in Naples, Florida. I am forever grateful to her constant challenges on my ideas and humour, along with her commitment to editing and rereading. I knew I was on the right track when I heard her laugh out loud.

I am grateful to Beth for her initial reading and comments on the first draft.

Huge gratitude to Gina Michelle of 'Life, Lens and Love' blog for critique, commentary, and suggestions.

Special thanks for the advice and detailed editing from Andrew Reid over a short intensive period of time to challenge some of the concepts and to get the novel ready for publishing. Thanks for giving up a month of your busy life.

Thanks to Sandy Jamieson of Ringwood Publishing for his encouragement and comments.

Appreciation and thanks to Isobel Freeman, Chief Executive, of Ringwood Publishing for moving the novel from the submission to publishing stage and finally, I am grateful to Nelli Bergen, Managing Director, for editing and supervising the end process and Grant Simpson for supporting her.

DEDICATION

For Barbara, my lovely wife who supported me for three years with this project.

PART I

Chapter 1 Fitba' – More Important Than Life or Death

The answer that remains unquestioned, strong gravity the singer hears
Between the poppy and the means, the dancers of the spheres

The Song of Villadedino, Saint Dino 240AD

Touching the lapel of his faded retro denim jacket to find his lucky brass badge with the hammer and sickle missing, was the first forewarning to Rab Lennon of the portent that things were not going to go well. It was a stark omen for his upcoming football match. Rab had been meticulous, some might say obsessive compulsive, about his rituals and superstitions in preparation for playing the beautiful game. He had woken up that morning with the usual sense of hopeful anticipation that precipitated a match, successfully resuscitating back to life the two-week-old lard in the frying pan and cooking an historically accurate full Scottish breakfast of two eggs, bacon, sausage, black pudding, and potato scone with a side of turbo-charged baked beans. He saturated his being as he embraced a serene contentment from his deep-fried heaven, while at the same time taking a couple of yards off his pace and a decade off his lifespan.

Following his worship at the altar of crispy, carcinogenic sustenance, and with a sense of occasion, Rab continued to prepare in his usual fastidious and ritualistic manner for the game. First he dressed, careful to wear his lucky underpants with the patterns of shamrocks and leprechauns (he had scored a hat trick in these); then he packed his kit bag, placing items in the order required, with his boots last in the bag; humiliated the cloned budgie by kissing it three times; rubbed the head of the statue of Mary; gave the double thumbs up to the poster of Karl Marx; and, finally, waited till he was outside the door of his apartment before tying the laces of his lucky 3D-printed trainers.

It was only when he was on the driverless bus and his hand, with comforting habit, reached for the lapel of his faded denim jacket to absentmindedly rub his small brass badge with the red hammer and sickle, that he found it had gone. Immediately, he had that sinking feeling in the pit of his stomach, triggering the premonition that misfortune would befall him on that fateful day. Whenever Rab experienced that sensation, his superstitious emotions came to the fore, inevitably stimulating conflicts between his humanist and religious upbringing, his mortality and the randomness of fate. Rab had been absorbed in campaigning for a change in the law concerning assisted dying with a group of people affected by long-term complex conditions. *Snap out of it*, he checked himself, *there are more important things to think about than death.*

The annual football match had been re-enacted like an ancient battle over the last decade since 2023 between Glasgow Communists FC and Glasgow Anarchists United of New Scotland. It was just the type of activity that transcended Rab's mind above and beyond the daily grind of churning over one of his assisted dying campaign issues. Today's game had more than its usual enmity riding on the encounter. The reason for the increase in malice was the envy felt by the Communists towards the surge in popularity and recruiting power of the Anarchists. This upturn in the fortunes of the Anarchists stemmed from the actions of one person, Billy McGlinchey. Billy had joined the Anarchists just six months ago, but in that time he had transformed them from a haphazard rag tag outfit into a smooth, disciplined and incongruously effective organisation. Billy's capability originated from the two years he had spent completing a Master's Degree in Business Administration and Redundancy. His ideas for hierarchies of authority, systems, processes, and corporate marketing were disliked at first within the Anarchist group. However, no one could argue with the increased recruitment to their cause achieved thanks to Billy's slick virtual advertising campaign: *'BE PART OF A BIGGER ORGANISATION – JOIN THE ANARCHISTS'*

Billy had also organised and coordinated impressive marches through the streets of Glasgow, in contrast to the Anarchists' usual sorry sauntering style, carrying one or two giant tablet placards (when they remembered to bring them); occasional chants that petered out as soon as they began; and depletion of the ranks as, bit by bit, the marchers dropped out for a visit to the pubs dispersed along the route. Now, following the skilful leadership of Billy, their organisation was awe-inspiring. Different tasks had been allocated to the various groups of Anarchists. The marchers provided rows of coordinated giant tablet banners in the 'corporate' colours and style he had adopted. Different sections of activists chanted coordinated slogans with delegated responsibility to a group leader with a megaphone. For added glamour, attractive females at the edges of the marching formation handed out glossy 'speaking' leaflets to watching bystanders. Not permitted was the drinking of alcohol, bad language, delinquency, graffiti or vandalism. The overall effect was similar to an American high school marching band rather than a troop of violent agitators. While this might have been as far as one could get from the Anarchist ideology, it felt safe and welcoming. And so, recruitment to the group really started to take off in a big way when the professional marchers were accompanied by television commercials and inviting hologram billboard adverts:

'GOT FREE TIME ... JOIN THE ANARCHISTS!

Value for Money Joining Fees Apply. Loans available – 2,355% APR'

Billy, with his financial acumen, had also increased the bank balance of the association through strictly administered financial exchange processes for collecting weekly subscriptions from the growing ranks of members. So, as well as being organised, the group was flush with virtual money that could then be used to fund a range of activities including bankrolling their football team. The needle for the annual football match was in no small part due to the defection of some members of the Glasgow Communist Party, drawn like moths to the substantial resources of the Anarchists by the bright light of Billy's candle.

It just so happened that, by predestination, the pull of the moon on earth's gravity or a comedic ruse by the gods, the Communists had all hailed from the Irish Catholic persuasion while the Anarchists came from the Protestant tradition. In the city of Glasgow, this meant that when it came to choosing the football strips that each team wore, there could only be two choices. So, the Communists played in the green of one half of the city's major teams, while the Anarchists played in the blue of the rival outfit. These two teams had an historical rivalry that mirrored the sectarianism of the two religions. The fact that a few former Communists had crossed the divide between the two political philosophies was compounded exponentially by the wearing of the rival's strip.

It was into this tense 'theatre in the round' that the now agitated Rab Lennon arrived, minus his lucky brass hammer and sickle badge, to take part in the anticipated grudge game of football.

Rab, at this point, was semi-aware in a disinterested way that his parents had gone off on holiday to a destination they had, as usual, omitted to inform him about and that he had, with indifference, failed to enquire after. This lack of concern from Rab had more to do with his parents than the nature of Rab himself who was normally conscientious and sensitive when engaging with his fellow human beings. The parents had been more committed to activities that promoted the Communist cause than spending time with the upbringing of their son. Left to his own devices, or 'dumped' unceremoniously for days at a time with his grandparents, there was little relationship between the boy and his uncaring parents. As an emotional coping mechanism, Rab remained detached from the activities of his parents' holiday was considered by him distantly as just another of their

Communist Party jaunts.

Rab was, therefore, completely unaware that they had in fact travelled to the notorious Hotel Euthanasia in the Principality of Villadedino, a quiet little backwater located in Central Europe. They were now also irretrievably deceased, having been deceitfully, by the Glasgow Communist Party, persuaded to partake of assisted suicide. The Communists were desperate to get their hands on Mr and Mrs Lennons' pensions to finance their plans for combating the Anarchists' successful marketing and recruitment scheme. The Communists' values concerning the inviolability of life or death meant that they had a detached view in encouraging the demise of Mr and Mrs Lennon if it was for the greater good of the Party.

Changing into his football strip triggered Rab's memory of the discord of his upbringing and the conflict between his parents as Communists and his grandparents as second generation Irish Catholics. He had always felt torn between them, with his parents lambasting his grandparents for taking him to church on a Sunday and making reference to the 'opium of the masses'. As a small boy, he had thought about this and concluded that the thurible, a metal censer containing burning charcoal and incense that the priest swung from side to side in ritual fashion at mass, must be the 'opium' referred to by his parents. The disharmony was exacerbated by his grandparents, who filled him with religious indoctrination along with a litany of saints to pray to. '*Saint Gianna, we pray for the sanctity of all human life. Amen!*' They also defied Rab's parents by covertly smuggling in religious statues and pictures into his bedroom to immerse him in the artefacts and memorabilia of Catholicism. He remembered his father 'going bananas' when he found the Sacred Heart of Jesus cushion hidden under his pillow.

Rab was allowed, and still managed to keep, a statue of Mary, the mother of Jesus, on top of his chest of drawers; another lucky charm in the life of Rab Lennon. For some reason, possibly through some deep-seated pagan worship of a mother figure or the calming blue vestments trimmed with gold and her non-threatening virginal smile of acceptance, his parents allowed him to keep the statue regardless of the number of crucifixes and prayer books that ended up being returned to his vexed grandparents. The grandparents also fortified Rab's young mind with the doctrines and moral order of the Church regarding the sanctity of human life and the immortality of the soul reaching a heaven full of singing angels and eternal happiness.

Rab had long since internalised and intellectualised his parents' atheistic and humanist view that when you die you cease to exist. But, he still had some vestiges of an emotional tie to guilt when using a condom or working with his campaign group and national supporters to lobby for changes to the law on assisted dying. The only thing that his parents and grandparents could agree on, to the delight of the young Rab, was the gift of a new football strip of their favourite team every year that had led to Rab's love of the 'beautiful game'.

The excuse posing as the 'beautiful game', planned between the Communists and the Anarchists, took place on the Glasgow Green Municipal Football Parks containing six genetically modified grass football pitches, contrasting with fetid changing facilities, a shower that didn't work, and a toilet that never flushed. There did, after all, need to be some indulgence towards a 'traditional' football experience.

The two teams changed into their strips and headed out to the pitch to warm up. It became obvious to Rab and his Communist team mates that the Anarchists had adopted new disciplines in their brand-new and crisply laundered strips with each of the players' names printed on their backs and sponsored (Billy McGlinchey had negotiated and received £1,000 for the privilege) by Lendabuck Loans Company. In the past, the Anarchists' warm up consisted of the team making their way out to the pitch in dribs and drabs, standing around smoking cigarettes and drinking cans of beer (the matches took place at 10am on a Saturday morning – as good a time as any for a quick 'swally'). Now, there was a tangible difference as what could only be described as a group roar emanated from the Anarchists' changing room, heralding their arrival on the pitch. They entered the fray, jogging out two by two, their expensive new strips proclaiming superiority. They proceeded to undertake a group stretching session, followed by five-a-side practice, passing routines and group sprints between cones that had magically appeared on the pitch. The team manager, Billy McGlinchey, oversaw the game preparation, professionally kitted out in full football manager 'de rigueur' style, with hooded, quilted puffer jacket with the Anarchists' corporate logo emblazoned across the front and *Lendabuck Loans, the loan that never leaves you alone*' across the back.

The Communists, by comparison, stood dumbstruck

and agog on their half of the pitch, watching this precise synchronised session unfold before their eyes. Jolted out of their stupor by the referee whistling for the start of the match, the Communists moved into their usual formation, honed over the last decade by their 'cult of the personality' manager Big Tam (so named, in typical Glasgow inverse humour, for the reason that he stood 5 foot 1 inch tall). Big Tam preferred having the Communists' goalkeeper operate 'Relative Deprivation' of goals protected by a 'United Front' defence who would quickly get the ball to the 'Central Committee' of the midfield, then to the 'Left Wing' to cross to the 'Popular Front' forwards to score an 'Ideological' goal. The Anarchists, on the other hand, had adopted a formation which was the antithesis of the concepts of 'Horizontalism' and 'Hierarchy' since Billy McGlinchey had become the out and out leader and authority figure, who delegated actions and expected responses from his team. This resulted in individuals willingly giving up their autonomy to fulfil their specific roles within the team. There was no 'Revolutionary Spontaneity' from any of them as they followed the specific game plan revolving around the 'Social Centre' half and where all players were slaves to the control of Billy. They were also joined by 'Radical Cheerleading' from eight attractive and disconcertingly flexible female anarchists dressed in bright blue spandex leotards performing flying leaps, jumping jacks and human pyramids at the side of the pitch. The Communists were certainly distracted by the unusual sight of eight nubile young women as they threw their hands in the air, 'like you just don't care', shaking their brightly coloured pompoms and chanting, 'One, two, three, four, who are we for, An-ar-chy! Rah! Rah! Rah!'

Needless to say, the Anarchists capitalised on giving up their individual freedom for the governance, preparation, and organisation of the team by Billy and to the dismay of Rab and the Communist team quickly went three goals up. Their 'Berlin Wall' of a defence collapsed and they looked as rusty as a field of tractors during Stalin's five-year agricultural plan. The Communists were getting the run-around. Half-time saw a purge of recriminations, reflection and analysis of the reasons for their failure.

"We are gettin' annihilated here, boys. You lot will need to do better." Big Tam looked up and rebuked the subdued and chastened Communist Team gathered around him at the half-time break.

"Did you see their brand-new strips and every one of their players has a new pair of top of the range football boots? How are we goin' to keep up with this? I just knew when I lost my lucky badge that it was all going to go wrong today," Rab said.

"How can we compete with them? They are obviously rollin' in dosh! We've got no chance," the goalkeeper added, accompanied by groans and moans of acknowledgment by his beleaguered team mates.

Big Tam was feeling under pressure to keep up the spirits of his 'under siege' players. "Don't get too despondent, boys. I've heard we've got some money comin' to us," Big Tam reassured. "It'll no' be long till we are challengin' those Anarchists on an even playin' field."

"How is that then, Big Tam?" asked the now interested goalkeeper.

Big Tam, with a flourish to dispel the negativity and to bolster his authority, triumphal like a magician pulling a rabbit out of a hat, released the good news without thinking of the consequences, "We've accessed Maw and Paw Lennon's pension money."

"What … What did you just say? What are you talkin' about, man?" Rab queried, while retuning his hearing into Big Tam's disclosure.

Big Tam now started to feel his proud expansive revelation contract like a balloon with the air seeping out. Feeling suddenly even smaller and wishing that he had kept his mouth shut, he realised that Rab had been kept in the dark and was unaware of his parents' demise. He immediately regretted that he had to be the one to disclose the news. "I'm sorry to be the one to tell you, Rab, but your Maw and Paw are dead," Big Tam blurted out with the sensitivity of a fart in a crowded lift.

"Okay, what's the wind up? This sick joke's gone way too far," Rab said, searching with his eyes around the stony faces of his team mates and Big Tam for the punch line that would reveal the prank. However, the lowered eyes and the white face of Big Tam were starting to unnerve him. "Is this for real?"

"Yes, I'm sorry, man," Big Tam replied, the results of his ill-timed news leaving him feeling extremely tense.

"Shit, I'm phonin' John Davis right now," Rab shouted, heading off to the changing rooms to fetch his mobile phone to call the Chairman of the Glasgow Communist Party.

He was now incandescent with anger at his parents, Big Tam, his team mates, the Chairman of the Party, the Communist Party, and the whole damn thing.

*

"Calm down, Rab, an' let me explain," John Davis, the Chairman of the Communist Party in Glasgow, pleaded, now having to confront the conversation he had been subconsciously avoiding. John Davis had known Rab all of his life and liked him. He had qualities that were evident in his straightforward manner that assured people that he was sincere. Okay, despite being one of the brighter comrades, he could say some things that were a bit idiotic from time to time, but that just made him more likeable. John was regretting that he had put off dealing head on with informing Rab about the death of his parents.

"Just tell me, is it true? If this is a wind up then it has gone too far," Rab shouted down the phone while breathing in deeply the revolting air in the changing room.

"Rab … yes, it's true. Your Maw an' Paw made the greatest sacrifice they could possibly make for the Party. All I can say is that they wanted to do this and in my eyes, they are true heroes of the proletariat. They have become immortal now."

"Big Tam said you were doin' it to get their pensions. Is that true?" Rab shouted, wanting answers.

"Look, Rab, your Maw and Paw saw what was happenin' and they wanted to make this contribution. We paid for their travel and put them up at the Hotel Euthanasia. We're goin' to use the money for a big television commercial to promote the Glasgow Communist Party. You've seen for yourself the success of the Anarchist lot. Surely you can see that we had to do somethin' to compete with them."

It was now starting to sink in with Rab that the fates were truly against him today and the world had gone mad. His parents had undertaken assisted suicide so that the Communist Party could fund an advertising campaign. He found it hard to compare the incongruity of the death of two human beings with a capitalist means for the enhancement of nothing more ephemeral than an image. His initial reaction had been to disbelieve Big Tam's 'bombshell' about his parents' death. Now, after speaking with John Davis, he was certain that they had passed away. He still did not want to think that his parents had carried out this awful deed without letting him know of their intentions, but his defence mechanism for dealing with this as a buffer to the unexpected shock was fast dissipating as he came to terms with the first feelings of loss.

How could they have been so stupid, he debated with himself as he first became angry at them and then with the Communist Party for duping his parents into killing themselves. He started to bargain with himself and thought, *maybe I should have been a better son, been closer to them, found the money myself for the stupid advert*, but this line of defence was weak and he had to admit that it was not his fault.

A wave of sadness overcame him. He started to cry as if someone had opened up an emotional tap inside him, now numb to the world. Without any further words, he ended the call to John Davis. In a daze, he automatically made his way out of the changing rooms, his mind contorted by the strong emotions coursing through him and carving out a new course of beliefs about the Communist Party and eroding his support for assisted suicide.

Rab was lost in himself – standing crying and completely unaware of other games of football taking place that morning. He was also oblivious to the fact that the game between the Communists and the Anarchists had stopped and that there was much furtive discussion in whispered voices accompanied by badly disguised pointing towards himself.

The other game being played involved the Glasgow Rabbis versus the Glasgow Priests. The 'Dead Sea Strollers', as the Rabbis were called, wore skull caps and all white strips with the blue Star of David emblazoned across their fronts and with their backs proudly advertising, '*Abraham Cohen - Meeting all Your Bar Mitzvah Catering Requirements*'. The Priests, with their nickname the 'Virgin Fathers', were dressed in their all black strip with white round collar. Managing the 'Virgin Fathers' was Archbishop Romario who was well known for his support for the 'beautiful game' of football and for his team debriefings in the showers afterwards.

Archbishop Romario sensed that the young man standing in a stupor with tears running down his face was in distress and, given that his team was five goals up, approached him to see what the problem was.

"You look as though you have had bad news, my friend," the Archbishop intuitively offered as an introduction to Rab.

Rab initially gave no recognition of the approach but then blurted out, "Yes, both my parents are dead," and burst into tears. The Archbishop put his arms around him to comfort the grieving fellow.

*

It was following a period of pastoral care and comfort from the Archbishop that Rab came to acknowledge acceptance that his parents had agreed to the Communist Party's arrangement for assisted suicide. It was not his fault and he started to balance the experience of his grief with the triggering of a healing process. He was grateful for the support of the Archbishop, who offered him an opportunity to attend a bereavement support group operating from a church near his home.

*

Severing all contacts with the Communist Party, Rab, in the days and weeks that followed the news, attended the bereavement support group, which he found a helpful addition to the natural healing processes. Gradually, while continuing to oppose the reasons given for his parents' actions, he was able to accept their death and come to terms with his grief. The comfort and support of the bereavement group provided an alternative to the Communist Party and filled a gap in his life over this period.

At the same time, he was introduced to the zeal of the present Pope, Leo Sixtus I, in reforming the liberal ideas of the previous Pope, Hilarius II. Rab's first-hand experience, reinforced by the Catholic Church's 'counselling', then set him off on a direction that would have implications for his future actions. In particular, he changed his position on assisted dying from one where he had been an advocate for a change in the law to one where he was now against it. Rab resigned from his campaigning role in support of assisted dying, much to the annoyance of the relatives and people who had relied on him to champion their cause.

Rab's renewed but different revolutionary fervour provided him with a diversion from his sorrow and a focus for his passion for activism. He reflected that his grandparents would be proud that he had come back to the Catholic Church. His parents, on the other hand, would have been turning in their Lennons' mausoleum. Rab himself was able to rationalise the memories of hellfire, damnation, miracles, and virgin birth with happy memories of favourite hymns such as the May Hymn to Mary from his schooldays.

Archbishop Romario continued to keep in touch with the young man he had converted to the one true faith – and such a handsome young man too. While the Archbishop may have had some other objective in mind for his relationship with Rab, he came to see the many qualities he possessed as a means to promote his own ambitions within the church and, at every opportunity, he encouraged responsibility and leadership that had synergy with the social conscience in this eager convert. Over time, Rab was appointed to be the leader of a Catholic cell for Retribution and Inquisition, that would come to play a significant role in satisfying the barely suppressed desire for revenge Rab had for the death of his parents.

Chapter 2 The Journalist Interviews the Hotel Manager

The parable reflects the feeling that prepares the writer's sign

The Song of Villadedino, Saint Dino 240AD

"I would put the success of Villadedino's suicide industry and the esteemed Hotel Euthanasia down to the foresight of our beloved King Eugene III, who is a passionate supporter of the right to choose death over life. The King foresaw the emergence of a market for assisted dying in the early part of the twenty-first century when there was a shift in support for individuals who were testing the laws on assisted dying in a range of countries. He was an enthusiast for assisted dying and recognised that the influence of the Church was waning, along with the greater choices available to the most affluent and the middle classes of the world. The father of King Eugene III died 'imaginatively' at the hands of a wild bear, allowing his son to take forward his great ambition to open up the Principality of Villadedino as the assisted dying capital of the world. In the 2020s, as I was saying, the moral landscape was changing and if customers could afford it, then Villadedino would provide an outstanding product to satisfy their consumer needs. Villadedino has a unique history, dating back to 239 AD, and had the political will that made filling a niche in this emerging suicide market ripe for the plucking, and King Eugene III plucked it with gusto!"

That, anyway, was how the Manager of the Hotel Euthanasia presented his view of his country's recent history to Mark Goodwin, award winning investigative journalist with '*The Intellect*', a major broadweb publication of Olde England, a country with economic dependencies in the federal states of Wales, Yorkshire and Northern Ireland. Mark Goodwin thought to himself, *bloody hell, it is so simple, why didn't Olde England think of this, it's a bloody goldmine!*

Mark was visiting the Hotel Euthanasia, that most famous of Classic French Renaissance styled establishments, to write an article for the Sunday edition of '*The Intellect*', but he also had a specific personal issue relating to the Hotel Euthanasia that was a great deal more important to him and which was the real reason compelling his investigation. He surveyed the opulence in the Manager's grand and extravagantly decorated office and put his next question to Zeca Silva, the larger-than-life Manager of the Hotel Euthanasia, "So, Zeca, what is on offer at the hotel?"

Zeca stroked his ample black bushy moustache, leaned forward in his antique leather desk chair and swirled, with sophistication, the vinho tinto circling invitingly in his expensive crystal wine glass. Zeca was the epitome of the dapper European. His palest of blue suits was handmade of the finest cashmere and wool mix, alongside his contrasting darker blue double-breasted waistcoat. Everything about Zeca indicated refinement and charm. Those who knew him described him as a raconteur and joked about his never-ending wealth of folk stories and morality tales from his home region of Alentejo in Portugal. Zeca had answered this question about his establishment's special services many times before and he could replay effortlessly the fabricated myths that supported the inception of the Principality's singular enterprise.

"My friend Mark, we are unashamedly a theme park for assisted suicide. When you come here you enjoy the best of your life and the best of your death. It is the ultimate experience, the final trip to end all trips." Zeca rolled out his endless array of tried and trusted sound bites. "Your life … your choice!"

Zeca was regurgitating, with pleasure, some of the key straplines he had created for the most recent advertising campaign. He was warming to the sound of his own educated voice and, glancing over, analysed Mark Goodwin's face for the expected signs of admiration. Although Mark was short for a man, standing at five feet five inches, he made up for this with a trim build and broad shoulders sculpted from regular visits to the hypergym and body sculpting clinic. He had thick dark hair that flopped over his forehead, requiring him to frequently sweep it back. He wore white-rimmed computoglasses, as was the fashion of the day. Mark's clothing was of a casual shirt and slacks, but obviously purchased from the most expensive and fashionable of retail outlets.

Zeca sipped his wine and continued, "When a customer signs up for our experience, we provide the best luxury can afford, utilising our range of eXi-theme Departure Suites available within the Hotel Euthanasia. For example, we can provide you with your choice of personalised options, including last confession and absolution from specially trained Pope impersonators recruited from a pool of former priests and we can guarantee that there is no sin you have committed in your life that will not be forgiven in a customised style requested from our easy to complete on-line ticklist. Think how reassured you will feel, going to your death knowing that there is no hellfire or eternal damnation awaiting you. Damn good, if you ask me! From our pick list of options, our more sedate and demure paying guests can choose to pass away in our peaceful country garden picnic scene, consuming a superior assortment of sweet and savoury delicacies, the final course of trifle laced with brandy and our finest synthetic suicide potion, allowing them to ramble off into rural oblivion. Or, what about our Erotica option, delivered in one of our eXi-theme Departure Suites, where our customers can sign out of this life on the wave of an orgasmic tsunami administered by our disease-free prostitutes? I should also mention at this point that our prostitutes are all fully qualified social workers. We think of every aspect here. So, if there is any last-minute counselling or loose ends with family or estates required, they can get on top of that too. It's very personal care that we provide. You come, and we arrange piece of cake, piece of ass, and peace of mind!" Zeca was particularly pleased with that one-liner.

Mark noted down these phrases with a thought to the headline for his article. He was making a good show of conducting the interview conscientiously, but his mind was constantly calculating how he could introduce a line of questioning that would elicit information concerning the real reason he had come to Villadedino.

Zeca continued, "We also provide an Odyssey to the

East from our eXi-theme Departure Suites for those who want to exit in an enlightened state. We like to call our customers 'death's disciples', providing them with an enhanced and altered state of mind. We have the latest in designer drugs to make sure their brain patterns are manipulated to concur with the state of mind requested. To facilitate the experience, our own guru, Swami Riva, is available. He is renowned for having the longest resonating 'om' in the Eastern spiritual guru community. Yes, reach Nirvana way down upon the Swami Riva. Get it!" he chuckled, at yet another of his favourite one-liners.

He was experiencing a warm glow from the interview and his discourse coincided with finishing off the last glass from the bottle of vinho tinto imported from Alentejo in Portugal, which he had brought up from his cellar.

"Of course, the Swami, actually a fourth-generation Bengali Muslim from Birmingham, has had to brush up on his Indian accent. We had problems with authenticity initially, I think you call it a 'Brummie' accent, not to mention the difficulties trying to take on board all the Hindu/Buddhist terminology that our customers expect from their experience. But he has accomplished it now and sounds as if he is from West Bangalore rather than West Bromwich."

At least he is being honest, Mark thought, *quite refreshing*. "Can I use that bit about the 'Brummie' accent?" Mark asked.

"No way!" replied Zeca, realising that his talk was becoming loose as a result of the effects of the fine red wine. *I really need to be a bit more circumspect with some of our trade secrets*, he thought to himself.

"Okay, I will just say something about him having a background in the Indian sub-continent," said Mark.

Mark was wondering how he could raise the issue of Estrela and the broadcast of her assisted suicide reported on the news. "I was wondering about a recent news story about someone who used your services. What was her name again? Ah yes, Estrela Pure, the singer. Given her fame, would you like to comment on her final moments?"

"All I can say is that it was very beautiful."

Zeca and the hotel had a strict confidentiality policy regarding the nature of individual choices of death and their last words, particularly for celebrities. He was reluctant to reveal anything other than generalities about Estrela.

"I am sure you would understand, Mark, that we cannot disclose any confidential matters about people who choose to use our services. So, all I can say is that it was a wonderful experience for her."

Changing the subject to bring the interview to a close in order to avoid revealing anything else that might be considered contentious, he ventured to Mark, "You will want to take the tour, Mark." He was also looking forward to his afternoon nap. "I have arranged for Angela Deff, our Customer Care Manager, to take you on a tour of our eXi-theme Departure Suites, our central crematorium and our cemetery with its view of the Villadedino mountains and forests. Make sure you see the Rock Star eXi-theme Departure Suite, one of my favourites." Zeca lifted the phone, dialled, and asked for Angela Deff to be sent to the Manager's office.

"Angela is very thorough," Zeca said, now rather sleepily, "She has been here with us since we opened in 2021 and will be able to answer all your questions. She will take you to the main eXi-theme Departure Suites and explain how the process works."

"One last question," Mark intimated, "Have you ever had any resistance to your business, given it is still quite unique globally and other countries have labelled Villadedino … ," Mark paused, "I am only stating here what is out there in the public domain … Villadedino is a pariah state and that it is a parasite living off an immoral business that other countries refuse to pass through law. You will be aware of the assassinations in the United States of politicians who simply wanted to have a debate in Congress."

Zeca pulled his most serious face, stroked his ample moustache, and replied, "We are the future, Mark. We meet a need in society which other countries that do not have our courage simply refuse to meet themselves. I like to think of our operation as an ethical and sensitive solution for people who have an overwhelming desire to end their pain and suffering. We also provide a service to people who do not wish to be a burden to their families and simply want to die with dignity in a way they have chosen."

"Is it not a slippery slope that leads from people making their own choices to people being coerced?" asked Mark.

"But, Mark, my friend, we never force anyone. We are a comfort in a time of darkness. We eliminate the pain of living and we do this with sensitivity and with sympathetic methods. People coming here do not suffer the anxiety and stigma of illegal assistance, such as takes place in other countries; or prison for their poor relatives who assist individuals to die. We are not paternalistic and our laws about personal choice support our position. Our physicians and psychologists screen all applicants. Everyone has to have a completed '*Competent Adult Test*', signed by a physician, that indicates the customer is of sound mind and can make an informed decision. I can also say we are non-judgmental here, believe in the liberty of individuals and not in the state telling individuals what to do."

Zeca's voice was starting to get louder just as he had been tutored to do by the company lawyer when he reached this part of his prepared diatribe on the moral and ethical justification for the Hotel Euthanasia.

"Wherever possible, customers administer their own final dose, but we do have our physicians to assist, if necessary, and we always have freely signed consent. We provide the best in comfort, care, and control of pain while also making the final moments of life an enhancing experience. The figures speak for themselves; we are always full and have a waiting list. We are not all about profit, although we do have to answer to our shareholders. We have our renowned 'Subsidised Assisted Dying' or SAD places for those who cannot afford the fees. We also have contracts with a number of countries that understand what we have to offer to help with their ageing populations. Group bookings of 10 or more bring savings of 20% for commissioners of our service."

"Can I just stop you there," Mark interrupted, realising that his voice was also starting to get louder. However, before he could ask his question about the morality of paying for the privilege of assisted dying, there was a sharp knock at the door.

Saved from further questions, Zeca was relieved for the respite and shouted, "Enter!"

The door opened and Angela Deff marched, staccato fashion, into the room. It was quite an entrance. She was edging towards six feet two inches tall, elevated further by the highest of heels, athletically built, blonde hair in the style of French braided pigtail plaits, and the brightest red lipstick that Mark had ever seen. She was dressed in what looked like a dark navy military style jacket with gold epaulettes and tap details and her cool and detached manner made the biggest impression on Mark. It was as if she had not even seen him in the room and only acknowledged his presence when Zeca made the formal introductions.

"Angela, let me introduce you to the famous journalist from the renowned broadweb Olde English media sensation you will be familiar with, '*The Intellect*'. He is here to research a story about the hotel and the services we provide."

Angela turned to Mark and made what looked like a short bow of her head and extended her hand. Mark stood up, feeling his usual embarrassed lack of confidence when he was in the company of a taller woman. Mark looked up as Angela towered over him by nine inches.

"Angela is a remarkable woman who has a genuine aptitude for this job. She really understands what we are trying to achieve at the hotel with our outstanding care of customers who make the journey here for the purpose of assisted dying. You could guess that, to a certain extent, we here at the hotel require to maintain a professional detachment in relation to our role. There are so many things we have to take into account to make dying a meaningful and life-affirming choice, which reminds me of a pertinent story from my home in Portugal."

Angela at this point, recognising that Zeca was moving into his story-telling mode, powered down to a state of hibernation as she had become accustomed to doing while waiting for one of her boss's tales to take its course.

Zeca proceeded, "There was once a young man called Luis, who decided to spend some time on the beautiful beach of Porto De Mos in the south of the country. This beach had soft clean sand washed by pure salt water and was bordered by falesias (high rock cliffs) which had been eroded over many years by the bleaching sun, the south westerly winds, and the winter Atlantic Ocean. The beach was also famous for the various sizes of rocks that toppled from the cliffs to the sand below. On one particular quiet area of the beach visitors would, for diversion from the sun, the sea, and the sand, balance rocks one upon the other to form various conical towers of increasingly smaller rocks rising to the smallest at the top. The more artistic visitors to the beach would form small statuesque effigies that looked like miniature human figurines, two to three feet high, sitting still looking out to sea. For example, there would be a large stone to represent the legs with a slightly smaller stone balanced on top that represented the torso and on top of that, a smaller stone to represent the head, this one selected for its features that approximated the representation of a human face with the indications of eyes, a nose, and a mouth. Just like a little man made of rock. Some of the better ones were very realistic indeed. So, Luis liked to sunbathe at this spot where the large rock cliff, weathered and sea beaten, had formed crevices and natural shelves and ledges on which the rows and terraces of conical towers and little sculptures were displayed and which Luis appreciated very much.

Now, a most unusual happening occurred on the beach every 534,000 years, when the fallen rocks on this beach would wake up and come to life. When I say come to life, what I mean is that they woke from the long meditations that are in the nature of rock forms and were able to speak just for one day only.

Luis was lying back, enjoying the sun when he heard a voice, "Desculpe, excuse me?"

Luis raised himself up on his elbows and looked around for the person who had said this. He looked right to left, then up, and down; looked at the rows and terraces of towers and figurines; but could not see anyone. *That is strange*, he thought to himself, *I could swear someone just spoke to me*, as he lay down again to sunbathe, thinking that maybe it was a call of a gull or perhaps the wind that had deceived his hearing.

"Desculpe, excuse me?" he heard again.

Sitting up, now certain that he had not misheard the wind or perhaps a gull, he looked around but there was still no one to be seen.

"Desculpe, sorry, Senhor?"

This time, Luis was sitting up and could determine the direction and proximity of the voice, which was coming inexplicably from behind a little rock figurine of a man three feet tall. The head of this little figure had a spectacularly realistic, full-featured face, obviously from a stone selected for this purpose by one of the more creative sculptors. It also had a little flat stone on top of its head with a cylindrical one on top of that, giving the impression of a little man wearing a 'pork pie' hat. Luis, wondering how someone could be hiding behind the small statue, stood up and walked over and around the figure but there was no one there.

"Boa tarde, good afternoon. Desculpe, excuse me?" was uttered again. Because he was standing right in front of the sculpture, Luis had to admit to himself that the voice was coming from the little stone person. *Someone must have hidden a speaker in the rock for a joke*, he thought as he inspected the little figurine, listing through the friends he had told he was visiting the beach today and those who might come up with such a ruse.

"Can I ask you a question?" the rock said.

Luis, entering into the joke, replied, "Yes, but where is the speaker hidden and where are you watching me from? Is that you, Bruno, up to one of your jokes again?"

"I don't know what you mean, Senhor, as it is I who am speaking to you."

"I don't understand," replied the bemused Luis, not to be fooled by a practical joke.

"I can explain," said the rock, "We rocks at the foot of

29

the cliffs are able to speak today and only today as this is the time we awake from our meditations. I am pleased that you have passed by at this moment, as I wanted to ask you a question that I could perhaps meditate on for the next 534,000 years."

Luis thought to himself that this was a good trick and the person operating the speaker must be watching him from a secret location laughing to himself. But, he thought, he would enter into the joke anyway. "Okay, what is your question, little rock?"

"Obrigado, thank you, Senhor. As I have explained, we rocks spend a long time meditating. We have been here for millions of years – long before you humans appeared on the scene. We spent our time meditating on the sea, the wind and the air contemplating deep and profound thoughts. Then, when we are eroded and fall from the cliff as rocks, we meditate on the purpose of erosion as we roll about in the waves, rubbing together as we turn to sand. I particularly like to mediate on how such a soft little substance as a drop of water can erode the strongest, mightiest cliff or mountain range over time. That thought has entertained me for many millions of years now. Desculpe, sorry, I am not getting to my question, please forgive me. So, for millions of years we have reflected and meditated before there was life on earth, when there were only creatures in the sea, when they crawled onto the land and when birds made their home in our cliff faces. However, now we have been presented with a new phenomenon that has appeared in the last six million years. It is your type, Senhor, humans. You first started to wander on the beaches, moving up the coasts, settling further and further around the coastlines until the present day.

We hear from the wind and the sea that you are present now in every part of this planet. Nowadays, visitors like yourselves come to the beach and we have noticed that you formulate the stones into shapes some of which, in a peculiar way, simulate yourselves. As you can see, I am a strange representation of a little human with the large stone representing the legs, the next large stone the torso and the smaller one, I am speaking from, the head of a human. So, this is my question. Every year, humans come and form us and every year the winter storms and the tides and the winds knock us down only for the humans to return the following year and build us again. My question is: Why do you do this? I would like to meditate on this issue for the next 534,000 years and would be extremely grateful for your thoughts on this."

Luis became so engrossed in the speech from the rock to the extent that the remarkable nature of the event had predisposed him now to believe the rock was transporting him to a reality where rocks came to life and spoke. With this sentiment, he felt compelled to answer the rock, forgetting his previous scepticism that the occurrence was a hoax. And to the best of his ability, Luis tried to answer the rock's question.

"We human beings, other than palaeontologists of course, generally think nothing of the timescale of rocks or cliffs, that you say meditate for hundreds of thousands of years on a single issue. Our time on this earth is short by comparison with yourselves. The reason we create images of ourselves, such as the figurine you have been formulated into, is because we just want to leave some impression of our passing. It entertains us to see little figurines of ourselves or to see rough nature tamed into a familiar shape or pattern that our mind takes geometric or mathematical pleasure from, such as a cone. The winter storms are like our deaths that return us to our basic state which are the chaotic components scattered randomly on a wild beach."

"In some respects we are very similar," replied the rock, "My brothers, the mountains, also like conical shapes and our own cliffs, which have formed into caves, take great pleasure from the sea dancing in and out to the rhythm of the tides. However, where we are different, is that for the cliffs, their final incarnation if you like, is after we have been released from the cliffs as rocks and then when we have been ground together for millions of years by the waves and tides to become sand. We then become one with the sea, travelling up and down the coast, making distant journeys to other continents and dancing in the deep. When we are in this state, we are at the pinnacle of our evolution by being split apart into our smallest component, whereas if you were reduced to dust, you feel this is a diminution of your existence."

Luis, now convinced of the authenticity of the rock, was moved by the idea that being broken down into its component parts might not be a death but just another form of existence. He thanked the little rock figure for its revelation and peacefully returned to sunbathe on the sand. And, as Luis lay there for the first of many future times in his long and fulfilled life, he meditated with a renewed appreciation on each grain of sand under his body.

"It is a good story, is it not?" Zeca said as his eyes

sparkled quizzically, "Angela, can you explain the meaning of the story to Mark?"

"Yes, Zeca. It is clear that the man would have been better to sunbathe further away from the rocks and then he would not have had his sunbathing time interrupted."

"I would recommend that you mull it over in your mind a little more, my dear, and consider other possible interpretations and the mysterious opportunities that death may offer," Zeca concluded, aware of Angela's difficulty in assimilating abstract concepts. He then nodded towards Mark and said, "I think it is time for your tour of the Hotel, Mr Goodwin."

"I will show you round, journalist. Follow me!" Angela instructed with a mechanical intonation, making her sound somewhat robotic. Mark noted that she missed out the usual social niceties of introduction. He was also intrigued and bemused by Angela's interpretation of Zeca's tale ... *Bizarre response! Where is this girl coming from? How could she miss the point of the story?*

Zeca, seeking the comfort of his afternoon siesta, ushered them out of his office and Mark, still considering the randomness and the chaos of life and death, found himself in the foyer, his elf to her Valkyrie, following compliantly behind Angela Deff to embark on his guided tour of the Hotel Euthanasia.

Chapter 3 The Catholic United Network for Transgression of Sins

In best laid plans of mice confused to measure meaning or define

The Song of Villadedino, Saint Dino 240AD

Two years after what he considered was the unnecessary death of his parents, Rab Lennon had ended his support for assisted dying. Rab opened the meeting of the Catholic United Network for the Transgression of Sins, this being the rather grandiose name thought up by Rab for the Glasgow Inquisition and Retribution cell. The meeting was taking place at 6:30 p.m. on a Scottish spring evening and there was a sense of positive anticipation from the group, both from the light starting to return to the dark wintered city and the enthusiastic and committed leadership that Rab provided.

Rab stood just short of six feet tall; he had piercing blue eyes and a slim build. In conformity to his communist-socialist background and despite the incongruity of his choice of clothing to the fashion of the times, he insisted on wearing the uniform of the 'working class hero' – ragged, patched blue jeans, ancient trainers, unironed t-shirt, and faded denim jacket. His only concession to frivolity was a small gold earring in his right ear.

Rab welcomed the two most recent recruits to the cell, Malky and Shug. "Welcome Malky, welcome Shug, we're most blessed to have you with us, comrades. Sorry! I mean brothers." Rab thought to himself, *I'll have to stop using that Marxist terminology. I sound more like bloody Lenin than Lennon!*

How could my parents have been so stupid to fall for their lies? The thought that kept replaying over and over in his mind about the perverse set of factors that had led to his parents' demise kicked in again.

The starting point had been the local Communist Party's campaign to raise funds to keep up with their rivals, the Glasgow Anarchists, who were becoming more organised. This had led to the Communist Party targeting the pensions they paid to Rab's father and mother as the means of funding the Party's advertising campaign to challenge the Anarchists. Rab's father had been sold on the plan from the moment he had laid eyes on the design for the May Day parade banner as it was shown to him. In the style of Samokhvalov, the words proudly proclaimed 'VICTOR LENNON – HERO OF THE GLASGOW COMMUNIST PARTY', encircled by red flowing flags of the Union of Soviet Socialist Republics surrounding the image of Rab's father with his fist in the air, taken from the 'Speech and Dinner Dance Night' at the Communist Club.

This simple exercise in negotiated coercion was all it took for his parents to embark on the all-inclusive (with drinks) trip to the Hotel Euthanasia. It didn't hamper the Communist Party's efforts either that Maw's favourite soap opera had been axed from the television, so she didn't have anything to live for anyway. Mr and Mrs Lennon would take the ultimate test of their belief that a life was only worth living if it could serve the greater cause of the Party.

Rab had subsequently been angered to hear that the hotel where they had met their end did not even arrange his parents' final moments to their specified requirements. As planned, the maXiviewalls had been playing the Moscow Red Square military march-past with its rousing music from the 1960s. But the hotel technicians had then got it quite wrong as his parents' terminal culmination had not delivered, as requested, the planned readings from the works of Karl Marx to commemorate their sacrifice, but, instead, had put on a showing of 'A Day at the Races' starring the Marx Brothers.

The effect of the strong emotions associated with his parents' debacle caused a complete change of heart on Rab's view of assisted suicide. Instead of being an advocate and campaigner for a change in the law on assisted dying with a reasoned opinion that individuals have the right to choose what they do with their own lives, this was now replaced with revulsion for the pointlessness of the whole absurd undertaking. Rab had been filled with anger, loss and an unquenchable thirst for revenge against both the Communist Party and the Hotel Euthanasia for what they had done to his parents. In the days that followed his discovery surrounding the conspiracy to coerce and defraud his parents, he resigned from the Communist Party, leaving a gap the size of Joseph Stalin's paranoia in his life. The Catholic Church of Pope Leo Sixtus I, with its campaigning zeal, stepped in to provide the motivation, opportunity, and cause he needed at that point in time to fill the vacuum.

Rab had become the cell leader, appointed by Archbishop Romario two years ago in the hope that Rab would be as active in the work of the Holy Church as he had been as campaigner and activist in his role as a community worker for the local government and as dedicated unpaid contributor to the Communist movement before his conversion.

Archbishop Romario himself was a direct appointment by the Holy Father, Pope Leo Sixtus I. The Archbishop thought of himself as a humble soul whose only desire was to serve the Church as best he could. Obviously, given his ability, this would require to be in as lofty a leadership role as his colossal ambition could attain. Of course, this required some minor necessity, '*for the greater good*' he would repeat to himself, to lie, cheat, and stab others in the back to accomplish his noble goals. Such were his altruistic aspirations in taking on the burden of power and position. In this selfless endeavour, he had served the Church and had been actively seeking an opportunity to raise his self-sacrificing profile and enhance his modest reputation and standing with the Pope. Archbishop Romario saw Rab's appointment to lead one of the cells for the Inquisition and Retribution as providing evidence of the strong leadership and drive that was required to fulfil his own plans to raise his 'unassuming' profile and achieve his 'simple' ambitions.

Rab looked around the room occupied by the small group of eight members now augmented by the two new recruits. The room was a typical standard municipal accommodation, booked for meetings of small community groups, sparsely furnished with hard-backed chairs and an antique formica-topped table at the front for, in Glasgow parlance, the 'heid bummer' taking the meeting. Rab did not, as designed, sit behind the table separating him from the others, but rather sat relaxed and engaging, a natural leader of men and women, on the front edge of the table. He had an ability to make eye contact with everyone in the room and when he spoke, each of the participants felt he was talking directly to him or her. Conscious of the need to place the meeting in an historical context, he outlined the chronological background to the cell for the benefit of the two new recruits.

"Right, let me tell you new guys why we came into bein'. Pope Leo Sixtus I, after his ordination in 2032, grabbed the Catholic Church by the cassocks and forced it to take a good look at itself. You'll remember this was followin' the death of Pope Hilarius II. Remember that laissez-faire dumplin'? He was responsible for presiding over 14 years of moral decline that brought the Holy Church to its knees. Lookin' back, people can see how it crept up on us ... it was wee bits at a time. It seemed fairly pragmatic at first because Pope Hilarius II had the 'recruitment of priests' crisis, which resulted in him allowin' married priests, but then it got totally out of hand when he allowed women priests, ... no offence to the sisters present ... followed by openly homosexual and lesbian priests. Things started to really go downhill fast when Pope Hilarius II threw out centuries of Catholic moral certainty and started to undermine the authority of the role by reporting paedophile

Priests to the police, allowed contraception and supported gay and lesbian weddings in the church. It was the last straw when he wouldn't even oppose the development of … ," Rab paused, turned his head to the side and feigned a simulated spit, "the Principality of Villadedino's euthanasia industry."

Rab seemed to grow two inches in front of his small attentive audience as he entered into his demagogue zone and continued, "Then, after Pope Hilarius' death, came the backlash led by Pope Leo Sixtus I. Thank God he took us back to a more civilised time where men were men, women were women, and priests remained in the closet of their confessional. Pope Leo Sixtus I returned the balance to somethin' more principled. This could be attributed to his historical revisionist position on the Spanish Inquisition. His mother was Portuguese and his father was Spanish. It also helped that they were pro Franco and Salazar, givin' their boy the strict upbringin' that has stood him in good stead to push through all the changes we needed. The congregations were fed up with too much democratic involvement and cryin' out for an increase in ignorance in order to have a pure heart and a back seat. Leo Sixtus I was unanimously elected as Pope on a mandate to return the Church to the security and sanctity of medieval morality. Thanks to him, women returned to the role that God ordained for them and recognised their place as submissive to their husbands. Finally, Pope Leo Sixtus I gave us back our worship of Mary the Mother of God and, most importantly, returned us to the important spiritual truth and discipline of not allowin' the eatin' of meat on a Friday. Fish on a Friday terminated the decline, improved

39

moral discipline, and also led to the fish and chips shops across the city experiencin' an economic boom."

"Can I ask a question?" said Malky, who had been intently digesting Rab's engaging presentation.

"Aye, of course," answered Rab.

Malky continued, thoughtfully, "Where is the nearest fish and chip shop, anyways?"

"Good question," Rab replied, his mind connecting to the pangs emanating from his stomach and making a mental note to grab a fish supper on his way home from the meeting. "If you turn left as you come out the front door of the buildin', you go past the pub, the hairdresser's, then the bettin' shop, till you get to the bus stop beside the other pub, then cross the road and it's beside another hairdresser's. If you pass one more pub, you've gone too far."

"So, that, comrades, sorry, friends, is the background," Rab continued, "We've great things planned for this cell. I cannot give you all the details yet, but what we've prepared is goin' to skelp the arses of that euthanasia lot in Villadedino. So, I'm lookin' for volunteers to form a small Retribution Action Group. Any takers?"

Malky and Shug immediately put up their hands, filled with the enthusiasm of the newly converted (Malky) and newly recruited (Shug). Malky wasn't too sure what Rab was talking about, but the fighter in him felt the excitement and adrenalin associated with getting up to some yet to be comprehended mischief. Malky also liked the call to battle he heard in Rab's tone, while Shug, after debating with himself and changing his mind five times within the three seconds from the end of Rab's request, finally and randomly raised his hand.

"Me too," said Magdalene and Rashona almost in unison, while both making meaningful sideways glances at the handsome Shug.

"Great, so that's Malky, Shug, Rashona, and Magdalene, brilliant and fantastico," Rab responded, filled with delight.

"Let's finish with a wee hymn … altogether now … " Rab handed out the song sheets and they all sang a rousing rendition of the recently revived Catholic song in adulation of Mary Mother of Jesus, at least, for Malky, up to the line where there was stumbling and mumbling in relation to the bit which said 'all the world is gay'.

> *The sun is shinin' brightly*
> *The trees are clothed wi' green*
> *The beauteous bloom of flowers*
> *On every side is seen:*
> *The fields are gold and emerald*
> *And a' the world is gay*
> *For 'tis the month of Mary*
> *The lovely month of May.*
>
> *O Mary, dear Mur-rer*
> *We sing a hymn to thee*
> *Thou art the Queen of Heaven*
> *Thou too our Queen shalt be*
> *Oh! rule us and guide us*

Unto eterniteeeeeeeee!

Rab had a warm glow from the pride he took in his leadership skills and the anticipated portion of oily battered fish and chips he would soon have dripping through the wrapping and onto his hands. *You deserve a pickled onion*, he thought to himself as he looked forward with intensity to avenging the death of his parents through the plan for the destruction of the focus of his outrage, the Hotel Euthanasia in Villadedino.

Chapter 4 Opening Doors on a New Enterprise of Death

Life flows from the mountain streams while precious metal weighs the body deep

The Song of Villadedino, Saint Dino 240AD

Yes, this place is like a benevolent friend, thought Zeca, *not the predatory vampire feeding on the lifeblood of the sick and vulnerable, attributed by the various media consortia that were opposed to its noble endeavours.* Zeca's mind drifted as he pondered the character of his beloved hotel, imbibing his afternoon glass of vinho tinto. Today was no different from most, as he used his precious private time for reflecting on the nature of the hotel surrounding him. *Benevolent friend,* the mental image evoked by the enticing main entrance, grand windows, ornate balconies, high turrets and solid fabric of the impressive building, its temperament and disposition. *Why, even some of the very stones used to build this edifice are certainly steeped in their own history,* he thought, *perhaps some even recycled from the original villa of the ancient founder of the Principality, the exiled Roman Dino Dormus.* Zeca imagined the Roman nobleman seated at his desk, his scroll laid out in front of him, peering at the page through the candlelight, writing his thoughts on mortality. If those stone walls that surrounded the Roman could observe Zeca now, they would see a manager whose role was to lead an enterprise solely devoted to the

43

commercial activity of death. The hotel was both ancient, like death itself, but also modern, like a Lazarus raised from the dead, with its refurbished halls, lounges, rooms, spas, and new state of the art technology; the conveyor belts leading to the crematorium at its centre, the living flame of death, and its sacred beating heart. Zeca smiled at the symmetry of his thoughts that further invoked the spirit of the hotel. This intellectual satisfaction was, however, tempered for a fleeting second as he felt the ghosts of guests past, reaching out from the walls behind him. In retaliation, he lifted the vinho tinto to his lips, providing a comforting reassurance, as its familiar taste consoled him, dispelling his spectres, and replacing them with his reasoned and logical views on the afterlife.

He had always been something of a scholar and had studied at the best universities in Lisbon, Paris, and Rome. He had honed and weaved his accomplished knowledge, together with his leadership skills and natural charm, to rise rapidly through the ranks of the hospitality industry to be manager of the best hotels in mainland Europe. He had of course been recruited by none other than King Eugene III of Villadedino himself for the crowning achievement of his professional life. Yes, from humble origins as the bastard son of a single parent, he now held the most prestigious hotel manager's post in the world. He was certainly grateful for the inheritance left by his deceased uncle, who had stipulated that it must be used for the purpose of his education.

It was this intellect he now applied to his meditations on the hotel. *Death or life, it doesn't really matter in the grand scheme of things*, he thought as he overlaid his previous ruminations on the personality of the institution he perceived to be a benevolent aristocrat. *This hotel is superior, privileged and has a detached disdain for generously relieving human beings of their common lives. Death is the fiefdom to which the grateful cheering peasants happily submit their life for the privilege of serving their lord and master. Okay, the fundamental driving forces are the successful economic and commercial objectives of the business, but who better than the hotel with its solid character and ancient reasoning to deliver these objectives successfully in a most right and proper way.* In addition, in the same way as a father would feel for his child, Zeca enjoyed a sense of pride as the one who had breathed life into the creature.

Oh, how we laugh now when we look back, Zeca thought to himself as he sipped again from his much deserved early afternoon glass, reflecting on the hotel's new beginnings as it took its preliminary steps, awaking like a sleeping giant from the slumber of obscurity to be the successful enterprise now known as the Hotel Euthanasia. He smiled as he recalled the first recruitment of staff and some of the more humorous answers to the question 'What is your view of assisted dying?' posed to the stream of eager applicants interviewed for the various posts on offer at the hotel.

'*I've never dyed clothes before, but I'm sure I could learn*,' answered a serious young man, who had obviously not read the job profile properly.

'*I would definitely recommend it for my husband*,' a

45

middle-aged woman had responded with a nervous straight face, serious, sincere, and with no humour in her answer.

'*It is eminently sensible for ending your life if it is of no use to you,*' answered the tall blonde woman, Angela Deff, who came to be employed by Zeca as his Customer Services Manager.

There had been something about her, even then, that Zeca had felt was a personal challenge to his ability to explain the moral issues surrounding the subject of death. Angela's direct forthright thinking had also made him consider whether he was in fact overcomplicating the process of assisted dying in his own mind. It was when he saw how the customers responded to her somewhat idiosyncratic and matter of fact approach that he was forced into modifying his thinking. He had then fine-tuned the operation processes to reflect the uncomplicated transactions between the customer seeking death and the hotel meeting their request.

'*I think I've changed my mind and I am not going through with it,*' he had overheard one guest say to Angela, only to hear her responding, in the detached way that only she could deliver, '*You have paid your fee, it would be a waste of money not to get the full service.*' To Zeca's surprise, the guest acknowledged that he thought she was right and resolved to get his full money's worth and, in so doing, completed the final act of the assisted dying process.

It was during these early encounters with Angela that Zeca developed his method of relating inspirational tales in an effort to both test his own values about death and dying, whilst also reaching out and trying to understand Angela's unusual mind. Zeca wondered if, in a sense, he had used Angela's personality, devoid of emotion, to project onto the hotel something that reflected the cold detached nature of death. Such detachment had enabled him to resist 'beating himself up' over the constant moral challenges that existed within the services that were provided. A certain level of detachment in the culture of the hotel had been an important factor in its commercial success.

Zeca recounted to himself, with a creative pleasure, one of the tales that he felt encapsulated the crux of the problem with the business of death.

There was once a farmer who lived in a small farm in the hot dry land of Alentejo. The farmer was familiar with the cycle of life and death through the rotating seasons of the year, working with animals and on the land. As with all farmers, he had slaughtered many animals, which he personally did with kindness and in his heart and mind, he was grateful to the creature that was giving itself, however compelled, to enhance his life, his pocket, or his dinner table. Having this experience, the farmer held the strong belief that, if ever an animal was suffering, it was better and more charitable to end the poor creature's life rather than for it to undergo unnecessary pain and suffering. It was in this sorry state of distress that the farmer's dog now found itself. It was old, half blind, and fell over from time to time. Worst of all, it was subjected to the indignity of vicious attacks by the farm cat. Now, the cat was jealous, as only cats can be, of the farmer's affection for the dog and took every opportunity, since the dog had become incapacitated, to exact its revenge on the dog. It would wait in ambush and then rush out and inflict scratches and bites to the poor hound. The farmer, on seeing the deteriorating life of the dog, felt saddened, but compelled to put it out of its misery. He settled on the necessary action, fetched his gun one day, and summoned the dog to the courtyard. The dog hobbled obediently to its master, watched inquisitively from a wall by the cruel cat. The farmer raised his rifle, took aim, and, with tears in his eyes, made to end the poor creature's life. He stood like this for half a minute, but, instead of firing, he adjusted his rifle. He could not end his companion's life. Instead, he turned and dispatched a bullet that used up the last of the farm cat's nine lives. This left the cat blood-soaked and with a most surprised look frozen to its face, lying at the bottom of the wall where it had fallen from its watching position. The farmer had had a revelation: his dog could live a debilitated but undisturbed life if the farmer disposed of the cause of its misery ... the cat! This all worked out fine for a few days, until a rat, who now lived unopposed in a cat-free farm, bit the dog on the nose, thereby causing a serious and painful infection that spread through the dog's body and resulted in a death of extreme agony.

'*Angela*,' Zeca recalled saying in the hope that she would see the moral duty the farmer should have exercised in managing the death of the dog, avoiding the death of the cat, and also in the hope of drawing out the lesson that sometimes choices resulted in unintended consequences. '*Angela, what is the moral of this tale?*' Angela had replied instantly and with serious intent, '*It would have been better for the farmer to have taken a liking to the rat, then the cat would have become jealous of it and killed it, thereby relieving the dog of a miserable and painful death.*'

As ever, Angela's eccentric answer, born from a brain wired differently than most, confounded Zeca. But this only increased his resolve to influence the mind of his Customer Services Manager. Angela had poured cold water on Zeca's reasoning that had catalogued the randomness of death into the sort of order that assuaged his conscience, whilst also prompting him to surmise that death and assisted dying were even more absurd and chaotic than his logic could imagine.

The challenges to his intellect that these absurdities generated caused him to reflect on another contentious issue he had had to deal with in the early days of the hotel. He recalled, with some discomfort, the assimilation of the older members of staff who, like the refurbished hotel, had difficulties making the transition from the establishment's previous incarnation as the rather run down Hotel Villadedino to the new regime as a centre for all things 'assisted dying'. They had approached him as a group claiming they found it too distressing and against their moral principles to serve people that they knew were arranging their deaths. Some were of the religious persuasion that held life to be sacred and were troubled by their part in the self-induced affiliation of others to such a sinful act as taking their own life. Zeca regretted giving them the benefit of the doubt and not sacking them before the hotel opened, which was the eventuality in any case.

It had come to a head following a series of incidents and complaints from guests that these particular staff were harassing them, pleading with them to change their minds, slipping them inspirational prayer tracts promoting the sanctity of life, and generally making them feel guilty. On one specific occasion, one of the more creative personnel, with a penchant for dramatic effect, resorted to dressing up with a skeleton mask, wearing a black cloak, and jumping from the closet of a guest in order to instil in him a profound fear of death itself, thereby shocking him into changing his mind on his planned suicide. It ended ignominiously when the guest keeled over and died of a heart attack brought on by the trauma of the cloaked evangelist jumping out of the wardrobe shouting, '*It is not your time to die!*' As fate would have it, on this occasion, it was!

The teething problems continued, Zeca recalled, with establishing the new processes for the smooth operation of the hotel. Much like the vital systems of the body, the Frankenstein of a hotel needed to be kick-started in order to truly come to life. The initial tranche of guests produced a litany of errors by the newly appointed staff group coming to terms with the procedures, including the technicians mixing up the subject matter for the eXi-theme Departure Suites.

The most incongruous incident involved a little old lady who passed away to the roar and vision of motorbikes rumbling through the mean streets of the city accompanied by ear splitting heavy metal rock music, while in another eXi-theme Departure Suite, the motorcycle gangsters, high on a cocktail of drugs and alcohol, had to content themselves in their last rebellious contemplations before death with gentle thoughts for the day provided by a saintly white haired priest surrounded by puppy dogs and bunny rabbits frolicking in a peaceful garden with a soft focus for the priest that made his silver hair glow like a halo.

Doctors failed to turn up to administer the deadly dose at the right time, resulting in one guest complaining that '*you could die waiting in here for assisted suicide*'. There were problems with erroneous routing of the coffins, meaning that some mourners were left by the empty grave waiting to pay their last respects for their loved one, while their dearly departed had been redirected to make their last hurrah in the hotel crematorium, burning brightly and contributing to the carbon content of the planet.

The initial advertising campaigns launched to a worldwide audience and using a multitude of mediums had not fared much better in introducing the concept of assisted dying to the public at large. A number of publications were commissioned to place an advertisement. One of the publications, after receiving the request by phone from the hotel, failed to write the request down at the time and, working later from memory of the phone conversation, inserted the wrong contact information for the enterprise for assisted dying. After interrogating the listings of local businesses, the publication, instead of identifying the Hotel Euthanasia Villadedino, selected by mistake the Hostel de Youth operated by a Mrs Viola Dino and her husband Dennis.

Mrs Viola Dino was, as you might expect, pleasantly surprised by the considerable increase in requests for reservations at her modest youth hostel high in the Villadedino Mountains. She would reply back to the applicants with a warm letter and welcome leaflet describing the male only and female only dorms, outside cold showers, ten mile treks through the mountains, and singing around the campfire accompanied by Mr Dino's 'enthusiastic' guitar playing. For one or two applicants, this was their hearts' desire and they signed up gladly for the pleasure of what they took to be the Hotel Euthanasia 'Youth Hostel Experience', but it all ended badly with fisticuffs round the campfire when their requests to be administered assisted suicide were fiercely rejected by the Youth Hostel owners, who misconstrued the request and took umbrage at what they interpreted to be an adverse response to Mr Dino's 'enthusiastic' but barely discernible three chord guitar playing skills.

The most successfully memorable advertising involved the internationally distributed television commercial of a sultry, shapely female in a satin slip leaning forward enticingly on the silk sheets of a luxury bed, looking directly into the camera lens, smiling suggestively, and uttering the now immortal phrase that had entered into the modern idiom, '*Come and die at my place*'. This was followed by a beautiful sunset over the turrets and cypresses of the Hotel Euthanasia and the now familiar coffin, spires and neon logo for the enterprise.

This commercial was of course considered successful, owing to the notoriety that it stimulated as it fanned a wildfire of debate and online furore about the use of sex to sell death. On one side of the debate were the feminists in an unholy alliance with the religious right wing that coalesced around the reduction of the female to a stereotypical objectified sex symbol enticing males to lascivious licentiousness, not least that this Jezebel was encouraging a sin at odds with the blessed gift of life. On the other side of the argument were the 'anything goes' brigade who supported the right of the individual to do whatever they wanted. After all, the actress was only earning an honest living.

However, the death threats and lucrative modelling jobs dried up for the poor actress as agencies, worried about a religious backlash, wouldn't touch her with a bargepole with an undertaker at the end of it. She ended up in a giant billboard parody of herself, dressed as a giant lobster on a bed of French fries now inviting the public to 'Come and dine at Joe's Seafood Place'.

The least satisfying part of the job, reflected Zeca, were the underprivileged sufferers with all sorts of multiple morbidities that turned up at the border each day begging to be assisted to die. Zeca was a kind-hearted man and a part of him wanted to help, but, after all, this was a business. He did have the Subsidised Assisted Dying (SAD) schemes to assuage his conscience. *The hotel has a clear ethical approach*, Zeca thought to himself, recalling how he and the King had introduced the assisted places scheme for the underprivileged.

The arrangement for the SAD scheme was a necessary evil. This arose out of the need for compromise with the Socialist Left Wing Party in alliance with the Sanctity of Life Over Nihilism Group (SOLONG) that had lobbied against the assisted dying law when it was being debated in the Villadedino parliament. They had managed to secure some of their objectives and a sliver of control over death as compensation, when they recognised the inevitability of the introduction of the new law on assisted dying and that they would lose the vote. A pragmatic settlement was agreed to provide some charitable support for people who could not afford the overpriced market tested fees anticipated by the hotel-planning group.

The idea that had given Zeca the most pleasure had been the 'Work to Die' internship scheme, that allowed him to both meet his responsibilities and to provide free labour from the willing trainees who undertook some of the more straightforward waiter or porter roles and tasks required by the hotel. The arrangement involved the trainee working for free for a period of six months, at the end of which they would be recompensed with a free assisted dying place.

Much better, thought Zeca, than the essay competition that he had to read and judge each month for a SAD place on the subject of 'Why I Choose to Die And How I Will Make My Departure Fashionably Interesting'. It had been a long time since he had come across anything that remotely resembled an original thought on the subject. Although, he had to acknowledge a certain artistic appeal concerning the imaginative fellow who proposed he dress up as a giant mouse and meet his demise in a cheese laden mousetrap.

At least now Angela deals with the begging letters using one of her two standard replies. One reply pointed out that the hotel provides its SAD schemes and proposed that the recipient apply to take advantage of one of these; the other simply advised the person that there was insufficient evidence from their request to indicate that they had the capacity to undertake assisted dying and that they might be better taking up a fulfilling hobby. Angela had a ready-made list of hobbies that she tried to match to the writer. If she could not decide on a suitable hobby, she simply inserted skydiving as she thought this would have a high probability of ending their life in any case and, therefore, reduce the number of follow up letters she would have to deal with.

Governments that had legislated against the practice of assisted dying within their own countries were keen to collude with the Principality to use the services of the Hotel Euthanasia. There were various reasons why they continuously declined to introduce a comparable law to that which operated in Villadedino yet at the same time wished to utilise the services of the hotel for their own purposes. The main reasons for their intransigence was the irrefutable fact recognised by even the most stupid of politicians that dead people don't vote. The second reason was the considerable lobbying power of the Catholic Church. However, these self-same governments all had a dilemma owing to the growing populations of older people who placed increasing pressure on health care and social support.

Zeca's introduction of the foreign cultural exchange scheme meant that governments could get around the law by paying for their older people to visit the museums, churches, and other variable landmarks in Villadedino. Once comfortably ensconced in Villadedino, it was straightforward to apply the

Competent Adult Test. It was then only a short step on to a pain-free process that removed a burden for the sponsoring government 'disposing' of a problem usually in collusion with immoral relatives eager to get their hands on property or bank wealth. Zeca recognised that this was somewhat underhand, but he was first and foremost a businessman and comforted himself with the thought that, as the farmer in his story should have done with the sick dog, he was relieving people of their pain and suffering.

Each multi-faceted thought in his meditations accumulated in the mind of Zeca and conspired to conclude that the nature of the hotel was in fact death itself and that he, Zeca, was its agent. He had to come to terms with the unwelcome idea that the hotel had, like death, a duplicitous uncaring and greedy nature. He had come to terms with the fact that, as well as the slightly aloof benevolent aristocrat that he would have preferred, the nature of death, while offering a welcomed relief, was somewhat more unedifying than he would have liked. It grasped greedily from the pockets of the living to serve its own purpose, while refusing to reveal the mystery behind the ambiguous stage curtain separating the recipients from their fate.

*

Chapter 5 Family Degeneration

Towards another travelling onwards sliding down the steep incline

The Song of Villadedino, Saint Dino 240AD

Robin Mitchell from Oxford had been as surprised as any young man would be when he was diagnosed with Motor Neurone Disease eighteen months ago. He was only forty and had known nothing about neurodegenerative diseases, but was soon to find out. Weakness in his arms and legs was the first symptom that he put down to overwork in his successful but time consuming business of supplying and installing the very popular maXiviewalls (wall vision technology) across the south of Olde England. It had been getting near his summer break from the moneymaking enterprise that he had built up over the last twenty years. He just thought that with a bit of relaxation in the Seychelles he would soon recover. However, when his legs started to feel like dead weights and, more and more often, he had to drag them to make any progress walking and his speech started to become slurred, his wife Bethany forced him to visit a doctor. Robin was at least compensated with a quick and accurate diagnosis, made within a two-week testing period. Doctor Vernon, a highly knowledgeable physician in the area of progressive degenerative diseases, was able to eliminate other possible causes quickly, identifying the symptoms as caused by Motor Neurone Disease. Doctor Vernon spent a considerable amount of time talking with Robin about all of the potential progressions and outcomes of the disease. He was honest and frank about the effects the disease would have on Robin's body, including the likely timescales for each stage. Yet, he was comforting and consoling during the consultation as the increasingly despondent Robin revealed his growing anxieties and fears, realising that there was no cure and overcome with thoughts of the ways his body would disintegrate, he would become increasingly helpless and dependent on others and, finally and inevitably, he would die.

Just as the doctor had described, the disease progressed very quickly, eventually resulting in Robin being unable to walk or use his hands and arms. He also lost most of his ability to speak and swallow food. Muscle weakness and atrophy spread to other parts of his body in a short space of time. Although communication was more and more difficult, his brain still had its full functioning. He could still manage a few lugubriously slurred words, could point at objects and nod and shake his head.

At first, his family, Bethany and his twenty-year-old son Ian, were supportive. They had to adapt their mansion for easier accessibility to wheelchair usage and also to enable Robin to remain downstairs to sleep. But the use of equipment for moving Robin was becoming more and more difficult for Bethany and Ian. They were attentive to the risks of chewing and swallowing, making eating extremely onerous and having the potential for choking or risk to the lungs. They also increasingly had to manage his continence. Ian had soon had enough and, feeling embarrassment and disgust, he refused to assist with changing continence pads and became unable to cope with this his father's most basic of functions. Then there was the pneumonia event that developed and the loss of weight which traumatised them as much as it did Robin.

As Robin's breathing weakened, so did the resolve of the family. The maXiviewalls business was impossible to oversee and Robin had to put plans in place to sell it off. This was difficult for Robin in his condition, but he still had a good business brain and with the help of his lawyer he made progress with this task.

The involvement of expensive care workers and nurses also added to the complications within the household, as their continuous presence started to feel like a constant intrusion of strangers into the lives of Bethany and Ian. A ventilation machine had to be used to support breathing, initially at night, and later during the daytime as well. The tracheotomy recommendation was the final straw that broke the weakened back of the family's fragile coping mechanisms.

The brief talks between mother and son about the difficulties they were having showed up their small changes in attitude at first, but these soon escalated to what felt more like therapeutic discussions between Bethany and Ian, which involved full-scale confessionals between them, sharing their anxieties, frustrations, anger, and guilt about how much a burden Robin had become to each of them. The family began to have less and less direct communication with Robin as his condition deteriorated, initiating a depressive state that became progressively worse and worse. His will to attempt any positive acts to live a meaningful life, rich in purpose and fulfilment, was decreasing. After what had been initially a manageable and sympathetic period with Robin's condition, the family were now feeling under constant pressure with caring or arranging support for this person who was becoming a real inconvenience in their lives and disrupting them getting on with their own.

With the business sold and the money in the bank, Ian saw an opportunity to access his inheritance sooner rather than later. It was his girlfriend, Melanie, who had first put a potential solution in his head.

"Have you heard of a place called Villadedino, with a Hotel Euthanasia that specialises in assisted dying? They help people, who are suffering, to die there. Wouldn't that be a great place for your dad to go if he is in such misery? It would be so much better for him in the end, don't you think?"

There was much discussion in the household, out of earshot of Robin of course, about 'needless suffering' and with the doctor having given the prognosis of another two years to live, the prospect of the pressure extending beyond their coping mechanisms was weighing heavily on their shoulders. They could not put their lives on hold any longer. Something had to be done. So, with these thoughts, the family embarked on a campaign to convince Robin, drip feeding subtle hints, encouraging him to consider an alternative solution as a preference to another two years of suffering, anguish, and pain. Discussion with him would involve questions such as "Why would you want to undergo such a cruel and unnecessary condition?" There was much talk of human dignity and the quality of his life, not to mention the crushing impact his condition was having on the family.

Bethany, in her hours of need, had been receiving sympathy and comforting support from her concerned tennis coach, regarding the difficulties she was enduring. Melanie continued to support and counsel her boyfriend Ian. And all the time there was a big fat bank balance from the sale of the business awaiting the colluding mother and son.

Despite his physical difficulties and bouts of depression, Robin's brain still remained active; he had, after all, managed with the help of his lawyer to successfully sell off the business, ensuring that a good market price was achieved. He also had some insight into the pressure his family was under, although his hope was to continue for as long as he could. But his resolve, combined with the pressure from his wife and son, was waning. *The money in the bank will pay for my long-term care and also be enough for the family when I am gone*, he thought. In between the discomfort and pain, he did think about his family, who did not seem to be coping with his condition or the burdens he was placing on them, and he took some satisfaction that they would probably only have to cope for another couple of years.

Bethany and Ian, augmented by Melanie, continued to discuss the future and how much better it would be if only a merciful end could be found to Robin's predicament. The costs of palliative care were also mounting up and with the prospect of these continuing to increase over the next two years, a dent in

61

the bank balance would soon become evident. Although not substantial, relative to the overall size of the bank balance, any reduction at all in the anticipated inheritance was becoming increasingly resented by Bethany and Ian (not forgetting Melanie).

"How long can we go on like this?" Bethany conspired with Ian and Melanie.

"Look, at the end of the day, maybe you just have to recognise that he is being selfish," Melanie accurately articulating the resentment held by Bethany and Ian.

"I spoke with Doctor Vernon yesterday, Mum, about whether there was some drug or something that they could give him that would put us out of his misery," Ian announced with an unintended but appropriate slip that reflected what they were all really feeling. "The doctor was sympathetic to the pressure we are all under and said there are drugs you can get on the Internet, but it is illegal and it would be treated as manslaughter or something. Fourteen years behind bars, the doctor said. The doctor did confirm Melanie's idea about the Hotel Euthanasia in Villadedino, though. He told me, a requirement in Villadedino is that a patient must be able to give informed consent and has to undergo some sort of test to prove this. The doctor said he would be willing to help Dad if this is what he wants, by conducting and signing off the test that says he is able to make that decision himself. The doctor also said there was no way the law in this country is going to change. There is a powerful lobby from the Catholic Church against assisted dying, slippery slope and all that. He said the politicians know where their votes are coming from and will not change the law to allow assisted dying. He said that with the pressure we were obviously under, he is willing to help us out with our problem, sorry, I meant dad out of his misery."

"So, if that's the only help we can get," Bethany said firmly, "then we need to go ahead with it. Let's get the test done and get your father off for a nice stay at Villadedino," she said, comforting herself with the delusion of Robin going on something akin to a holiday.

Robin was not sure why he was at the doctor's clinic, as he had only recently had his situation reviewed, but Bethany was insistent, so the best form of defense with his wife, given his condition, was just to go along with it. What harm could there be anyway.

*

"I just need to carry out some tests, Mr Mitchell," a smiling Doctor Vernon ventured, "I will need to get your wife to acknowledge your response to the questions. If you can just blink your eyes or point to the letters on the alphabet board, then that will suffice."

Doctor Vernon proceeded to undertake the Villadedino 'Competent Adult Test' used to assess suitability by the Hotel Euthanasia. Doctor Vernon had accessed the paperwork for his clinic. There was a small fee to the Hotel Euthanasia, of course, payable for registration, administration, and copyright. The purpose of the test was to assess whether someone is competent to make an informed decision to reasonably choose the 'life changing' act of assisted dying. The format of the test was simple, but Villadedino had had it verified independently and objectively by an army of eminent psychiatrists and research universities across the world. Villadedino's contribution to research programmes and building projects had not gone unnoticed by the esteemed and distinguished institutions that had authorised its validity. In a case like Robin's, because of difficulty with speech, the patient is provided with some multiple-choice options and a board with the letters of the alphabet to elicit understanding and help the patient make his or her responses. The test starts with the patient being told a story as follows:

The Principality of Villadedino Competent Adult Test

As per the 'Conduct of Assisted Dying' Act 2021

A man takes his dog for a walk on the beach. During the walk, the dog sees a branch floating in the sea, jumps in to get it, and retrieves the branch in its mouth. It brings the branch back to its owner. The dog likes the branch. The owner then uses the branch as a walking stick. The man and the dog return home. The man is not sure what he should do with the walking stick. He ponders whether he should keep the stick or put it in the garbage. He thinks the dog will feel bad if he puts it in the garbage and eventually decides to keep the stick.

1. *Can the patient remember the story?*
    Yes/No

2. *Can the patient describe what the story was about?*

    a. *Was it about a woman, a rabbit, and a carrot?*

    b. *Was it about a man, his dog, and a stick?*

    c. *Was it about a child, a toy, and a banana?*

3. *If the correct answer is given to Question 2, can the patient say what factors the man is likely to have used to make his decision about the stick?*

    a. *The time it took for the walk?*

    b. *The proximity of any shops to the house?*

    c. *His and the dog's feelings?*

4. *Can the patient tell what decision the man made?*

    a. *Keep the stick?*

    b. *Give the dog away?*

    c. *Call the garbage service?*

5. *Can the patient see what might be the consequences of the decision?*

    a. *The dog steals the stick and puts it in the garbage?*

    b. *The man puts the dog in the garbage?*

    c. *The man keeps the stick and uses the stick on the next walk?*

6. *Describe how you are going to get home from the clinic.*

    a. *Bus?*

    b. *Train?*

c. *Taxi?*

d. *Car?*

7. *What day of the week is it?*

8. *Where are you?*

9. *Spell 'Hannah' backwards.*

10. *Draw a polygon.*

11. *Repeat 'a bird in the hand is worth two in the bush.'*

12. *What is 3 multiplied by 15?*

13. *Which way would sugar fall if the sugar bowl is turned upside down?*

14. *Can the patient remember the story after 5 minutes? Yes/No*

15. *Remember three words from the story.*

If the patient can answer twelve of the fifteen questions correctly, then this will be an indicator of competence to make an informed decision about whether to partake of assisted dying. In his case, Robin would indicate his answers by blinking, which would be interpreted by Doctor Vernon with some help from Bethany.

The outcome was that Robin was able to answer twelve of the questions of the 'Competent Adult Test' correctly. This allowed Doctor Vernon to verify that Robin was a competent adult and would be able to use the facilities of the Hotel Euthanasia in Villadedino. Bethany was overjoyed with the result, which surprised Robin, as she had never shown this level of cheerfulness with the range of other tests he had undergone.

Throughout the test, Robin kept wondering what

the point of the exercise was. He understood that, in some cases, people with Motor Neurone Disease did develop Alzheimer's disease and he thought that perhaps Bethany was getting apprehensive about anticipating yet another decline in his condition. Her enthusiasm with the result, he guessed, was probably due to relief that he, at least, did not suffer that complexity from his condition. On a positive note, the doctor had said he had passed the test with flying colours and in Robin's mind this commendation that he was 'declared sane' was some consolation. *So*, he thought to himself, *the trip to the clinic wasn't wasted after all. At least I can go on living at home with my family and with my current condition.*

Chapter 6 With Choice and Free Will, the Only Thing You Can be Sure of is Uncertainty

And the careless wind blows random thoughts through the minds of saints

The Song of Villadedino, Saint Dino 240AD

"Assisted dying is no laughing matter," Archbishop Romario pointed out to the five assembled souls making up the cell led by Rab Lennon, who were sitting around his lavish drawing room, lounging unceremoniously on his expensive imported Italian armchairs and sofas. He needed to emphasise the importance of their mission that would send shock waves of respect for his initiative through the corridors of power at the Vatican. It had been necessary for him to keep the scheme under wraps in case some other Archbishop muscled in on his glory. *It is just as well that I do not suffer from the sin of pride*, he reassured himself as he humbly envisaged kneeling at the feet of the Pope. He imagined that same Pope offering him an elevated position in the Vatican hierarchy, *perhaps right hand man to il Papa himself*, he thought, preparing mentally for taking over the most noble of positions at some point in the future, as his most modest of ambitions desired and envisaged. For maximum effect, he adopted his tried and tested serious expression, honed to perfection after hours of practice in the mirror, for the benefit of the gathered band of intrepid agitators and proceeded to enlighten them on a higher understanding of their mission.

"I want to congratulate you all on your willingness to take part in this most important of missions. You will be led by Rab to ... ," he paused for effect, " ... blow up that den of iniquity known as the Hotel Euthanasia that operates out of the ungodly state of the Principality of Villadedino."

The soon to be saboteurs were 'all ears' now as the enormity of their mission became clear.

"You are vital to the work of God and I know that you will carry out your tasks to the highest standard. It is your destiny to fulfill God's purpose to fight for the sanctity of life and ensure that Holy Mother Church, acting as God's agent here on earth, is the one that controls the point of death and not the individual. We also have a duty to ensure that the numbers in our congregations are kept as high as possible so that they can contribute economically to the glory of the Church. God himself has predestined that we should take up this good fight."

Surveying the eager faces before him, Archbishop Romario thought to himself as he continued to speak, *it looks as though I am getting through to my recruits. I can't leave anything to chance. Okay, it is a bit of manipulation of their innocence, but I can't let their ignorance get in the way of this most splendid plan and I do have to protect them from themselves. It is my role, on behalf of the Church, to help the poor less enlightened souls to think in the manner God intended. Things are going well with getting them on board.* However, the inconvenient thought of the recurring dream he was having over the last few weeks leapt uninvited into his mind causing him to pause.

"Free will and choice, this is what is at stake," he heard himself say to his assembled recruits, more spontaneously than he would have planned, mirroring the scenes of the dream that replayed in his mind. In the Archbishop's dream, he saw himself as Abraham talking to God, who, as was his predilection, requested Abraham (the Archbishop) to take his son to the mountain and there to kill him as a sacrifice to his God. In the dream, the Archbishop (Abraham) took his (Abraham's) son, who bore a remarkable resemblance to Rab, up the mountain and proceeds to fulfil his destiny and God's will by killing poor Rab on a stone altar. Just at the point in the dream when the Archbishop/Abraham, happy to have done his duty to his God, is staring down now with mixed emotions into the dead eyes of his departed son, God appears saying, *"Abraham, you didn't actually do it, did you? I was only joking. I meant to stop you before you carried out the act, but was caught up with something else and didn't get back in time to let you off the hook. So, oops, sorry Abe, but what can I say?"* at which point the Archbishop always woke up sweating and with a disconcerting feeling that his certainty about predestination had been replaced by something that was a good bit more random.

Fully conscious now and aware of being in the presence of others, his control and certainty returned as he tried to dispel the chaos of the dream and repeated, not quite knowing where he was going with it, "Misappropriation of free will, this is what is at stake."

"Is that the film about the big black and white fish?"

70

Malky couldn't resist making the joke. While the prospect of blowing things up had an obvious attraction, all this free willing and choice stuff had the potential to get just a bit boring.

"Now, now, Malky," said the Archbishop, "Let's keep this under control. Assisted suicide, I say again, is no laughing matter."

"I'm no' laughin'," Rab corroborated, "I wasn't laughin' when they told me my mother and father both took their lives in an assisted suicide pact, was I? The Archbishop is absolutely right," he also confirmed, "I should know, as I've been on both sides of the argument."

Before his conversion to the church and before his parents' demise, Rab had been employed as an activist in the local community in a role that suited his campaigning skills. Paradoxically, one of the community groups he was supporting had wanted the law on assisted dying changed. The sons, daughters, husbands, and wives of very ill or disabled relatives, that were suffering extreme pain and wanted to end their lives, had come together as a group of like-minded individuals. They were highly motivated because of their frustration and anger at not being able to do anything about their sick relatives' plights. The law was an ass, as far as they were concerned, when it came to assisting your relative to die.

There had been much reporting and debate about the uncertainty of the law in relation to relatives assisting their loved ones to end their misery. Cases had hit the headlines and become much publicised when the poor relative had been arrested and jailed for 'taking the law into their own hands'.

Rab had been convinced of their collective case to change the law, of course before his parents' own actions, as the reasoning seemed to him to be self-evident. All his training had promoted self-determination and the rights of a human to take control over their own lives or in this case, consistent with this perspective, their own death.

While there were one or two genuine supporters in the political classes, he had been disgusted with the majority of politicians who postured and performed with self-righteous piety during parliamentary debates about the difficulties for their constituents, promising duplicitously to vote for a change to the law. However, all the time, these politicians knew they would not be voting for choice. They appeared to be taking on board the views of the activists for a change in the law about assisted dying. But, all the time, lobbying from religious groups, disability forums, certain right wing media moguls, and businessmen, for the sanctity of life meant that for the politicians, a vote for uncertainty in the law was a vote for stability. Not least in their minds was an over-riding concern to ensure the stability of their own personal re-election to represent dutifully the will of the population. So, they waxed lyrical about the importance of palliative care, hospice care, drug-induced freedom from pain, and the role of the voluntary sector to support those in need.

Rab, listening to the Archbishop, kicked his reasoning into gear and assimilated his own thoughts about choice. He decided that there was an importance to responsibility that goes along with rights to make choices, and in the feelings of empowerment and disempowerment that emanate from either being able to choose or not to choose. He had been badly affected by the experience of being disempowered when he heard that his parents had chosen to die. The emotions released as a result of this act had made him feel anger, disappointment, and a loss of control and self-esteem. This had thrown his usually reasoned and rational approach to choice into confusion, particularly where assisted dying was concerned. He had gone from being an advocate of assisted dying to being diametrically opposed to the idea. Now, he was hell-bent on taking revenge on the agents of his parents' death.

"So, let me get this straight in my head," Malky's voice interrupted Rab's reflection, "You can choose to do some things but it is wrong to choose some other things? I could choose to jump out of an airplane with a parachute and that is okay, but I can't choose to kill myself if I am in agony, although both actions might lead to the same result?" The thoughts were starting to pick fights with each other in Malky's brain.

"And what if I chose to get into a fight with three blokes that were bigger and stronger than me," … this was not an unknown event in Malky's life … , "and these three blokes gave me a good kickin' and I ended up dead. Would that have been me choosin' to die? And would that have been wrong? Or okay? Because I might have been totally drunk and been totally out of my head with regards to makin' that choice?" … again, not too dissimilar an event that Malky would have engaged in.

For sure, Malky had a 'death wish', although he wouldn't have called it that. He would have thought that it was only sensible to get into as many fights as he could to reinforce his self-image as a 'devil-may-care' type who wouldn't shun an act of intimidation such as someone glancing his way in a bar or accidentally bumping into him in the street; or for that matter, walking on the same street at the same time as him. Once Malky got to know you, he was a different person. He was loyal to a fault, single minded, and willing to take a risk of appearing foolish by disclosing his ignorance. Okay, a lot of the time he was foolish, but again, his own personal view of himself was that life was too boring not to crack a joke. Personally, he could never take his own life because that was being a coward; in truth, he did not have the personal conviction and strength of character to take this step in the cold light of day. If he had ever thought about his own mortality, he would probably have preferred to follow the death route of getting drunk and losing his life in a knife fight. In saying all that, he had been impressed by Rab and this had had a sobering effect on his life. So, for his part, he was willing to go along with the plan to blow up the hotel as this would be a '*pure mental thing to do*'.

"It's all a bit complicated, isn't it?" Malky concluded.

"The difference in your examples, Malky, is that with the risky sports you mention, the intention is not to take your own life, whereas it is the opposite with assisted dying. Intention is everything. God has made it very simple for us," the Archbishop intervened, "He has told us about the sanctity of life, that life is sacred because God has bestowed on us an opportunity to fulfill his plan here on earth. This is a blessed gift from God and no human being has the right to take this away.

That is all we need to know. If God has given us life, it is a sin of the most selfish proportions for us to take that life away. Life is a gift."

Magdalene suppressed a sob that she skilfully converted into a cough. All this talk of the sanctity of life was dredging up unwelcome memories for her. She had been only fourteen and it was just the one time that she had done it. If truth be told, she didn't even enjoy it, but it was enough for her to add one more number to the teenage pregnancy statistics through the subsequent abortion by the time she was fourteen years and seven months. '*It is the best choice,*' her mother had coerced her, '*You don't want to be tied to bringin' up a baby at such a young age*'. The immature Magdalene had gone along with it and she had sleepwalked into the clinic, undergone the procedure, and then 'carried on with her life'. However, at the back of her thoughts, secreted away in a dark part of her mind, was this little girl person that she continued to have conversations with. Now, all this talk of choice and free will was opening the casket, opening the door in that dark cupboard of memories to distinctly hear her dead baby girl say, '*You got to choose, mummy, but nobody asked me*'.

"That's a bad cough you've got, Magdalene," Rashona offered, as Magdalene moved her hand swiftly to wipe away the tear and quell the emotions swelling up in her chest.

"I'm okay," Magdalene countered abruptly before trying to get back into a better emotional frame by diverting her darkest thoughts towards her least admirable qualities – and harassing Rashona. "What about you, you fat fuckin' cow. Why do you choose to eat so much? Don't you know that you are killin' yourself? All this talk of choice and all you choose to do is reduce your life by eatin' too much. You are going to end up with a heart attack, carryin' all that extra weight. What kind of stupid choice is that?"

"Don't you call me a fat fuckin' -C-O-W-," Rashona replied taken aback, spelling out what she interpreted to be the most salacious element of the insults that cast aspersions on her character and trying to demonstrate some deference to the Archbishop for the uncalled-for profanities exiting from Magdalene's foul mouth. "That was very hurtful and you know that I am constantly dietin' to get my weight down. It is just my nature to be big. I can't help it."

Magdalene regretted that she must be appearing to be so mean in front of the others, in particular Shug. "I'm sorry, I don't know what came over me. I just got a bit emotional."

Rashona for her part was always quick to forgive Magdalene. There was a natural pecking order that had been established between the two females. However, at the back of her mind, the unprovoked attack and the discussion had her thinking that she lacked the resolve and will power to get thin. She had had a good upbringing from her mother but her father had been very strict with her. She could not do anything right in his eyes and when the weight started to pile on as a young girl, he had set about undermining her confidence. She was unaware that the eating had been the method she adopted as her only means of gaining some control over her life. Now this had somehow translated itself into an obsession with diets.

Rashona had spent most of her teenage years in her bedroom in self-imposed exile from a cruel world and harsh father. She had studiously read every available book about diets, but there was something conflicting in her nature that subliminally subverted her conscious efforts to see snacking as a contradiction to her diets. If truth be told, Rashona had a dysfunctional brain where the left temporal lobe operated independently of the right one. In effect, she was unaware that she was constantly snacking. She was certainly in denial about the impact that her nurture had in blocking her painstaking efforts to achieve her desired body shape. She had read somewhere during her anthropological studies phase that it was just natural for people to have an almost constant urge to eat due to the survival instincts developed when homo sapiens were evolving. This proposition and theory eased any prospect of confronting her denial and gave her some respite from guilt as she returned to a state of equilibrium, with the thought of herself as a hunter-gatherer in the wild savannah, tracking down and gorging on a party-sized pizza. As she played with the idea, the thought also seemed to cavort alongside a gratifying fantasy in which a lion was eating her father. All the calorie reducing talk of free will and choice at the end of the day was making her hungry.

Rab, sensing that the two females' flare up of antagonism was triggering disintegration in the proceedings, changed the subject to an area he felt would be more rewarding. "Being able to make your own choices is the most empowerin' of actions we can make as human beings. Because I choose to

77

take part in this mission, I feel I am going to achieve somethin' worthwhile and that gives me a great deal of satisfaction. I can avenge the deaths of my parents. Magdalene, what choices would you make that would make you feel empowered?"

"Well, it would be the most empowerin' moment in my life if I was able to marry the man of my dreams," Magdalene responded glancing coyly over to Shug.

"That's funny," ventured Malky, "that's exactly what my ex said to me when the divorce came through, that it was the most empowerin' moment of her life."

Everyone laughed, clearing the air around the conflict that had raised its head between Magdalene and Rashona.

"I really felt empowered when I took up hang glidin'," said Shug, "there was somethin' about the freedom and control that I felt up there."

"Wasn't it a bit frightenin'?" Magdalene asked, concerned that the focus of her loving attentions and intentions might suddenly fall out of the sky through his choice of extreme sport.

"Well, yes, it was. The problem was that I couldn't really make up my mind. I had chosen to take up the sport but, as soon as I was about to try it, I got cold feet and thought about what might go wrong. It was while I was ponderin' this on the edge of a high hillside, fate took matters into its own hands and this big gust of wind came out from nowhere and I was up in the air. So, I suppose that I had chosen to do it but then changed my mind and fate or somethin' like that chose for me. Sorry, that sounds a bit random."

"That's what I was trying to tell you earlier," interrupted the Archbishop, glad to get the discussion onto a surer footing for himself, "We all have free will, but for some of us, and I mean this group of noble souls, God has a higher destiny. As it says in Ecclesiastes, 'there is a time to die'."

"There is a time to embrace and to refrain from embracin'," Shug added under his breath, remembering the verse from his time in the seminary and taking a sidelong glance at Magdalene.

The Archbishop continued, "You are predestined to do God's will to preserve the sanctity of life and eliminate the sponsors of assisted dying and so it is right that we destroy the abomination of the Hotel Euthanasia."

Shug was getting that familiar feeling that he had when he entered the seminary to train for the priesthood as a teenager. Somehow, he had felt sure that God was telling him to take up his true vocation. However, no sooner was he committed than he had doubts. Had he chosen to do this or was it the pressure of his family, teachers, and priests in the Catholic Church that were deciding for him? There was also the attention he received from the female of the species who all saw in Shug the embodiment of desirable masculinity. These doubts had led to his exit from the seminary, which of course he had deep regrets about. *Am I doing the right thing or should I stick it out?*

It seemed to Shug that he was on a constant cycle of making choices and then wishing he could turn the clock back and choose the opposite. But here he was and he was sure that this was a most noble mission. *But what if it all went wrong?*

"So, are we all agreed in choosing this mission?" Archbishop Romario focussed the group on his main objective, "I can promise you that you will be saints in Heaven because of this and I see a great future for us all if we succeed. The Holy Father will be highly pleased with us." He looked around the room and saw enough in the eyes of the assembled rebels to feel sure of the settled consent he desired. *I think I can actually pull this off*, he thought.

"One final thought on free will and choice," proclaimed the Archbishop, calculating that he needed to reward his agitators, "Who is for fish and chips from the chippie, because I'm paying?" A brief incongruous thought swam through his mind concerning thirty pieces of deep-fried cod but he quickly disposed of the absurdity of this fleeting rashness.

Of course, they all agreed, in particular Rashona, as the primitive side of her brain 'kicked in' to the ancient instinctive worship of a deep-fried indulgence. Who wouldn't?

They left the palatial surroundings of the Archbishop's home with some of the honest donations for the upkeep of the church from the various congregations of the Archbishop's diocese, now commandeered for deep-fried sustenance and secreted in his pocket for safekeeping. Rab reflected on how perverse it was that he had been an advocate of assisted dying and here he was now about to lead a mission to destroy the very inner temple of assisted dying, the Hotel Euthanasia. *I'm pretty sure about this*, he thought.

Chapter 7 The eXi-theme Departure Suites

The act plays out the role concludes the dance of life as ever thus

The Song of Villadedino, Saint Dino 240AD

Angela Deff looked down condescendingly on Mark Goodwin from her superior height as they started their tour of the Hotel Euthanasia. She did not suffer fools gladly and hoped that Mark would listen carefully to her most excellent descriptions of the hotel and desist from asking any questions. Angela was border autistic spectrum disorder, resulting in a manner that could be perceived by others as ranging from humourless, cold, and distant, to overly direct, arrogant, and rude. In her own mind, Angela was straightforward, conscientious, and as honest as her condition would allow about her role. Unfortunately, her interpretation of situations resulted in an obscure logic that leaned towards taking things literally and that contributed to an unconventional response to social intercourse.

Angela gained a great deal of job satisfaction from her work as she was clear about the hotel's function in providing a service for customers to die. She considered this to be eminently sensible and practical as she could not understand the purpose of her jobs in previous hotels, where people wanted to, in her practical way of construing social actions, waste time in activities for the sole purpose of enjoying themselves. *What was the point of that?* she often thought to herself. Ms Deff simply could not enter into the idea of 'fun'. This job suited her better. While initially all the customers participated in the fun and delights provided by the eXi-theme Departure Suites, they always ended up dead. Within her complex mental configurations, this objective made eminently more sense to her as there was a concrete conclusion to their hotel stay rather than some philosophical outcome of a personal nature that she failed to understand. She was ideally suited then to the role of Customer Care Manager because of her dispassionate detachment to the bereavement processes and the sometimes emotionally charged atmosphere generated by the guests at the hotel.

She was conscientious and took a sense of achievement from fulfilling the detailed job description and role, which, with a typical Angela sense of eccentric priority, she had framed and hung in a prominent position in her own quarters. At times, however, she felt that her ability to connect with people was not always as satisfactory as she would have liked. She had read books on customer care where the strange concept of communication had been repeated again and again. She resolved to diligently explore the forms of interaction mentioned and had been trying to build better communication skills with members of the public. She thought she would try out a newfound conversational mode with Mark.

"I had a very satisfying time in the shower this morning shaving the hair from under my arms. How about you, journalist, do you shave the hair from under your arms?" she said.

Mark was taken aback at such an odd question,

especially as this was the only time she had spoken since they had left the office of Zeca Silva. "I've never really thought about it," came the uncertain response from the wrong-footed Mark before he had time to figure out any context or logic for such a strange question.

"You really should, as it will improve your personal hygiene," Angela offered, thinking, *that was a successful interchange. I am really improving my communication skills.*

Bolstered by her progress and logging the subject of exfoliation as a productive form of social intercourse, she explained to Mark about the layout of the hotel, "Journalist, you will listen carefully. I am going to explain the layout and processes of the hotel. Do not interrupt as this will increase the time it takes to explain the systems here and I do not want to spend any more time with you than I need to."

Charming! thought Mark, who had other ideas planned. He wanted to see if he could tease out of Angela Deff some answers concerning the real reason for his visit. "Have you ever had any famous people come to the hotel to die, Angela?"

"My contract of employment states that I am not allowed to discuss any of the guests and, as I have said already, I am here to give you a tour of the hotel," Angela responded plainly, getting a little agitated there might be some interruption to the scheduled programme for the day she had spent two hours constructing.

Angela directed Mark through the corridors and reception rooms of the grand hotel that, since its period of decline in the time of King Eugene II, had been fully refurbished with the richest of fabrics, surfaces, and stylish antique furnishings. Special attention had been afforded to the gold leaf cornices of the magnificent ceilings throughout the building that set off the sparkling crystal chandeliers. The grandiose marble entrance, nicknamed the pearly gates, included a series of interlinked high arches, fountains, and further marble stairways with ebony and wrought iron banisters that had been lovingly restored to their former glory. There stood some original Rodin sculptures, acquired with no expense spared from the Glyptotek in Copenhagen. Expensive restored wooden floors in the lounges, adorned with Persian rugs, complemented the marble walkways. Marvellous panoramic views towards the forests, lakes, and snow-capped mountains were captured from every grand window or terrace accessed from French windows. Further afield in the distance could be seen the pastoral farmlands and small rural hamlets of the neighbouring country of Figas. Mark was shown through comfortable bars, dining rooms, reception areas, and lounges; each one more elegant than the other and with more sparkling chandeliers than he had ever seen. As well as the antique charm of the old hotel, every modern provision was accounted for from the maXiviewalls in each bedroom and lounge to the state of the art hypergymnasiums, pools, spas, and piazzas. They wandered outside the hotel and admired the koi-filled ornamental ponds, ornate fountains, sculptures, impressive towers, high spires, and solid battlements of yellow sandstone. They walked across the manicured lawns, well-stocked gardens with their topiary hedges, laurel maze, and interspersed cypresses, tall sequoias, and mature oaks. They looked beyond the hotel and up the hill to the mountain, where the forest at first thickened and then started to thin out as it neared the remains of last year's snow. A flickering memory drifted through Mark's mind of his time with Estrela in the Highlands of New Scotland as he gazed up towards the snowline beyond the forest.

Mark managed to restrain himself to accommodate Angela's dictats and kept quiet throughout the tour. Finally, after viewing the green undulating lawns, monumental tombstone and cenotaphs of the hotel cemetery, Angela brought him back into the building .

"Ah, now here we are, journalist, at the eXi-theme Departure Suites," she was glad to say, returning to one of the unique features of her tour, "We have a range of choices for our clients."

She opened the door to one of the suites and into a large room in which there were no windows, a couple of fashionable leather sofas, marble tables with exotic flower displays, a large bed, and a table laid out with an enticing range of foodstuffs, sweetmeats, and fruit for the next recipient of the suite. Large maXiviewalls were evident on three sides of the room, with the potential to fill the space with film images of the guest's choosing. The incongruous parts of the room were the stainless steel medical cabinets and what looked like an extra-large elevator door against one wall. Angela pressed the button beside the elevator doors and they opened to reveal an easily accessible coffin lying on a conveyor belt, two feet from the ground, with its lid open on ornamental brass hinges.

"Once the death process has been completed, the body is placed in the coffin by the family, mourners, or our technicians if requested; the body is then transported to either the crematorium or the cemetery. We find this a very efficient way of disposing of the body." Mark was lost for words but also moved to think that this might have been the last place the love of his life had spent her final moments.

"So, to the range of choices," Angela began, as she embarked on her favourite part (she liked lists) of her tour itinerary, "Men tend to select our erotica themes before the others and so we provide for them a range of sex acts including fetish and sadomasochism if desired, with our trained prostitutes who, being qualified social workers, can provide a range of essential services. You are a man, journalist, which sexual fantasy could you see yourself buying into if you chose to die here at the hotel?"

Mark, embarrassed by the forthright question, mumbled, "That is very interesting but please go on and tell me what other choices are on offer."

Angela was surprised by this response, as the men she had tested this question on before had always been enthusiastic about letting her know about their sexual fantasies, some of which, she was led to understand, strangely involved herself.

"If you are more inclined towards religious themes, we have the Jihadi martyr theme, where we use our game consuls linked to the maXiviewalls to help you destroy Crusader armies, who all bear a striking resemblance to a former American

President. Death is induced at the point where seventy-two dark eyed virgins are paraded on the maXiviewalls before your eyes to keep this image clearly in the mind of the client.

We also have a confessional in another of our eXi-theme suites and this is very popular with Catholics, who receive their final confession from a Pope impersonator. As far as Catholics and impersonators go, the Pope is almost as popular as our Elvis impersonator singing '*Crying in the Chapel*' to the supplicant as they drift into death.

Finally, in our religious portfolio, is the Odyssey to the East with our permanent resident guru, Swami Riva. The disciples are issued with orange robes and chant 'om' while sitars evoke the mystical east. The maXiviewalls are filled with imagery of Buddha and Krishna. Sometimes we have to suspend the activities midway through the process as the participants have an irresistible urge to eat a curry before they die. I don't quite understand this, but when they return, they exit very peacefully to the sound of 'oms' accompanied by uncontrollable flatulence. Very peaceful, but the cleaning staff tell me that they do appreciate there has been incense burning during each event.

Our other options include 'Rock Star in Woodstock', where the eXi-theme suite is arranged for the client with the choice of electric guitar, drums or organ. The maXiviewalls come into their own as we project images of the one million adoring Woodstock fans, who are programmed to cheer at the appropriate spots in your performance while chanting the client's name. There are drugs of your choice available to enhance the performance. In our experience, guitar players are very complicated, as it is difficult to get them to stop playing once they start and they always want to go on forever playing extraordinarily long guitar solos. We now offer an option for any relatives in attendance to electrify the guitar player using a specially customised instrument. This option, we have found, is very popular with the relatives of guitar playing clients and significantly speeds up the throughput.

Or, there is 'A Round of Holes in One', using our maXiviewalls and the digitally enhanced golf clubs. This one finishes off nicely with a whisky flavoured suicide potion at the nineteenth hole.

For the ladies, we have a range of choices. The most popular, 'Chocolate and Food Heaven', speaks for itself and 'Forever Young', which calibrates the maXiviewalls to synchronize the reflection of the female client's younger self back to her no matter what angle she sees herself from; very clever use of technology and extremely popular with the older lady.

Other popular choices are 'Counting Your Money', 'Fit and Vibrant' for our younger suicides, and the 'Party to End All Parties', which, for the men, always tends to end up linking to our erotica themes. So, you can see, we have many choices."

Mark had only vaguely heard what Angela was saying at the end of her diatribe. At one level, he had taken in the unique facilities available at the hotel, enough to form a half decent article, but at another level, his proximity to the place where Estrela had died evoked a sadness and guilt that were hard to displace. Angela, for her part, was satisfied that she had fulfilled her task efficiently. Looking at Mark, she interpreted his silence as compliance with her instructions to listen carefully and not waste her time. Mark, however, was deep in thought, focused on his beloved Estrela and how she might have spent her final moments. This was the place where it had been arranged that death would whisper enticements in her ear convincing her of the merits of oblivion and then steal her away from him forever.

Chapter 8 Final Orders

The pious hand in the riddle's glove deviously prays for a brotherly love

The Song of Villadedino, Saint Dino 240AD

Archbishop Romario had put all the finances for the trip to Villadedino in place using the tried and tested method of skimming off the money from the Sunday collections of the good and generous people of Glasgow. To all intents and purposes, it was just a devotional trip by a group of pious pilgrims. Rab laughed to himself when he remembered Malky's reaction to being called pious by the Archbishop.

"I take offence at bein' called a pie," complained Malky in response to the blessing by the Archbishop, "I know I'm a wee bit on the heavy side, but that's just pure cheek, so it is!"

He did calm down once the definition of the word pious was explained to him. However, not sure that he was being told the truth, he was still heard later murmuring something about pies under his breath.

Archbishop Romario had arranged for the explosives necessary to blow up the Hotel Euthanasia to be passed to the Glasgow group by the cell for Retribution and Inquisition in Figas, the country bordering Villadedino. This was to be at a secret rendezvous following their arrival. Rab recalled his final meeting the previous night with Archbishop Romario.

"You'll have a drink of whisky, Rab," the Archbishop said welcoming him. "Here, try this one-hundred-year-old MacShoogle single malt. I understand it to be quite rare."

"Do you mind if I put some of my can of fizzy drink in it, Your Holiness?"

"No problem. I'll have a wee bit from your can myself if that is alright. Sit down, Rab, and we'll get the business matters over with so we can spend some time relaxing together. Here are the tickets for yourself, Malky, Shug, Magdalene, and Rashona for the flight to Villadedino along with your bookings for the rooms. In the duffle bag is enough cash to see you through your 'pilgrimage' and don't be austere with your spending. I am sure the parishioners will be appreciative of your efforts on my ... er, sorry ... their behalf. Right! That's that now settled. The next issue is the tricky matter of getting the explosives. I have arranged for the Cell for Retribution and Inquisition in Figas to supply these to you. You know – Figas, the country bordering Villadedino. You will meet with them at the farmhouse of a Mr Müller. The farm is one mile west of the border, crossing on the main road between Villadedino and Figas. You will be met there by our contact in the Figas Cell for Retribution and Inquisition, Father Marionatta, who has arranged for another person called Sasha to make the transfer of explosives to you. You will say the code words to Sasha, '*July is like a goat with a lot of grass.*' Sasha will answer in response, '*My watch says mid-day.*' You will complete the introductions with, '*I would miss your July apples for a glass of beer.*' Sasha will then pass over the explosives. So, ... simple, eh?"

Rab repeated the secret code words in his mind as he added more fizzy drink to his whisky, while the Archbishop allowed himself a small congratulatory thought, *I just can't wait to see the look on the Pope's face when he hears about how I covertly shaped and consolidated my little band of saints to carry out a most daring act on my own initiative. My integrity will, of course, not allow me any distinction. I will be a reluctant hero with no thought of personal honour on my humble enterprise.*

"Pope Leo Sixtus I is a true saint," Archbishop Romario continued, "He has stopped the rot of modernisation that has plagued the church in the time of Pope Hilarius II and has inspired and spiritually guided the Cells of Retribution and Inquisition that are now starting to bear fruit. These give all of us encouragement. The successes the church has achieved so far, such as the closure of all gay seminaries, excommunication of married priests, and the closure of the casino in the Vatican in the Holy City of Rome, are only the first step. The pin holes we secretly inserted into the production line for the condom industry in Bangladesh means that no one can be sure if they are going to work or not. The same sabotage to introduce flavoured condoms by using red-hot chillies worked well too. Unfortunately, it did backfire in Mexico, where the entire batch was sold out in days once word got out. You can't win them all I guess.

We now need to attack the repugnant and sinful efforts to exploit susceptible innocents who are tricked into succumbing to the sin of euthanasia. We are pleased with the progress made in all countries that have banned euthanasia of any kind, but for some reason we could not persuade Villadedino to follow the guidance of our Holy Father in Rome. They must now pay the price for their iniquity.

We need to continue the good work started in the church. There is nothing like good old-fashioned fear to save the soul. The videos of Hell with the horror of devils whipping and torturing shrieking naked human souls with fire, transmitted to our Catholic Primary School children every morning, along with the viewing of a full and gruesomely detailed crucifixion after lunch, has put the fear of God in these young minds when we need it most and at the impressionable age of five. Parents are complaining about the increasing instances of bed-wetting in their little ones, but they will soon come around to the idea that fear is not only good for the body but is also essential to the edification of the soul.

On top of this, the separation of the sexes at church on a Sunday has helped focus the mind of the congregations and kept them away from impure thoughts; how much more natural for men to mix with men and women to mix with women. The devil has work for idle hands. I particularly like the Vatican's re-introduction of castratos for the choirs. Oh, how their voices soar, filling the soul with heavenly thoughts. I am pleased to tell you that the sackcloth and flagellation marches are gaining popularity and have overcome the slight problems we had with the infiltration by masochists. The beatings inflicted by our Catholic Pretorian Guard unit soon stopped them in their tracks.

My own favourite is the banning of girls from altar

duty. I am pleased to say that we now have an all-boys arrangement. That particularly pleases me. 'Altar girl' just does not sound right, whereas 'altar boy' really trips off the tongue. Give me twenty or so of these altar boys and I will guarantee at least five of them for the priesthood and further services to the Church. So, Rab, I am very pleased that we could relax together and all this talk of altar boys has made me think we should now say a little prayer together ... Oh, I have left my prayer book in my bedroom ... I wonder if you could fetch it for me as I am afraid this whisky has gone to my head some."

"No problem, Your Holiness. Where do I go?"

"It is the room just at the end of the corridor."

Rab ventured off to find the Archbishop's prayer book. During his search for the prayer book in the bedroom, the Archbishop entered announcing, "Rab, silly me, it was by my side all the time. Never mind, since we are here let us just pray as we sit on the side of the bed."

They both sat down and the Archbishop read a prayer from his book while placing his hand on Rab's knee.

Blessed are the knights of the Church and those who serve it,

Bless this knight with whom we will sail together on a sea of blessing,

May we sow the seeds of agape as we join together this night in prayer.

The Archbishop squeezed Rab's knee and continued, "As brothers in the church we must love each other as brothers in arms. Do you wish to be loved as a brother in arms, Rab?"

"I canny wait to get goin'," Rab said enthusiastically, and with this got swiftly up from the bed and headed for the door grabbing the duffle bag with the money and tickets on the way. "Thank you, your Holiness. I won't let you down."

Rab left the Archbishop looking somewhat disappointed as he heard the oblivious but encouraged Rab close the front door behind him. The Archbishop opened the drawer on his bedside table next to his bed and reached in for his book with telephone numbers of priests as he thought to himself, *I wonder who I should call to come around for evening vespers tonight.*

*

Philomena O'Shaughnessy, the eighty-seven-year-old housekeeper for the Archbishop, thought it extremely considerate of the priests who stayed over with the Archbishop at the house. Sharing a bed saved her the bother of making up another bed. It reminded her of her childhood in Ireland, where her four brothers had to share a bed. She was getting old now but prided herself in being able to rise at the crack of dawn, at six in the morning, to prepare and serve a full English breakfast to the Archbishop and the young priests he so conscientiously mentored.

"Just let me know, Your Holiness and Father, if you will want any more bacon or eggs. How about another rasher? Perhaps you would like another wee sausage, Father?"

The Archbishop and the priest thanked Philomena, "I think we have more than sufficient, Philomena."

"Sorry, Your Holiness, what was that you said?"

"Thank you, Philomena. We are very grateful, Philomena, for what we have."

"Ok, I'll just get you some grapefruit then, Your Holiness."

"No, I said grateful, Philomena. Now, you must get on with your work, Philomena, and stop fussing over us," pleaded the Archbishop.

"Well, all right, Your Holiness." And with this, Philomena dragged her old bones off to get on with her first cleaning task of the morning thinking to herself, *now isn't that Father just such a lovely boy and so devoted to His Holiness. He would bend over backwards for him, so he would.*

Chapter 9 The Death of King Eugene II

*As the dance of bears give birth to death the vault of crowns
superfluous*

The Song of Villadedino, Saint Dino 240AD

King Eugene II looked admiringly at himself in the ornate
full-length mirror; or rather he looked at the handsome bear
that stared back at him. This was certainly the best bear suit
yet, made by the Royal tailors and designed to give the King
maximum flexibility for his performance while looking suitably
terrifying. It was just after lunch and the King was in his
dressing room at the royal palace. The occasion he was looking
forward to was the Royal garden party to celebrate Saint Dino's
day in memory of the life of Dino Dormus, the patron saint of
his kingdom, who was celebrated as founder of the Principality
of Villadedino two thousand years earlier, and for his legendary
fight to the death with a ferocious bear. The legend of Saint
Dino and his triumph over the wild bear had become the most
famous tale in Villadedino and, over time, had been embellished,
with the bear becoming increasingly larger and more ferocious
as the story was handed down from one generation to the
next. The king of the day, as custom dictated, was expected
to dress up as the bear to entertain the guests and dignitaries
attending the garden party. King Eugene II was renowned
for his increasingly enthusiastic portrayals of the bear, and it
was now his only source of pride in an increasingly drunken

and morose life, not to mention his affliction of constipation, which was becoming an ever more frequent inconvenience.

The King was progressively losing touch with reality. He was drinking a bottle of whisky each day, interspersed with what was left of the fine wines from the royal cellar. In his more despondent days, he had toyed with the idea of suicide. While one didn't talk of death as such, the subject being far too crude for the dignified discourses of Royalty, there was some traditional precedence to taking one's own life, mainly due to the narrow gene pool available to their exalted rank. The King was ambivalent about undertaking the act and, while his depressed state and reducing funds gave him an incentive to do the dastardly deed, he was, by nature, weak and lacking in the gumption to take that course of action. His ongoing discussions with his son about the Crown Prince's proposals for setting up some sort of business model based on assisted dying had some appeal but was also a source of annoyance to him. While his son's idea had some merit in theory and he was generally supportive, he had difficulty in coming to terms with what he considered to be the 'vulgarity' of an assisted dying scheme open to any Tom, Dick or Harry. The tradition of the Royal families of Europe, which he subscribed to, was that suicide was a much more dignified, private, and individual affair. Money is the problem, he rationalised to himself. *If only my esteemed ancestors had left more 'dosh in the kitty', then the country and myself would not be in this predicament.* He had gone, begging bowl in hand, to the rest of the Royal households in Europe and had used up any good will he, his family and his country still had left.

The proposal his son, Crown Prince Eugene, had been promoting for some sort of 'death hotel' surfaced again for an instant. *It is just not tradition*, he reassured himself. *It just makes me so sad to think about this bitter decline in our fortunes*, he thought as he poured another glass of reviving whisky and steadied himself in front of the mirror again. The sight of the familiar tradition of himself in the bear suit, along with the temporary effect of the whisky, were giving him some slight respite from his depressed and suicidal thoughts.

His mind drifted as he surveyed the bear in the mirror, like the King himself, a Regal symbol that graced the flag of Villadedino. He imagined the inner thoughts of the original bear that had fought with Saint Dino and was now nobly represented on the Royal Standard. The King evaluated himself against it: *that bear was strong, but deep down I know I am weak; that bear had power to control his territory, mine is now all but gone; that bear had superiority over all other creatures, while my status has now reduced to mediocre insignificance; that bear cultivated the riches of the forest whereas all that is left to me is poverty*; and finally thoughts of the loss of that bear's life at the hands of Dino Dormus prompted the King to subconsciously associate this as a foretaste of his own demise. The King shed a silent tear, that rolled pitifully down the inside of his mask, the product of his hopelessness regarding the finances, the randomness of death of St Dino's bear and the inevitability of his own mortality.

His thoughts brightened grudgingly, his mood swinging back, as it did uncontrollably these days, returning to happy thoughts of his anticipated upcoming performance: how he would enter the garden party to the cheers of the gathered crowd; the expectations of the children and their mothers feigning terror to incite their offspring to snuggle closer for protection; and, most of all, his newest trick, which was to enter on his bicycle roaring like a bear through a megaphone. He laughed out loud at the thought of it and, with another glass of whisky, was content to put his financial woes, suicidal thoughts and his son's assisted dying scheme to the back of his mind for the time being.

Before encasing his head within the giant growling bear mask and zipping together the bottom and top halves of his costume, and following some deliberation about whether he would try one more time to evacuate his bowels to avoid any interruption to his performance, the king made his way to the Royal bathroom. After five non-productive minutes, he stood up, stamped to get the blood flowing back into his legs again, and reconciled to leave for the garden party where all of the royal household were already in attendance along with the invited dignitaries from across the Principality; of course, not before downing another couple of whiskies. So, King Eugene II, suitably inebriated and wearing his most excellently fashioned bear suit, set off on his bicycle with another bottle of whisky placed, for Dutch courage, in the basket.

*

Meanwhile, at the 'World Famous Most Fabuloso Circus', which was encamped close to King Eugene's palace grounds, Bern, the performing bear, was being led back to his cage by his trainer Pedro. Bern had been put through his paces by Pedro and was looking forward to sharing a couple of drinks with his trainer. Pedro had become accustomed to the bear and the bear to his trainer. Their friendship was cemented through their mutual attraction to beer and whisky. Pedro was well known as a drunk by the owner of the circus but as long as he was getting the performances from Bern that attracted the crowds then this was glossed over. The audiences loved Bern's act, particularly his drunken man impersonations, which in fact bore more of a resemblance to reality than fabrication. Pedro had trained Bern to drink beer and whisky and ride a bicycle, to dance and act drunk … which Bern was most of the time anyway.

Pedro had been drinking all morning and was feeling drowsy after his rehearsal with Bern. They made their way to the sizeable tent where some of the circus equipment, along with Bern's cage, was located. When they both reached the cage, Pedro gave Bern a bottle of beer and ushered him inside and, forgetting to lock the door, sat down for a much-deserved rest. It wasn't long before he had drifted off, enjoying a dream that centred on the lovely Delilah, the trapeze artist, gracefully performing high aerial swings in her alluring gossamer body suit and bestowing on him the most endearing smile.

Bern quickly swilled back his beer and settled down to examine the contents of the tent outside the cage. His eyes focused past the sleeping Pedro on the pleasing sight of more bottles of beer temptingly displayed outside the cage. Half in hope, he pushed the cage door and opportunely, discovering that his door was indeed open, proceeded to exit his cage and finish off the four bottles of beer that had been left there by Pedro, so generously albeit inadvertently. Bern now had the taste for alcohol and, although happy to imbibe, was disappointed that the four bottles had been exhausted. After an unproductive few minutes examining the tent for the possibility of another bottle of beer, Bern wandered off amiably in search of additional alcoholic beverage, filled with the hopes that only a circus bear that has drunk five bottles of beer can have.

*

King Eugene II mounted his bicycle with a great deal of difficulty, partly due to all the padding of the bear costume that encased him, but mainly from the effect of the alcohol blurring his vision while attempting to keep his eyes focused through the eyeholes of the bear mask manufactured by the Royal tailors. However, with some assistance from his personal manservant, he got up on the saddle and finally pushed off with a bottle of whisky in the front basket, pedalling in an uncoordinated fashion and zig-zagging down the path leading from the royal palace to the garden party. He had not even cycled half way down the road when a sudden and imperious pain gripped his stomach like a belligerent foe and, with the inescapable urge to empty his bowels, he dismounted his bike … or rather tumbled off it … and resigned himself to the fact that he would have to delay his entry to the garden party in order to relieve himself of nature's call. Once off the bike and realising that at least it was an opportunity to be rid of his oppressive constipation, particularly before his performance, he parked his bicycle beside a bush and, moving behind the shrubbery, proceeded to remove the lower half of his bear suit and squat in as kingly a way possible to expel his royal excrement.

As it happened, Bern, the bear from the circus, was wandering by this self-same spot on his search for more alcoholic refreshment and seeing the bicycle with the whisky bottle jutting out of the top of the basket he proceeded, naturally, to help himself to both and swigging from the whisky bottle, he happily rode away on the king's bicycle unbeknown to his esteemed highness straining royally behind the bush.

*

Pedro, Bern's trainer, awoke suddenly from his dream just as the lovely Delilah fell from her trapeze into a swimming pool filled with crocodiles, while at the same time, in the way we know that dreams acquiesce, Herman the Human Cannonball hit him squarely in his groin with the full force of his crash helmet after being shot from a cannon. A sharp intake of breath thus stirred Pedro from his sleep. Disorientated but grateful for the reality that it was only a dull ache in his head from the drink rather than Herman the Human Cannonball, Pedro sat up and turned to say something to Bern the bear. The fogginess of his sleep lifted sharply and the situation became instantly crystal clear in his mind with the discovery that there was no Bern, the cage door was open, and the bear and beer were gone. After calling out for Bern and furtively searching the inside of the tent,

Pedro ran to the circus boss's caravan to raise the alarm that a bear was on the loose!

Pedro's boss was nothing if not pragmatic and, although he knew Bern to be an amiable bear, he decided on a course of action that he considered would provide the optimum means of mitigating the risk of Bern lunching on a hapless human being. Much to Pedro's dismay, his boss barked out an order that dispatched a marksman to find and shoot the missing bear.

*

King Eugene II was oblivious to what was happening on the other side of the bush, so intent was he on his exertions. From his place behind the hedge there issued grunts, groans, girns, and bellows. The King, sensing victory was at hand, made one final roar of encouragement that vanquished the enemy resulting ... at last ... in glorious success!

Meanwhile, the marksman, having scoured the area around the circus tents, caravans, and cages, had moved his search towards the Royal grounds. Alerted by strange noises some distance away that he deduced were coming from the bear, he moved nervously closer to the sound and peering eagerly caught a glimpse of the top of the bear's head poking above the bush. From the growls that were now audible, his mind worked overtime to construct the scene in front of him. He interpreted the animal noises filling the air as coming from a bear engorged in the process of tearing some luckless human limb from limb and feeding on the flesh. He started to sweat as an uncontrollable fear coiled up his spine. Now shaking with terror, he crept forward as close as he dared go, took careless aim, and fired his gun while at the same time turning on his heels in case the bullet missed, and fled. His imagination was unhelpfully fabricating the image of a ferocious and now angry bear emerging with a roar from the bush to chase and attack him. He did not look back and ran for his life as a loud bellow emanated from the bush.

The bullet had passed through the bear's mask and grazed the Royal temple, dazing the King, who staggered from behind the hedge with the bottom half his costume abandoned at the side of the bush, and teetered down the road in the unconscious stupor of a somnambulist.

*

Bern the bear was as happy as a circus bear on a bicycle with a bottle of whisky could be as he entered the perimeter of the garden party setting arranged for King Eugene's performance and the awaiting audience of the fine aristocracy and citizens of Villadedino. As he had been taught by Pedro, he waved his paw in the air when he heard the loud cheers from the onlookers, just as he would do in his circus act. The whisky was going to his head and he was enthralled by his good fortune. Warming to the crowd, Bern the circus bear moved automatically into performance mode.

The audience collectively thought the King had really outdone himself this year and his bear suit was, by far, the most authentic they had ever seen. They cheered at each of the king's tricks and small children pushed closer to their mothers, who feigned terror at the proximity of such a wild creature.

Bern, spurred on by the adulation of the crowd, set to delivering his finale. This involved one foot on the saddle and a leg out behind like a ballet dancer, continuing with a jump from the bicycle, and finishing with a drunken dance ... more effective today as a consequence of finishing the bottle of whisky. Any conflict between Bern's animal nature and what he had been trained to do was long gone as dancing a jig, he milked the rapturous applause. He was in ecstasy. But, suddenly, he became aware of a change in the atmosphere all around him. As if in coordinated unison, and with expertly executed timing, there emanated from the crowd an instantaneous wall of ... Silence!

King Eugene II had waddled into the scene dazed and disorientated, wearing the bear mask, dressed only with the top half of a bear costume, and sporting bare (and not bear) Royal hindquarters.

The crowd, who had been enjoying what they thought was a splendid performance by the King, now fell into a shocked silence, trying to make sense of what their disbelieving eyes could see but which did not compute with their brains. Mothers, fearing lifelong trauma for their offspring, were starting to divert their children's eyes from the scene, when there was a loud bang.

The marksman, after regaining his courage, had returned to the bush and, realising that he must have missed the bear, had then continued on to the garden party in search of the dangerous animal. He arrived in time to see the spectacle that had unfolded and was as confused by the scene as much as the audience; but, with his returning fortitude, he fired a shot into the air.

Bern, on becoming aware firstly, of the 'wall of silence'; and then, secondly, of the loud shot, stopped his dance, turned around, and, through drunken eyes, fixed his focus on the King. The King, still dazed by the first bullet to his head, was jolted into wakefulness from the crack of the shot and, on seeing a bear in front of him, the shock immediately stimulated a sudden flow of adrenalin through his bloodstream, bringing his mind sharply into focus.

One small boy cheered enthusiastically in response to the spectacle but was quickly quietened by his mother.

Bern, through his drunken haze, did not see the King, but another bear. Not just any bear, but the most beautiful bear he had ever seen. Given he had not seen any bear for ten years, he did not really have much to compare it with but still, drunken bears, like beggars, cannot be choosers. Today, things really had taken a turn for the better: the beer, the bicycle, then the whisky, and then the adulation of the crowd. Just when he thought it couldn't get any better, in front of him arrives an attractive alluring female bear. Rising to the surface came waves of ardour as Bern's true nature broke through the years of enforced sexual abstinence.

With his excitement running high following all of the adoring adulation from his performance and with the effects of the whisky affording him abandonment from his human environment, Bern only had one thing on his mind. His whole being compelled him towards this beautiful female bear and

107

to embrace his mating instinct. King Eugene II, before he could figure out what was going through the mind of the bear in front of him, was caught in a loving embrace by Bern with all the intensity of a lover who has not seen his beloved for ten years, only to be thrown together by chance.

Someone had switched on the music as a form of distraction for the crowd. Appropriately, but unfortunately, it was playing the world-wide dance hit 'Bear Hug', sung by Bernadette and the Bears, as the lyrics blared across the sound system ...

> *'I wanna love you on a bearskin rug*
> *I wanna give you a big bear hug*
> *Hug, hug, hug*
> *On a bear skin rug.'*

The marksman now put two and two together, taking cognisance of the setting of the Royal garden party and the half-dressed bear, and realised that it was, in fact, the King who was now being, as he assessed, mauled by the bear. This time, the marksman had to take proper control of his emotions and save the King; after all, there was an audience. No mistakes! He took aim and fired a shot that this time flew accurately through the air and burst the passionate heart of the ill-fated but sexually fulfilled Bern. However, the bullet unfortunately then continued its cursed journey to pass through the hapless skull of King Eugene II. Lamentably, the marksman had managed to kill both Bern and the King. As the last vestiges of what had been the King surveyed the scene from above, a few notions occurred to him: disappointment that all this 'ballyhoo' had somewhat spoiled his traditional performance that he had so much been looking forward to; that his outmoded life, like his performing bear act had been one big sham; and finally, that death, with its heightened sense of reality that he was now experiencing, might well have been a worthwhile enterprise to cultivate with his son.

*

There was no time for bereavement, as Crown Prince Eugene enthusiastically made an immediate start to his plan. How convenient and timeous his father's death had been. He convened an emergency meeting of the, still in shock, Royal Family precisely one hour after King Eugene II had been declared dead by the Royal physician. Crown Prince Eugene, who had just five minutes before the meeting been sworn in as the new King Eugene III, made clear to the Royal Family the financial predicament the country was in. The late King, he explained, had drunk all that was left in the Royal coffers. The new King read out the last will and testament, which sounded like more of an apology than a will.

"I leave you, my beloved family, all my cherished country and palaces herein along with all my goodwill," declared King Eugene III to a background of sobs from the Queen and Princesses.

The new King continued, "I have no need to tell you that our state of affairs is indeed a catastrophe and action needs to be taken or we and the Principality will be declared bankrupt. All of us will have to move out of the palace. It is likely that we will also have to take up gainful employment which, given the princesses' lack of qualifications, will see you waiting tables or labouring in the fields."

More sobs heaved uncontrollably from the distressed princesses. "As well as all this, you can guess what kind of publicity Villadedino will receive. You will be a laughing stock among the aristocracy of Europe. Villadedino is only a tiny sovereign Principality in an area of 2.8 square miles and with a population of 26,000 people. Economic development and tourism have dried up and we have fallen out of favour with the rest of the aristocracy of Europe." King Eugene III knew that he had to be direct in order to extract even the barest chance that the family could survive this crisis. "So, I will now advise you all of my strategic plan to save our Principality and your Royal status."

The newly appointed King Eugene III was indeed ready for this eventuality. He was now in his fortieth year and had prepared himself thoroughly for the time he would take over the throne. The new King had received a Doctorate in Economics from the University of Glasgow, having spent his student days in the beautiful land of New Scotland, famous for its education, social policies, and progressive industries. He was, therefore, well aware of the financial problems of the Principality and had been for some time. Unfortunately, he had been frustratingly impotent in obtaining the 'green light' from his drunken father, the deceased former King. Now was his moment to finally execute the plan that he had been proposing, in vain, to his father for all these years. He had more recently received some concessions around support for assisted dying, in theory, from his father, probably brought on by the King's depression and suicidal thoughts. The sticking point though had been his father's stubborn attachment to tradition. Now was the time for the new King Eugene III to act and he rose to the occasion as he outlined his proposals to his grieving family.

"We are a small but uniquely placed Principality, both in terms of our autonomy and our opportunities. I am sorry to say that our father and your husband, mother, was a drunken depressive who was not up to the job. I have been considering our future for some time now. Due to the events of today, I am in a position to finally take action. You will have been aware that instead of living the sheltered life that you all chose to follow, I pursued a course of academic study and for this, even if you did not understand it, you will now be forever grateful. While undertaking my doctorate, which started with the research question of resolving how to deal with both the growth in older people and the lack of burial space in our small Principality, during my research, I stumbled across the economics of the industry of assisted dying."

This discourse was going over the heads of the grieving family, who had lived a privileged existence, had never done a day's work in their lives and had found it too tedious to be bothered with pursuing any higher edification from learning. The truth of the matter was that there was a certain amount of inbreeding within the Royal families of Europe and this, combined with their sedentary lifestyle, had resulted in a regressive and weakened debility in the esteemed but useless aristocratic classes. Unbeknown to Eugene III, the new King, he was the result of an unplanned addition to the Royal gene pool that followed an impulsive passionate encounter borne out of frustration by the recently married bride of an impotent drunken king husband. The handsome palace gardener had been taken completely by surprise by the pent-up ardour of his employer's new bride as he considered an alternative horizontal view of the orchid's display from the floor of the castle's hothouse. And so, the result was Crown Prince Eugene, the now King, who had an insatiable appetite for learning and cultivating (his gardener father would have been proud) his mind, which had now developed the kernel of an idea into a fully flowered plan.

"We are going to turn the old hotel into a centre for assisted dying."

The Queen and the Royal Princesses looked at King Eugene III with surprise and confusion. *Had he gone mad? What was he saying? What is this afflicted dying he is talking about?*

"This goes against tradition," said the Queen, trying her best to behave regally and repeating a phrase she had vaguely heard her husband uttering in relation to some new venture their son had been proposing. "We have never been involved in anything like this. I cannot understand why you are talking about this when my beloved husband has just suffered a most cruel end. Why are you upsetting us with all this talk of poverty and afflicted dying?"

"Let me explain it in terms you will understand. We will charge each guest who comes to the hotel $100,000 to undertake the procedure and we will earn $1 billion per year. You will be able to live a life of luxury and indulge yourselves in anything you desire. The alternative will be, at best, becoming dish washers in some god forsaken kitchen somewhere."

The Queen's and the Royal Princesses' minds panicked at the thought of washing a dish and glazed over at the numbers. But, the frosty cloud in their minds managed to thaw with the heart-warming words … '*life of luxury and indulge … anything … desire*'. Had they been cartoon characters, their eyes would have started to roll round like slot machine displays and then stop on the big dollar sign with the word 'JACKPOT' printed underneath. Having won over his family without too much challenge, the new King knew he would have a harder test – to convince the parliamentarians of Villadedino.

*

King Eugene III presented his new draft legislation, 'Conduct of Assisted Dying Act', to a hushed Villadedino Parliamentary chamber two weeks later. The constitution of the Principality meant that the King was invested with overall power but, over time, this had been diluted because of the inability of previous Royal incumbents. A strong democratic ethos had also grown as a result of the size of the Principality, where the population saw a direct connection between their wishes and the representation and laws developed by their Parliament. This due process was the environment in which the new King had to present his plans and he would have to marshal all his wits and influence to convince the Parliament Members. There were three main parties in the Parliament. The Socialists Left Wing Party, who were in actual fact more to the right than the centre, the

Conservative Right Wing Party, who were far to the right and held with tradition, and the Democratic Centre Party, whose position was considered by the other two parties to be mainly located up their own self-serving backsides. There were adversaries to the plan from all sides based on self-interest, including the Church and Physicians, who held complete influence with the Right Wing Party, and the Left Wing Party, whose members were philosophically opposed to anything involving the Royal family. The new King did have the support of a campaigning environmental group, who had been fighting for the law to be changed to facilitate the right to choose assisted dying. He had sought their advice while undertaking his doctorate and been convinced of the moral and philosophical arguments as well as the economic ones.

The plan was debated in Parliament and nearly everyone agreed that something needed to be done about the economic woes of the Principality. There had been a run on the National Bank of Villadedino and it was more than an inconvenient truth that the coffers were empty and that depositors were queuing outside the banks to withdraw the savings they had previously thought to be safe there. Despite this, there were the expected impassioned speeches by aged Right Wing members who cited the 'sanctity of life' and that it was a 'slippery slope' that would soon see themselves as an older vulnerable group being pressurised and shunted off to leave space for the next generation. There was much talk of God's will and how sacred each human life was. A further argument by the Socialist Left Wing held that the proposed legislation was more about profit than principles. This point of detail had the unintended consequence of alerting some of the Right Wing with money to invest. Thereafter, they took an unedifying interest in the economic outlines being tabled.

'*What about people like us?*' cried the throngs of people with disabilities, who lobbied outside Parliament with placards and mock coffins. The Left Wing Party argued their case strongly, recommending that there should be safeguards against devaluing the lives of people with disability, prompting King Eugene III to add his 'Competent Adult Test'.

The new King Eugene III had anticipated all of these arguments, having studied them intensely at university and having been advised by the 'dignity in dying' group that had been campaigning to change the law. He had prepared in the years of his father's mismanagement of the Principality for this event and he skilfully, authoritively, and articulately took the argument to the Parliamentarians. His main allies were those from the left and centre parties along with both the 'dignity in dying' and 'humanist and atheistic' lobby, who had long been advocates for assisted dying, and presented a rational and sophisticated understanding of the issues.

The King promoted the moral and reasoned arguments that people should die with dignity rather than be at the mercy of the ignominy, pain, and suffering of complex multiple conditions. The focus of his argument started initially with those who had terminal conditions. In this he had to counter the physicians who took up their positions on the high moral ground of their Hippocratic oath. In reality, this had more to do with

115

reservations that they would be out of work if there were no ill people who needed their clinical care. The physicians had fervently lobbied the Right Wing Party to argue, from an ethical position, the personal difficulty for them, where they would have to be the individuals who would assist people to die. Meanwhile, their private conversations were more about the side on which their bread was buttered and that much more money was to be made out of supporting people with palliative care. Until they could be convinced about the profit in assisted dying, they were set against the whole thing. They also had a nervousness that, despite a change in the law, the first physician to undertake the initial assisted dying procedure ran the risk of finding himself or herself behind bars. And so it went on, the lobbying from interested groupings and unholy alliances.

Over the period of debate, some of the futile examples of people who had tried to take their own lives were cited, where the outcome would have been better had there been an assisted dying service in place with the accompanying guidance and technical support of skilled facilitators: the poor man who had taken what he thought was an overdose of sleeping tablets, only to discover in the most dramatic fashion that he had overdosed on laxatives; the troubled young man who had shot himself in the foot while loading the rifle that was to end his life; the depressed housewife whose husband came home to find her unconscious but still alive following her efforts to poison herself with carbon monoxide by leaving the petrol driven lawn mower to run in the garage; and, finally, the person with mental health problems who, abandoning his medication, felt compelled to end his life in the lion's cage at the zoo. In this last case, however, the lion was a very friendly, docile creature who had just been fed twenty minutes before, so that his entry to the lion's den ended with no more than a bored and sated lion yawning lazily through the whole episode.

The Democratic Party brought forward a list of experts who tended to disagree with each other and thereby undermined any influence the Party had.

The Centre Party argued that people may not be in a fit state of mind to make a competent decision and they would choose badly if given the choice. Various circumstances were aired, including: people with depression, who might only need better medication; people at the end of life who cannot make an informed decision, with relatives having to make the decision for them; and misdiagnosis by medical professionals. But, countering these arguments came through descriptions of the existing practice allowing relatives and professionals to make decisions about switching off life support machines, which were used to good effect.

There was discussion about active self-termination of life, with people physically able to carry out the act, and passive termination, in which severely disabled people had to find family assistance or professional service to help them by carrying out their decision, that usually hit barriers to their self-determination. Questions about justice and fairness were raised and considered.

Over days of debate, the argument for a compassionate view to prevent needless suffering was building consensus across the Parliament. One crucial tactic by the 'dying with dignity and pro assisted dying' lobby had been to carry out a detailed survey of people who had been diagnosed as being in a terminally ill state. The key question asked of the participants was '*if the law allowed it, would you like to have the choice to take your own life rather than suffer pain and suffering?*' Ninety percent of those surveyed responded in the affirmative. This provided a solid basis for the pro assisted dying campaign.

The new law was drafted to reassure physicians that they would not be criminalised for assisting people to die. The King argued convincingly that it removed, for all time, any uncertainty in the law for physicians, allied health personnel, family, and friends acting honestly and with integrity in assisting people to make a clear choice to die.

With the moral and professional argument having been well defended, or in fact won by the King and his pro assisted dying campaign, it was the economic argument that put the final nail, so to speak, in the coffin. A financial working group had validated the King's initial economic findings that there was a market for assisted dying and that it had the potential to attract a worldwide clientele. In fact, the general resistance by other governments to assisted dying meant that this could virtually be a monopoly for Villadedino. The figures had been tested and the findings identified that affluent people would be willing to pay $100,000 for the privilege of being assisted to die and, if the business model was made even more attractive, there was virtually no end to the demand for the service. The number of rooms at the old hotel meant that this would bring in a billion dollars each year to the small Principality.

Physicians suddenly changed their stance when it became known that they would require to formally register every death and that a $500 fee was expected as recompense for their skills. Overnight, palliative care ceased to be the top priority of the physicians. There were a number of other compromises that the King had prepared for, including the need for informed consent to be validated by a qualified physician. He saw this as another money-spinning opportunity and he planned to sell the rights to this registration of consent to all physicians who wished to pay the fee.

However, the Right Wing and the Church were still to be convinced. The role of the King was a particularly difficult dilemma for the Church as it balanced the sanctity of life with the divine right of Kings. As God himself had appointed King Eugene III, then, if he was an advocate of assisted dying, they had to be pragmatic and come to terms with the proposal. '*One has to acknowledge the proper order of things and submit to those one should look up to.*' It helped that new church buildings would be required to be built in the Principality and more priests would need to be recruited to apply the last rites to accommodate the visiting guests who were making the pilgrimage to end their lives.

The Right Wing Party activists who decided to come over to the King's view were also to be repaid in the time-honoured manner available to Kings throughout history and he was happy to promise, during individual meetings behind closed doors with key protagonists, exalted positions, knighthoods, and honours for compliance.

One final compromise had to be put in place and this from an unusual source. It was the Left Wing Party, who campaigned that there should be a proportion of places be made available to assist people who could not afford the process but who had a debilitating complex condition with the associated pain and suffering. The King promised to introduced an assisted scheme for people who could not afford the fees.

The vote was taken and due democratic process came to pass. The announcement was made to the world media, that had been following the story. Drafted by Villadedino Premier Consulting, the country's leading public relations agency, the statement said: "Today, the new monarch of Villadedino, King Eugene III, is proud to inform the world that his government is now offering the investment opportunity of a lifetime – shares in a new enterprise within this beloved Principality, which will provide an essential service that is not available elsewhere in the world. We will provide the best assisted dying that money can buy. We are today looking for serious investors with capital to finance our planned assisted suicide activities and a portfolio is available for your deliberations. To all you who are tired of life, come to Villadedino to die. To all of you who want their money to grow, invest it here. You will all be welcome!"

*

Within two years from the law being passed, Villadedino had successfully established itself as the number one destination in the world for assisted suicide. There had been a stampede of investors who recognised, like King Eugene III, the potential financial rewards from the concept of exploiting an autonomous Principality with its own laws that could have a monopoly on death; an outstanding enterprise that brought together both the opportunity with the available resources. There were also some surprise investors in the enterprise, including a powerful investment group from within the City of Rome – but information about that particular investment could only be found in the small print on page 87 of a financial report under the name of an obscure trust fund, managed in a tax haven through an offshore account.

Chapter 10 Contents of a Suitcase for Travel Can Tell You a Lot About a Person

Contained within provides the clue that reveals a deathly hue

The Song of Villadedino, Saint Dino 240AD

Rab was a minimalist in his packing, much in alignment with a personality that had been honed in the image of the Communist Party by his parents. He was not one for excess or frivolity and this was in keeping with his whole life, where private property and gross materialism were considered an anathema in his household. Brought up in a strict family setting where both parents were signed up members of the Communist Party, a practical, utilitarian austerity had been drummed into him. There were no presents at birthdays or Christmas, no holidays, no pocket money for Rab as a child, and only the bare minimum of furniture in the family's modest functional apartment. This avoided the perils, as his parents saw them, of acquiring material private interests. Their propaganda preached that all things had to be sacrificed for the party, even your own body; what good is a body other than to work for the Party. His parents made a virtue of poverty and all things beyond the most basic living expenses were donated to the Party. Since it was the Communist Party in Glasgow, the proceeds of their labour were mostly used for such egalitarian essentials as stocking up alcohol for the drinks cabinet of the Communist Club and days out to the people's game, 'fitba'. Rab's father, Vincent Lennon, had been enthralled by the teachings of Vladimir Ilyich Lenin, who, he had once erroneously thought, was his namesake. When he finally realised the spelling of 'Lenin' was not the same as his own 'Lennon' and it couldn't even be a distant relative, he still adapted his association to take pride in having the same VL initials. He took guilty pleasure in the personal satisfaction when his comrades raised their glasses with a call for 'A toast to Lenin'.

Rab had made the transition from Communist to Catholic around the time of his twenty-second birthday, at the time of the Rise to the Papal Crown of Pope Leo Sixtus I. Rab made this move, to a large degree, as a reaction to the assisted suicide of his parents and because of the revelations he had been forced to acknowledge about the true values of the Communist Party. He was fuming, because the Party had, in essence, convinced his parents to undergo assisted suicide through a relentless campaign, through which they were persuaded that they were more interested in their own personal aggrandisements than that of the common good and made to feel ashamed of indulging themselves in selfish materialism. The Party succeeded in their appeal to his parents' ideals concerning the proletarian struggle and wheedled their pensions out of them by convincing the couple to take a one-way ticket to Villadedino and indulge in assisted suicide instead of capitalist ownership. It had been a difficult time for Rab and the Catholic Church had come to his rescue, offering him an alternative 'institution' that he could attach himself to, according to the dictates of both his upbringing and his nature. There was in his mind a resonance between the pontification of the pontiff and his own need for order and surrender to a higher ideal. The fact that the Pope's values were based on fascist totalitarianism and Rab's own on socialist totalitarianism only enhanced the harmonisation between his needs now and that of the Catholic revisionism of the time. The crusade, 'Make the Catholic Church Ornate Again', to take back the Catholic Church from the liberations and freedoms of Pope Hilarius II's reign provided Rab with the focus for his intellectual leanings and zeal bordering on fanaticism to be a foot soldier of the Inquisition Revolution. This, on top of his work as a community activist for the local government and his Trade Union shop steward role, made him the ideal leader of others. His conversion from campaigning for assisted dying to hating anything to do with the Hotel Euthanasia meant that he had now become, like a reformed smoker, assisted dying's biggest critic. He could rouse an audience with a charismatic fervor and energy that saw him quickly rise through the ranks of the congregation and become leader of one of the cells for Inquisition and Retribution. Now, he was able to bring together the disappointment of his parent's assisted suicides, his lust for revenge on the Hotel Euthanasia for facilitating this and his revolutionary zeal on behalf of the new world order envisaged by Pope Leo Sixtus I with a clear focused objective to destroy the very same Hotel Euthanasia that had profited from the demise of his parents. The one contradiction and irony of the situation was that he had been an advocate of assisted suicide before this and, perversely, this had been used by his parents to ease their conscience for leaving Rab in the dark about their intentions. Now, Rab's guilty feeling and passion for revenge had, in effect, overridden his reasoned position, resulting in a heightened emotional response and in a complete reversal in his views.

Looking around at his sparse studio apartment, Rab completed his packing. His last girlfriend had moved out three months ago and he was on his own again. She had said she found it difficult to live with someone who was always focused on his campaigns and not on her. It had come to a head when she wanted to buy a leather couch. He had refused. He had said that there was nothing wrong with the one he had inherited from his grandparents, even though it had seen better days and was over forty years old. He reflected that he was hard to live with and acknowledged that his 'all or nothing' nature, simple needs and the fermenting anger bubbling away never far from the surface for revenge against the Hotel Euthanasia could be challenging for any human being to understand. While close relationships were difficult, possibly due to the lack of an emotional connection between Rab and his Communist parents, his nature still made him likeable. Even the things he said that he later recognised as lacking in sophistication and could seem to be quite stupid and regrettable, made him endearing to those who knew him. It was his genuine humanity that shone through; he was an authoritative leader with the power to convince people, never hiding behind charisma or authoritarianism. These characteristics flashed, like the burnished metal of the fiery sword, which he obsessively polished for his lofty assignment to cut through the heart of Villadedino.

The content of a man's suitcase for travel tells you a lot about him and this was no less true for Rab. He carefully packed his shamrock-covered underwear and black socks, his T-shirts in various colours but with the same screen-print on each of them of the face of Pope Leo Sixtus I superimposed on the iconic image of Che Guevara. A spare pair of retro jeans, toothpaste, toothbrush, shaving gear, and the complete writings of Pope Leo Sixtus I running to five volumes, entitled 'An Inquisition for Today', completed the items he packed in his case.

*

The same singleness of mind could not be said of his recruit Malky. At the point where he could not put off any further the necessity to pack his holdall, he suddenly realised that all his clothes were in his 'washing basket'. 'Washing basket' is taking the definition a bit too far, as in this case the washing basket consisted of the pile of dirty clothes lying on the floor of his bedroom where he had last stepped out of them. This had been one of the many faults that eventually led to his ex-wife walking out. A visitor might consider the congealed socks – the sweat hardened into a representation of one of the invisible man's feet – as a piece worthy of a conceptual artist. *Oh, well*, he thought to himself, *I will just have to try and wash them when I'm at the hotel*, as he crushed a range of odorous garments haphazardly into his holdall. Of course, he forgot any toiletries, as he was still seething about the reference to himself and his brothers in arms as 'pies'. He could not get his head around why everybody else thought this was okay. It just made him mad!

Despite his detestations of the 'pie' comparison, Malky was in fact considerably overweight and, ironically, this was largely due to the number of pies he consumed in a day. No matter what Malky did to improve his appearance, he always looked scruffy and unkempt, as if he had just put clothes on straight from the tumble drier without ironing anything. Okay, so this was what he actually did but *hey ho, nobody is perfect*. He had increased his bathing from once per month to once per week and had recently discovered the esoteric art of washing his neck. This was only after the cheeky reference to the line of dirt that stopped midway round his neck as a 'tide mark' by the last girl he had tried to chat up at the pub. His initial solution, until he discovered the secret of washing his neck, was not to wash his face at all so that the colour of his face matched his neck.

Malky's recent conversion to Catholicism was also troubling him. He couldn't quite figure out how that had happened. He had been going to what he had thought was a support group meeting for anger management problems. This was part of his suspended sentence for getting into a fight with that 'wanker' in the pub. *The wanker should not have been looking at me that way and deserved to get a good kicking.* Malky recreated the incident in his head, when this guy had bumped into him – and it had gone on from there:

> Other guy: *Sorry about that, chum.*
> Malky: *Are you talkin' to me or chewin' a brick, pal?*
> (Other guy staring at Malky wth some verbaL
> incomprehension.)

127

Malky: *An' now, who exactly do ye' think yur lookin' at?*

Other guy: *Sorry, mate, I didn't mean to rattle your cage.*

Malky: *Rattle ma fuckin' cage ... are you callin' me a fuckin' monkey?*

Other guy: *I suppose we are all simians, mate.*

Malky: *And noo, you are callin' me a simpleton. That's it, ya fuckin' wanker.*

Malky shadow-boxed the right uppercut he had landed to the chin of the unfortunate paediatrician who had picked the wrong bar on the wrong night and standing next to the wrong person to have a drink after a hard day's work. Malky reflected that the wanker deserved it anyway, as he had heard the term 'paediatrician' at the court and felt a sense of pride that he had given a good kickin' to a child molester.

Malky sniffed his holdall, grimaced, and recoiled from the rancid smell. He proceeded to fetch his spray deodorant with the picture of the wildebeest on the label saying 'Essence of Serengeti'. Well, it had been going cheap at the local 'Cheap as Chips' shop. *That should do it*, he thought as he sprayed the contents of his holdall with what smelled like the sweat of every living creature of Africa and congratulated himself on his enlightened advancement of his sartorial attire. Or in his own words, *that's got rid of the mingin' honk from my kit*.

He then focused on the subject of the mission. He had realised only after two meetings that the group was not the anger management support group he had been advised to join but a *pure mad, lawless group intent on pure blowin' up somethin'*. He liked the way Rab got *pure dead mental when he was talkin' and the wee catchy song aboot Mary wasn't bad either,* although he didn't like the reference to poofters in it. He reflected that the association with Rab had been good for him. *It has calmed me down.* While Malky had a tendency towards aggression, once he got to be close to someone, he was extremely loyal. If anything, his aggression had been a survival instinct developed in the rough neighbourhoods, tough schools, children's homes, and the 'Short Sharp Shock Camps' of his childhood.

Malky did have trouble with all the talk of death. He liked to have a good laugh and he found all the discussions about death boring. *I can see how you would want to kill yourself if you are old and decrepit, but I can't understand why people want to go and kill themselves if they are fit and able. What are these people thinkin' about?* Malky had looked death in the face only once and survived. He had not been scared of it but rather treated it like an officious teacher who had caught him smoking behind the bike sheds. His near-death experience involved an incident with a guy he challenged to a fight, who unexpectedly pulled a samurai sword from the inner lining of his duffle coat. *This is it,* he recalled as his short life flashed in front of his eyes. The extent of the life in question consisted of a few memorable Christmases; scoring a goal for the school football team; the face of his ex-wife walking out the door; and waves of endless disappointments with job interviews, football results, and hangovers. It was his quick thinking that had him placing a strategic kick to his assailant's groin and neutralising the weapon by pulling the duffle coat down to trap his enemy's arms. Needless to say, the other guy ended up in hospital as Malky turned to look admiringly at the samurai sword taking pride of place above the cheap woodchip, circa 1968, electric fire surround in his flat. The thought of death, he remembered, had disappeared in the adrenalin rush as if he had been able to make a run for it from the teacher who had not been able to get a good look at the boy's face. *Anyway*, he said to himself, *enough of these morbid thoughts. A wee trip to 'Villadevino' sounds like the very dab and there would be the wee bonus of plenty of wine to drink and, after all, it will keep me out of bother!*

*

Shug had, like Malky, only recently joined the group. He thought it would be a diversion from his misfortune. The misfortune in question, for Shug, was that he suffered from chronic ambivalence that materialised from the dilemmas brought about by the major affliction and sheer bad luck of being extremely handsome. He stood six foot two inches tall, naturally muscular without being muscle-bound, and had glossy dark brown hair that radiated health. His intense sparkling blue eyes captivated whoever he was with, which always seemed to be young women. He always tried to dress inconspicuously, but no matter what he wore, he could not help looking good in it. Shug was a 'babe magnet'; women were immediately attracted to him physically. He had the additional attributes of broad shoulders and a trim waist that females just wanted to embrace. His only 'turn off' was his whiny high-pitched voice, but this did not appear to put women off, as to them there seemed to be a reasonable trade-off between his good looks and his voice. In any case, the reason they were interested in him did not require any speaking whatsoever.

Shug had spent one year training to be a priest. His vocation had, however, faltered as he had doubts about the chastity element. If females had been attracted to him before he entered the seminary, then this was nothing to the attention they showered on him when he wore his 'dog collar'. He was 'a good Catholic' and he believed one hundred percent in the sanctity of marriage. He was still a virgin and only resolved the conflict between his vows of chastity and his sexual urges by finally and after great difficulty making up his mind to leave the seminary. He recalled with distaste the hard-line view of Pope Leo Sixtus I that it would be better for a priest of the Catholic Church to have sex with a sheep than to have sex with a woman.

He winced at the thought and of the nightmares he had had before he finally gave up the priesthood and settled on being a good lay Catholic, waiting for the right woman to come along to form a sanctified partnership within the auspices of the Holy Church. He could not quite understand why he was always the centre of women's attention and that they were so forward in their requests. He attended the Catholic United Network for The Transgression of Sins as a helpful diversion and he was glad that he had recently joined. He thought to himself, *at least I can do the work of the Church*. He believed in the sanctity of life and had taken on board everything that the Archbishop had expressed. However, he couldn't help being plagued by the nagging thought, *what if I am wrong about the whole church, death and marriage thing?* He continued his packing by unpacking and then repacking again with his simple but elegant choice of clothes, his range of simple fragrant toiletries, his diary, and a book of prayers entitled '*Oh Father Keep Me Chaste*'. Unfortunately for him, there were a couple of females in the party who had more 'chasing' than 'chaste' on their minds.

*

Magdalene inserted the illicit packet of 'Catholic Condoms for Copulating Couples', a relic from one of the now defunct enterprises of the late Pope Hilarius II, into her case. She also placed two pairs of six inch bright red and yellow stiletto heels; her smallest two feet by one foot by ten inches' makeup case, leaving just enough room for her negligée; the smallest of her Day-Glo PVC figure hugging mini-skirts; a see-through blouse to enhance her 36 DD National Cosmetic Health Service breast implants; a boob tube; fishnet stockings and suspender belt; and the smallest size of G-strings before entering the category of dental floss. *At least I won't look too tarty*, thought Magdalene, in the belief that she was simply enhancing her better points in order to appeal to Shug. Magdalene was excited and looking forward to the trip, because the object of her desire, Shug, was going. She dreamt of him every night and her every waking thought was of Shug ... *What was he doing now? What was he wearing? Was he eating? Was he sleeping?* Her infatuation stoked the engine of her desire with red hot coals. Steaming plumes of longing followed her wherever she went.

Magdalene was naturally pretty and she had known it from a young age. That was what had got her into bother when she was a young teenager. The face of a small girl appeared in her mind again, saying, '*Mummy, don't forget to pack the christening gown you keep for me*'. Magdalene dismissed the mental image by checking out her most sultry pout in the mirror ... *now she was stunning! She could get any man or anything she wanted, just by fluttering her eyelashes. But Shug had been a challenge, as he always wanted to remove himself from her company.* This coolness, however, only served to make him even more desirable to her.

Magdalene had been brought up in the Catholic Church and her parents had named her after a famous pop star of her day that used Catholic imagery in her videos. Some of the pop singer Magdalene's songs were still played regularly on digital radio, the most famous of which were '*I Don't Need Your Absolution for Sleeping with Your Best Friend*', '*Tie me up with your Rosary Beads*', and '*I'm Gonna Rock Your Cassock, Baby*'.

Magdalene had gone along with Archbishop Romario's mission to Villadedino, but she was only barely able to understand what the objective was. She didn't like to think about death. It brought back too many painful memories to her. She had found that the only successful way to cope with distressing recollections was to transfer her overwhelming emotions on to an alternative object – and what better object than the focus of her desires.

Shug! The motivation for this choice of alternative object was, of course, not primarily radical, religious or fundamentalist but rather hot blooded and passionate. However, when she found out that Shug was an ex-priest, she felt the weight of predestination pressing down on her libido and she could not wait to be in Shug's company. In her mind, there was both the possibility of seduction and the added extra of absolution from her perceived sin concerning her termination as a teenager.

Once they were married, she would of course have to tell him, but he would be kind and forgiving and perhaps his pardon could lead to some reconciliation and release for herself.

Absent mindedly, she carefully double-checked the packed condoms again and, filled with hope and expectation, she hummed the words of '*I'm Gonna Rock Your Cassock, Baby*' to herself.

*

Rashona Winterbottom was also named after a famous pop singer of her day, an African American singer who was famous for her flamboyant dance moves. This is where the similarity between Magdalene and Rashona ended. In every other respect, they were the complete opposite. Rashona was squat, overweight, and extremely plain. She was better than Magdalene in school, but her application to books had not translated into sensible and practical behaviour patterns and she had been described rather cruelly as 'one sandwich short of a picnic', although it would be unlikely that she would have forgotten to pack something as important as a sandwich unless she had already eaten it. She suffered from acne, a problem at the best of times, but an additional nightmare at school, because her classmates had been able to shout across at her, *'Is that a rash 'ona' your face, Rashona?'* Because of these unattractive characteristics, Rashona was never, like Magdalene, part of the 'in' crowd at school. She went to the same school as Magdalene and lived in the next street. They were the same age, but none of the life opportunities that had opened up to the pretty Magdalene had come the way of the socially awkward, plain and overweight Rashona. Except for one opportunity. For some reason – maybe, for some strange reason, it was her erratic diet regime – Shug preferred to spend time with Rashona instead of Magdalene. Rashona was extremely jealous of Magdalene in so many ways and could tell that Magdalene was attracted to Shug. Rashona could hardly believe Shug seemed to prefer her. While being her 'friend', Rashona was not going to let Magdalene forget it.

Rashona was plotting how she could capitalise on what she interpreted as her attractiveness to Shug as she packed her case for the journey. *One pair of big pants, one pair of even bigger pants, one pair of very enormous big pants*, she was counting into her case as she thought about what she could do to usurp Magdalene in Shug's affections. *Sensible elasticated waist trousers, thermal vest, high waisted thigh, bum and tum shaper for elegant ladies, big miniskirt*, she continued, thinking how alluring this would look with her push up bra that would enhance, at least by one percent, her diminutive and unshapely breasts. She finished her packing with some chocolate bars and fought the case into submission by sitting on the top and shouting for her mammy to come and pull the zip round the case.

Rashona, or rather the part of her that still craved control, decided on a snack now, something that would keep her going till the next instalment of her current diet. The problem for Rashona was that she had an eating disorder caused by a father who ruled over the household with the proverbial rod of iron. Rashona felt crushed by his strict regime and constant discipline. Eating, it turned out, was the only way that Rashona could take back any control of her life. She had no insight into her condition and constantly struggled to both eat and diet. She had tried every diet available to modern female magazine readers and beyond this, in her attempt to research human metabolism, could not, no matter how hard she tried, lose weight. In her mind, it was as if her nature had predetermined her size, regardless of what actions she might take. She had followed each diet rigorously except for one disruptive flaw – she had an inner compulsion to eat whatever she liked in between the set menu for the diet. She had a multiple personality disorder where one aspect contradicted and was completely unaware of the other. To sharpen up her exercise regime, she had bought a bio-data activity tracker to monitor walking motion, calories burned, and heart rate analysis. However, Rashona, with own special brand of misplaced logic, attached her monitor to her parent's dog and sent it out to run around the garden, while she ate a bacon sandwich and drank a can of fizzy juice. Rashona was very pleased with the results her family dog provided for her that indicated she (or rather her dog) was reaching and surpassing all her exercise goals.

Currently, she was on the popular 'Ape Diet'. The premise of this current trendy diet was simply that apes were never fat and that those people who reverted to the primate diet found under the forest canopy and from the undergrowth of the earlier homo sapiens would be healthy, fit, and, best of all, thin! This corresponded with her reading about the evolution of homo sapiens. The practicalities of the diet involved eating large quantities of produce that is in season and available for ape consumption in the wild. For example, if there is a tree that is bearing fruit, then apes will eat that fruit all day, every day, until the supply is finished. Rashona had kept to the programme the day before, eating live ants for breakfast, followed by a kilo of apricots for lunch, and a kilo of radishes for tea. In between breakfast and lunch she had, however, mechanically – without thinking – consumed two chocolate bars, a bacon roll, a packet of chocolate biscuits, two sugary donuts, and a litre bottle of fizzy drink; between lunch and tea she had got through a deep-fried peperoni pizza and two chocolate éclairs; and between tea and going to bed she had six cans of lager, a bowl of sugary cornflakes, a packet of peanuts, a roll and sausage, and a carry out portion of Indian pakora. Finally, the 'piece de resistance' was the bedside box of chocolates from which she made frequent selections as she woke hungry in the middle of the night, like a somnambulant to feed her need. It was only by luck that she had not dreamt of eating a giant marshmallow, as she would likely have woken in the morning with the pillow missing. Apart from her mental gap about snacks, she stuck rigidly to her diet programme. This morning, before heading off to the airport, she had eaten a kilo of raw spinach.

She was now sitting on the bus to the airport, alternating between biting her nails and feeding contentedly but compulsively on a king sized 'Chocowhale' bar. She thought about the conversation that had taken place in the Archbishop's house about the life shortening risks from being fat. *Okay, I am a little overweight, but I am on a diet for this. I can't see how eating can kill you and I am naturally big boned.*

She imagined death, that she had died, and was now in a heaven full of fluffy clouds and blue skies. She observed herself, dressed in white and slim, with a table laid out with the most splendid feast. She ate earnestly knowing that she would never put on any weight. Yes. *Heaven*, she thought, *I could happily go there. But hold on, I don't want to die. Death might be painful and what if heaven isn't like that. What if I go to hell?* An image popped into her mind of herself in hell and of lifting a large slice of Black Forest Gateaux up to eat … *Oh no, I don't have a mouth!*

A trickle of sweat ran down Rashona's back. It is all so uncertain. She shut her mind off, as she was skilled at doing, to compartmentalise thoughts of death. *No, I don't want to die. It will be all right*, she thought as she discretely discharged two cubic feet of consumed spinach related methane gas into the atmosphere. Luckily, this did not result in any trees being uprooted or structural damage. She looked nonchalantly out of the window. In common with all of her compatriots, as they made their way to the airport, Rashona grazed over her own thoughts of life and death. Rashona swallowed the last remnants of her 'Chocowhale bar' and took comfort against her hidden eating disorder with her own personal but sublimated self-deceit – *at least I am on a diet.*

Chapter 11 Estrela – A Small Bird Sings of Snow

So, sing the snow's sweet pure life as words drift down from endless skies

The Song of Villadedino, Saint Dino 240AD

"Mark! Get your arse over to my office, now. You'll just love the assignment I have for you." Mickey 'Mad Dog' Smith, Deputy Editor of '*The Intellect*', put down the phone and waited with the SongTap video on pause setting. He wished he could get out and do some interesting newspaper work instead of kicking the arses of his overpaid and over-laid prissy journalists. Mark Goodwin, probably one of the better ones, had arrived at the door of his office.

"At your command, maestro," he announced to the Deputy Editor.

"Have you heard of Estrela Pure, Mark? She is the next big thing. More hits than anyone else on the Internet, apart from sexy Lady Deep Throat Twatcha, that is."

Without waiting for a reply – time is money, after all – he started the video that played on three of the maXiviewwalls of his office. Mark was astounded as he heard, for the first time, a voice, not just any voice, but the most haunting voice he had ever heard in his life. From the first pristine note, her tone seemed to etch an indelible and evocative snow white landscape on the core of his being. She was accompanying herself with some simple chord structures and finger picking on the guitar, but it was the connection of that crystalline voice with his very essence that had him transfixed. A petite natural beauty sat on a simple white stool in a film set devoid of any props other than the seamless white studio backdrop that 'washed' the scene, leaving the stark but pure image of the singer and her guitar. She had long, straight, jet-black, glossy hair, almost pixie like features, dark eyes, porcelain skin, and pale, almost blue lips. Mark made a semi-conscious professional connection between these features and the story he had written two years back concerning foetal alcohol syndrome. She wore a simple short grey dress and sang in a delicate and elemental minor key. She sang something about trees and snow and a longing that transported Mark's mind effortlessly, conjuring with her words, emotions, and intonations a forest in winter, pure and white, with a stillness that excavated long, deep memories and feelings experienced from his past.

A solitary snowflake drifts from above
As the sky to the forest declares her love
Night in the snowscape
Caught in a dream state
Softness of the mist and air
Of the falling snowflake and a pure white dove

This is not ice, this is snow
This is not fire, I know
This is not hard, because I can grow

It will take time, I know
I am here that was then
I am now until I am there again

A solitary star tracks across the sky
As the earth revolves on a still snow land
Night in the snowscape
The star projects its escape
Stillness and silence
Of the voice of the snowflake in my hand

This is not ice, this is snow
This is not fire, I know
This is not hard, because I can grow
It will take time, I know
I am here that was then
I am now until I am there again

A solitary night bird gliding through the higher boughs
As its wings map the snow laden pines
Night in the snowscape
Gliding through the treescape
Floating and knowing the lightness
Of the movement of snow in time

This is not ice, this is snow
This is not fire, I know
This is not hard, because I can grow

It will take time, I know
I am here that was then
I am now until I am there again.

Mark heard himself exclaim, "Wow!"

He was snapped back to the biting reality by Mickey 'Mad Dog' turning off the video and the maXiviewalls returned to their usual tinge of tobacco smoke white colour.

"Thought you would like it," said Mickey, "Here's her phone number, so now get your bum out of here and get me an 'artsy fartsy' piece for the Sunday WebMag. Something along the lines of … new sensation; rags to riches; writing songs in her loft till discovered on SongTap; lyrics deep and meaningful; makes a connection with her generation; and throw in some young male celebrities dreaming about marrying her … you know … why is she connecting with people? Try and include an air of mystery. Okay, now fuck off and don't be fucking late with the copy!"

Outside Mickey 'Mad Dog's' office and clutching the singer's phone number, Mark was still trying to coordinate the thoughts and feelings aroused by Estrela's soulful song of snow and trees as he took his phone out of his pocket and started to dial the number.

"Hi, is that Estrela? Mark Goodwin from '*The Intellect*' here. How are you? We would like to do a piece about you for our Sunday WebMag and I'm phoning to ask if we can arrange to meet."

"Hello Mark, I seem to be popular with the media these

days. You are the third journalist this week to call. I have to say I have turned the rest down, but I do like '*The Intellect*' and I suppose if you do a piece then maybe that will stop the requests from the others."

Mark was noting the timbre of her voice ... almost childlike, sing-song, strange whisper to words ending in 's', unusual accent that he couldn't quite place.

"You won't regret it, Estrela, and thanks. I have your address, when can I come over?"

Estrela thought for a second and replied, "Lunchtime tomorrow is fine for me. If you check in with the commissionaire at the front desk, he will let you in."

Mark responded, "Great, see you then and thanks again." *This will be interesting*, he thought to himself as he headed back to his desk. As he recalled Estrela's voice, he tried to catch the butterfly of her accent in the net of his brain. He got so close, but at each sweep of his intelligence, the accent fluttered away from capture.

*

Mark was sitting in the kitchen of Estrela's apartment in a posh part of Islington Green. The decor was simple and unpretentious and the layout, open plan – white walls; white kitchen units; pine work surfaces; pine floors; a white leather couch; white coffee table; three guitars on their guitar stands; a wood stove; cut logs; paintings of forests; and most unusually six (he had counted them) eight-foot cypress trees almost touching the ceiling in enormous white, glazed pots.

"Green tea, Mark?" There was that voice again with the unusual accent.

"That will be lovely," he replied, thinking, *is she American?* while consciously analyzing her height – around five foot three. Mark couldn't help comparing his own height to the woman through the eyes of one with a troubling inferiority complex related to his own diminutive dimensions.

"I honestly don't know why I am so popular, Mark. It has been a roller coaster, ever since my neighbour Martha filmed me singing on her Camspecs and then posted it on SongTap. I swear I didn't know she had done it and I was the one who was most surprised when I saw myself on the News. I was shocked when the newsreader use the word viral and said that the song had the highest number of hits on the Internet that week. And someone has tracked how that happened ... some kids at a University in the United States started the interest and from there it spread all over the States, into Asia, and then into Europe. And then, after a few days, I noticed people staring at me in the street, which made me a bit paranoid. And that news article. Believe it or not, I'm supposed to be a phenomenon!"

Estrela giggled in a light-hearted, self-conscious, self-deprecating way that was both charming and genuine. Mark was hooked!

"So, that was a fortnight ago and I now have the top music agent in London – or that's what I have been told he is. And I've recorded two of my songs for Digital Music Express and sold downloads all over the world."

Estrela took a deep breath. She could hardly believe what she was describing. "The plan is to go into a music studio and record an album. Oh, and a film crew is going to make a film of me singing to upload onto the Internet. It is really quite amazing, but I just love to sing, ever since I was a child in the Yukon."

"Is that where you got that accent?" Mark asked quickly, using an opening to fill in the gaps his curiosity had created.

Estrela realised that she had said more than she intended for the interview and quickly changed the subject.

"Do you like my new guitar? You have no idea how much it cost but my agent said that I am going to be a very rich young woman now."

Mark's journalistic experience recognised that he was being diverted but he made a mental note to check out the curious Yukon connection.

The interview continued with some more discussion about the lyrics she wrote for her songs; did she have a trained voice or was it totally natural. Mark felt compelled to disclose the effect her voice had on him. He revealed to her the connection he had with the song about the trees and snow and how it evoked feelings he had had as a child on a winter holiday in the Highlands of New Scotland.

Estrela was a bit embarrassed by the attention, but she recognised there was something genuine about how this journalist was explaining his response to her song. Gradually, through his personal revelations, and for the first time, Estrela began to understand what people might actually experience from her song. Mark's insightful and profound explanation of his personal experiences in the winter forests touched a part of her that had been hidden and locked away for many years. Now, from deep within her frozen, ice-cold heart, born of the Yukon wilderness, there was the start of a thaw. She was surprised to find that something within had begun to melt and she began to examine Mark in a new light.

*

Mark researched Estrela's background following the interview and was most surprised and delighted when she agreed to his request for a second interview. He came prepared with some of the information he had discovered.

Mr and Mrs Pure had adopted Estrela in Canada when she was twelve years old. The family then moved to Olde England when Estrela was fourteen. He had read articles about their tragic deaths in a car accident when Estrela was seventeen. *The poor girl had certainly experienced tragedy and adversity in her life*, he thought. Perhaps that was the source of her song voice. He sensed she was fragile but discerned that this was an important dynamic to the story of 'Estrela Pure, the woman with a voice as delicate as a snow flake'. He liked that line and made a mental note to use it in his article.

Estrela was waiting for him at the open door of her apartment as he stepped out of the lift. "Hi Mark, good to see you again, I've been thinking about you." Mark sensed that she really was pleased to see him, maybe just as pleased as he was to see her.

They talked about her day and Mark waited for a

suitable moment to raise the tragedy of her adoptive parents. It was when she was talking about how much support she had had from her family with a distant look in her eye and an almost imperceptible tremble in her voice that Mark said, "Look, I apologise in advance, but I did some research last night and I know that you have experienced some real trauma in your life." He softened his tone and continued, "I would completely understand if you didn't want to discuss this and I will stop right now if that is what you want. But look, I really, genuinely believe you have a unique talent and I think that something about your background history will help people understand why you affect them the way you obviously do."

Estrela felt herself start to freeze over once again. It had been going so well. She liked Mark. But this was so intrusive. *How can I trust him with anything personal and who are the 'people' he is talking about?* She was in two minds, ambivalent about this situation she found herself in. *Mark seemed sincere; he wasn't pushy. She had not met anyone before that she thought she could trust sufficiently to discuss her loss.* She took a deep breath, readying herself to fly over the precipice of her bereavement, and said, "Okay, Mark, but when I say stop you must stop. This is hard for me to talk about and when I've finished, then that will be all I am willing to reveal. My parents, my adoptive parents that is, died in a car crash when I was seventeen. They were the best thing that ever happened to me and I loved them deeply." Estrela wiped a small, crystal tear away from her eye as she continued, "They died instantly, I was told. The road had some ice on it and a lorry slid across the barrier and there was a head-on collision. They wouldn't have had time to think and, I suppose, that was it. I was on my own again."

Mark was trained to keep quiet when someone was revealing intimate feelings and consciously resisted the urge to interrupt.

For the first time in her life, Estrela talked freely about her loss and Mark responded sensitively. She felt she had made the right decision in talking with him. But she was controlled enough to remind herself that she did not want to share anything about her lost pre-adoption childhood in the wilderness of the Yukon.

Mark was skilled enough to understand the effect his behaviour had on people. This was partly what had made him a successful journalist, working for the most prestigious media outlet in Europe. He asked Estrela, "Do you want to talk about your life before you were adopted?"

Cautiously, Estrela then took a further giant leap, trusting Mark enough to tell him about her life in a number of Children's Homes across Western Canada, but, of course, only telling him that the reasons for moving were due to the closure of the Homes. Whilst initially wary of Mark, she felt increasingly safe about confiding in him about her feelings of loneliness, sadness, hopelessness, and helplessness during her time in care. All the time, she was growing closer to Mark and despite his professionalism, Mark felt touched, like the first flakes of winter snow, by this beautiful woman's life in a way that no other woman had ever touched him before.

Chapter 12 Pilgrimage to Villadedino

To confuse the poor pilgrim's path confounding where the journey lies

The Song of Villadedino, Saint Dino 240AD

The intrepid five met up eventually at Glasgow MacSporran International Airport. The plan had been to meet at the Glasgow Coat of Arms beside the escalator. This was mixed up due to Malky and Rashona meeting, as if by osmosis, at the shop that sold coats beside the lift, where Malky entertained Rashona with renditions of the various fights he had been involved in, while Rashona munched amiably on a sandwich she could not remember having prepared for just such an occasion. The other three had waited at the correct place for forty-five minutes without any sign of Malky and Rashona. Rab had decided to go in search and found them, both starting to doubt their chosen location and looking more dejected than when they had first arrived at the coat shop. An accumulation of food wrappers obscured the floor at Rashona's feet and Malky was, for no apparent reason, remonstrating with the shop manager.

The group, having nearly missed their flight because of the mix-up, eventually passed through security that involved full naked body x-ray scans. The female transport security team operating the monitor asked Shug to repeat the procedure four times as they were not sure about something in the x-ray images. This necessitated escalating the issue and calling other female security staff to view the screen, which generated a great deal of discussion before they reluctantly approved his admittance. Rashona heard some tittering as she passed through, but apart from having to part with her prohibited two cans of lager, there were no problems for her. Magdalene was stopped as a routine random check and asked some questions.

"Have you packed anything suspicious?" asked the serious man wearing a sombrero and sporting a drooping moustache.

"Only some Catholic condoms," was all she could think of replying.

"Has anyone given you something to carry in your bag?"

"My mum gave me her hairbrush," Magdalene was wondering why the airline would want to know about her mother's brush.

"Are you an international terrorist?"

"No, I'm in a temporary job as a hairdresser," replied Magdalene, at which point the security guard was more than convinced that the uninhibitedly dressed female would have had difficulty being a terrorist in her own bedroom never mind internationally and, sighing, let her proceed to the next stage of the concourse. Little did he know that she was part of a rebellious group that did not have any suspicious materials on their persons, as they had arranged for the explosives to be picked up from the Retribution and Inquisition cell in Figas, next to Villadedino.

They were travelling with Mayan Airways, the successful, no-frills, low-cost Mexican airline that had made its name in Central America and the Caribbean before capturing the European market with their cheap, chihuahua, and cheerful travel philosophy. Particularly popular with the Glasgow traveller were the deep-fried tortillas, tacos, and cheesy chili chips served on board. Perversely, these were twenty-five percent more expensive than the flights themselves. Glaswegians knew they could gorge themselves on the deep-fried delicacies and Rashona, in particular, had undertaken her culinary research and anticipated the double helpings she would buy to alleviate the possibility of suffering some form of malnutrition on the three-hour flight.

Mayan Airways had a strict rule on the weight of passengers and suitcases and they had marketed themselves on ensuring that the cheap cost of the flight was balanced with a ritual public humiliation of the passengers being rebuked by the sombrero-wearing ground crew for any excess human or baggage weight. At peak times, the experience was doubly enhanced by the music of a live Mariachi band as flyers were asked to unpack, redistribute items of clothing to other accompanying passengers, and repack their cases. The heavier passengers required transferring items of clothing to their fellow travellers in order to beat the £10 per kilo over the standard weight limit per passenger. Glasgow was a goldmine for the Mexican outfit, as the passengers, with their 'healthy' diet of deep-fried chocolate bars and fizzy drinks, were mostly overweight. Some passengers had taken to wearing bikinis and swimming trunks in order to beat the limit (the much publicised problem of hypothermia associated with the practice had now dissuaded travellers from undertaking this ruse).

Flyers could also be seen running on the spot as a precursor to stepping onto the scales in order to lose a few grams before the weigh in.

This was the situation encountered by our gang of five. Rab and Shug got past the weighing machine unscathed apart from the traditional Glasgow humour from the other passengers waiting in line. The other three faired less well. First, Malky had to open his honking holdall and take out his assembled collection of fetid socks, rancid boxer shorts, malodorous vests, and noxious shirts and ask Rab and Shug to take some of these items in their luggage.

With a gentle retort of, "You can stick them up your arse first, pal," Rab declined the odious opportunity, while Shug, struggling with the thought of calamitous contamination, had to throw up in a recycling bin nearby. Magdalene and Rashona faired no better than Malky with their perambulations crossing through the gauntlet of ritual humiliation and had to empty the contents of their suitcases. This did, however, entertain the waiting travellers as they compared Magdalene's microscopic floss G-strings and Rashona's enormous passion-killer knickers:

All the while, the Mariachi band in the background was singing '*La la la la la Bamba*', accompanied by catcalls from the waiting Glasgow crowd of, "You should have sent your big knickers in advance by articulated lorry, hen!" and, "If your G-strings were any smaller, you would need to get a magnifyin' glass to put them on!"

Malky overcame the problem by simply taking all T-shirts and shirts he had in his holdall and depositing them in the recycling bin that was holding Shug's vomit.

"That smell is pure fuckin' mingin'," came from the waiting and increasingly uncomfortable crowd. Shug had no way to avoiding helping out Magdalene and Rashona and had to accept the tarty clothes from Magdalene and the exceptionally large knickers from Rashona and stuff them as best he could in the sensible pockets of his jacket.

Some wag shouted, "Why don't ye give that Mexican violin player your G-string!" and another chimed in with, "Aye, and then he could play the Mexican version of '*Air on a G-string*'!" This banter calmed the growing impatience of the crowd. Rashona looked forlorn as she stepped off the weighing machine with an additional bill for £40, much to the amusement of the crowd, who followed her step up on to the scales with a compulsory low chant of 'aaaah', rising to a crescendo 'aaaaaaaaAAAAAAH', and ending with the exclamation 'aaaaaaaaAAAAAAAAAAAAAAAAAH BROKE THE SCALES!' This traditional razor-sharp humour was applied to all who participated in the humiliating scales. Particularly the wee skinny guys with their pockets bulging with assorted holiday artefacts. No 'fat shaming' for the egalitarian Glaswegian passengers, as all were subject to the playful but merciless wry humour that cut through any pomposity or pretentiousness like a fart in a royal carriage.

*

On the flight, the formidable five were now becoming

increasingly uncomfortable with the collective smell of Malky's many sweating layers and were only too glad when the Mayan Airways air hostesses came along with the food and drinks, complete with sombreros and bullet belts, holding miniature bottles of tequila strung across their chests and with their trolleys overflowing with deep-fried tortillas.

After a few bottles each, the passengers were getting cheerfully inebriated, when one happy soul leaned over to the five friends and laughingly appraised them, "That was the funniest thing I've ever seen. I nearly wet mysel' when you started pullin' out your knickers and boxers. And when you put all your dirty clothes in the bin, big man, that was the funniest thing I think I have ev ... "

The happy reveller had not finished his sentence, when Malky placed his dense forehead on his tormentor's nose causing it to burst open, with blood projecting effortlessly throughout the cabin.

The air hostesses descended on Malky with a speed of response honed to perfection over years on the Glasgow to 'anywhere' flights.

"Right, pal, if you don't calm your jets, you're gettin' locked in the lavvy and you'll not like it because somebody has left a big Greyfriar's Bobby in the bowl and we cannot flush it away!"

"But that bastard was laughin' at us," Malky protested.

"I don't give a flying fuck," the air hostess responded, summoning the best choice feedback from her customer care training, "Any more of that and I've got a parachute in the back of the plane with your name on it."

"All right, hen, I'll just sit here quiet and drink ma last five wee bottles of 'terkeeler'."

The air hostess sensed just enough contrition in Malky's voice to allow her to transfer her attention to the bloody-nosed comedian, who had succeeded in covering every passenger in the tightly packed seats around him with copious quantities of his lifeblood, while making occasional incoherent utterances of, "fuckin' … I only said … fuckin' nose … fuckin' head … thanks, hen … it's sore … nose … bastard … fuck … nose fuck!"

The scene quietened as Malky and the bloody-nosed comic fell asleep to dreams of giant Mexican bandit mice, wearing sombreros, riding Chihuahuas through the cactus desert, and firing their guns into the air.

To the strains of '*La Cucaracha*' the flight landed in Villadedino.

Part II

Chapter 13 Welcome to the Hotel Euthanasia

We will gather at the dance of death, lives entwined in fate and time

The Song of Villadedino, Saint Dino 240AD

Zeca Silva, the Manager of the Hotel Euthanasia, and Angela Deff, his Customer Care Manager, were waiting in the reception lounge of the hotel to meet and introduce themselves to the anticipated new tranche of arrivals to the Hotel Euthanasia. The state of the art monorail from the airport was estimated to arrive in ten minutes' time. So, Zeca, welcoming the opportunity to hear the sound of his own voice, turned to Angela and proceeded to inspire her waiting time with one of his tales of the Alentejo region. *Here we go again!* Angela thought to herself, *I suppose I better listen carefully, so that I can respond appropriately to the point of the story when Zeca asks me as he always does.*

"When I was a boy in Alentejo, the area I came from was famous for producing wines and olives. Now, there were two owners of vineyards, João and Paolo, that were positioned side by side. The quality of the land was virtually the same for both owners, an unusual yellow ochre colour and very fertile, with a good composition of minerals, and well disposed to the growing of grapes. They used the same scientific techniques to analyse the soil, they stored the grapes in the same way, fermented them using the same processes, and bottled them using the same size and shape of bottle. Anyway, there was only one important difference between the approaches of the two owners. João picked his grapes at any time of the day, while Paolo always picked his grapes overnight and only during a full moon. That was the single difference.

Now, a very rich owner of a supermarket chain came to their local town and was informed about the two vineyards by the local innkeeper. It was the very rich supermarket owner's intention to buy the wine from one vineyard only.

He visited João and spoke to him about his processes and he tasted the wine. He was pleased with it and left after shaking hands with João and thanking him for his attention. The very rich supermarket owner then visited Paolo and entered into the same dialogue as he had with João. When Paolo came to that part of the process where he informed the very rich supermarket owner about gathering the grapes during a full moon, the very rich supermarket owner asked him to repeat this part of the process three times.

'*Why do you do this?*' asked the supermarket man.

'*It is part of our tradition,*' replied Paolo, '*and we have always used these techniques in our vineyard, my father and his father before him and, as far back as we know, the grapes have been gathered in the same way, always at the dead of night during a full moon. The death hour we like to call it.*' The very rich supermarket owner asked to taste the wine from Paolo's vineyard, which Paolo was pleased to offer to him. The very rich supermarket owner drank the wine and smiled a sweet smile of contentment. It was the smile reserved for those who have achieved their objective."

Silva stopped for breath and enquired, "Angela, can you see where I am going with this story?"

"Why yes, Mr Silva, the very rich supermarket owner wanted to know what the cheapest method for gathering the grapes was, so that he could buy the wine from the owner with the most economic costs and, therefore, make the biggest profit."

"Let me continue and perhaps it will become clearer," Zeca interrupted with a bemused grin on his face, "The supermarket owner not only smiled, but also made a very good offer there and then to buy every bottle of wine from Paolo and said he would repeat this every year in perpetuity."

Zeca explained to Angela, "You see, this is where I learned that to be successful in any business, you have to be unique. That is what makes me the successful Manager of the Hotel Euthanasia that I am. Uniqueness is something I pride myself in having. My hotel management provides a unique service that is not available anywhere else in the world and my distinctive style is finely tuned to serve its purpose. My advertising campaigns are legendary; my communication skills are akin to an art form; and my commitment and dedication are second to none.

Returning to my story," he continued, "The supermarket owner bought the wine because he could market it as 'uniquely harvested in the dead of night during a full moon' and also one more important factor ... the wine tasted better!"

"So why are you telling me this story, Mr Silva?"

"As the Customer Care Manager here, my dear Angela, you have to sell the customer the unique elements of the hotel. I hope you have understood the meaning of this story and I hope you can translate this into your practice."

Just then, carried by the monorail from the airport to the hotel, the guests, creating an upsurge of activity in the foyer, started to stream though the doors to the reception area. Zeca and Angela greeted them smiling (or, in Angela's case, a spookily fixed grimace that she assumed to be a smile), shaking hands with them, and handing out glasses of champagne, while instructing the various bellhops to take the guests' luggage to the bedrooms reserved for them.

Mark Goodwin, who was still hovering around in the background collecting information for his newspaper article, joined the group discretely at the edges of the throng and observed the pleasantries in action.

Zeca spoke to each set of guests in turn. "Hello Mr Mann, I obviously recognised you because of your little friend.

"Yes, this is Jiki, the best friend a man could have. Jiki give Mr Silva a high five."

Jiki, a capuchin monkey, followed the simulation of the high five movement of Hugh Mann's hand. The monkey raised his own hand up into the air, copying his master's movement to give a high five to the Hotel Manager standing beside Hugh. Angela Deff looked on not knowing quite what to make of the small primate or whether she should allocate it the pleasure of her smile. She did anyway.

Bethany Mitchell introduced her son Ian and husband

Robin to Zeca with something akin to a look of fatigue and relief. "We are so glad to be here, Mr Silva. It has been hard to support my husband in building his confidence to come here, but at least we will now be able to get on with our lives after the eh … you know … process."

"Your husband is most welcome here, Mrs Mitchell. We will be happy to ensure that we meet all his requirements," Zeca replied, making a quick computation in his head matching the Mitchells to the list of which guests arriving with their spouses used a wheelchair.

Zeca leaned down to stroke Mrs Merger's Yorkshire terrier, which growled a warning and snapped at a safe distance from the hand of Zeca, who gingerly removed his fingers before they were chomped. "What a delightful dog, Mrs Merger," he lied.

"He's a little shit," responded Mrs Merger, "He won't let anyone near him unless it's to give him food or treats. Anyway, Tyson, that's his name, won't be able to bite anyone anymore, after we both kick the bucket."

"Is that so?" said Zeca, trying to keep the atmosphere from getting morose.

"Are you married, Mr Silva, by any chance? You know, I've been married seven times and I'm getting a bit bored with it, but if you're game for it, and if you have enough money to support Tyson and myself, then who knows, I could maybe forego this suicide palaver and give it another turn."

"Why, Mrs Merger, I am just a poor hotel manager and could not possibly give you the lifestyle you so richly deserve," replied the cornered Zeca.

"Oh well, probably best I get rid of this old bag of bones then, son. Can you top up this champagne?" said Mrs Merger, before shouting a sudden, "Why don't you just shut up you moron!" as Zeca jumped back in surprise and Tyson began to bark and scurry about in agitated circles.

"I am so sorry, Mrs Merger, but what have I done to offend you? Is the champagne not to your liking?" Zeca responded.

"Apologies, Mr Silva. It's just these stupid ghosts of my seven dead husbands that keep following me about and I can't get rid of them. They never miss an opportunity to harass and insult me."

Zeca thought it better to say nothing more. Obviously, the woman was deranged and delusional.

However, the fact was that the ghosts of her seven dead husbands did constantly plague Mrs Merger. It had started after the death of her last husband, whose spirit turned up accompanied by the ghost of husband number six. The two of them had started hanging about and shouting abuse at her. Over the weeks that followed, spectres of each of her first five dead husbands joined in the fracas. Everywhere she turned, she was confronted by one or more of the ghosts hurling insults at her and complaining about how miserable she had made their lives when they were alive.

Whether this was an actual psychic occurrence or merely the unusual neurological workings of the synapses of Mrs Merger's deteriorating brain, it is difficult to say.

What was certain was that she had undoubtedly experienced something which manifested itself in the form of incessant haunting. She hadn't even been able to go to the bathroom without them crowding in beside her and it was just so exasperating and not least embarrassing to be getting out of the shower and to be accosted by seven ghosts pointing at her sagging body and tutting loudly. Visiting a restaurant had become a nightmare. Other diners would start staring at her when she could not contain her frustration and seemed to be shouting into thin air, '*I don't need your opinion about the size of my waistline, thank you very much*' and, '*Will you please stop screaming at my ice cream*' and, '*Take your foot out of my soup*' in response to the antics and gibes from the apparition of the moment. The comments were always the same and took the form of complaints about what she was buying or snide remarks about what she was wearing, the state of her make up, or her hair. It was escalating now to a constant bombardment of malicious remarks. This was what had resulted in her decision to end the torment she was enduring. And, along with the fact that she was no longer able to ensnare husband number eight, these were the circumstances that had forced her into seeking a resolution to her problems through the services of the Hotel Euthanasia.

On this occasion, the apparitions had been hanging about observing her during the welcome reception while she talked to Zeca. They had burst into a collective guffaw of laughter when they heard her asking the Hotel Manager's marital status and their shouts had included, '*You've got to be*

165

kidding us. Why would he marry an old harridan like you? Bag of bones ... most likely dinosaur ones.' This had been the final straw and she had yelled at them to shut up. At that point, the spectres merely dissolved into the ether, before regrouping to make obscene hand gestures and hound their tormented victim further.

"What did I ever do to deserve you lot?" the exasperated Mrs Merger seethed through her clenched teeth, "I've had enough!"

As Mrs Merger continued to battle with her invisible hostile forces, most of the other guests were doing their best to avoid staring at her and were turning their attention elsewhere. Many gravitated like metal filings towards a magnet, drawn to engage with the most charming man in the room.

A rose among weeds, Mr John LeMaistre was entertaining the throngs packed around him with tales of business success and namedropping associations with famous celebrity friends. He was using his significant intelligence to identify and target the most vulnerable within the group.

John LeMaistre sensed, with superior acumen, that he could have some fun manipulating the particular little group of Scottish guests, despite not being able to understand a word they were saying. His assessment of Rab was of somebody who not only lacked good dress sense, but who also sounded like a Neanderthal when he spoke. Looking Rab over, he thought, *obviously, someone with no class or capacity for intelligent thinking. He looks like a no-hoper, a dead-end dosser and probably weak and incompetent to boot. His friends don't look much better and where did they find those sluts with short dresses? Oh no, I don't believe it, the fat fellow smells like the armpits of a gorilla who has sprayed himself with a can of camel dung. I could have some fun with this lot!* True to his psychopathic nature, LeMaistre was unable to resist one final narcissistic manipulation before his carefully calculated suicide.

General Mustapha Sultana was splendid in his army uniform, wondering how to get away from the camel smelling Scotsman who had attached himself to his eminence.

"I just love your Michael Jackson outfit, General," intoned Malky, using his encyclopaedic knowledge of pop music.

"This is my honourable army uniform, sir, and not a Michael Jackson outfit," growled the offended General.

"Well, I just love the colour scheme on your pockets. I hope that is not a gay pride rainbow ensemble there, General?"

"These, my man, are campaign awards for the many honourable battles I fought for my beloved country Kushara and there is nothing gay about them," the general exploded, getting redder in the face, "We do not have homosexuals in Kushara!"

"Cool it down, man, no need to take offence," Malky replied in a measured response, seeking, unusually, to keep out of bother and seeing how red in the face the general had become, "You don't want to get yourself all steamed up there. You could do yourself serious damage with that blood pressure. Maybe we got off on the wrong foot. Let me introduce myself, Malky's the name."

"Okay, Mustapha," replied the General trying hard to keep his cool.

"Sorry, mate, must have a what?"

"There you go again, you little imperialist shit, just like all you English and American shits that shit up my country and spread it everywhere, shitting here, shitting there, shit, shit, shit, SHIT!"

"Sorry, I couldn't get you what you wanted, but no need to take it out on me and I'm Scottish not English."

"SHIT!" yelled the furious and indignant General as he stormed off.

"What did I say wrong, man?" Malky leaned over to Rab, who had been observing the interchange, "Folks here are really up tight, don't you think? Euthanasia? It's not as if it's life and death!"

"I think the General doesn't like America," offered Rab, "I saw a news article about him, that said he blames MI6 and the CIA for all the problems in his country Kushara. I also understand that he has 'done a runner' out of the country just as they were about to arrest him and try him for crimes against his own people. So, I just guess he heard your accent – and the Stars and Stripes on your T shirt didn't help. He took offence from the word go. He probably thought you sounded like a Scottish spy."

Mrs Merger, seeking solace from the spectral seven, had now approached the two Scotsmen and asked, with her usual opening gambit, "Hi you two handsome hunks, I was just wondering if by any chance either of you were single?"

Unfortunately, the seven abusive apparitions, materializing in front of her just at that moment, leaned in towards the two newcomers and sang a splendid barber shop rendition of '*Will You Stop Your Tickling, Jock!*'. This was just too much for Mrs Merger, who once again lost her composure and shouted out in response, "Can you pains in the rear end just get lost and stop annoying me!" – unsurprisingly confusing Malky and Rab.

Zeca, wishing to divert attention away from the mêlée created by Mrs Merger's manifestations of madness, managed, at an impeccably timed point in the proceedings, to ask the guests to please take a seat with their drinks.

"My dear guests, welcome to the Hotel Euthanasia and the beautiful Principality of Villadedino. Can I say it is a real pleasure to meet you all and I sincerely hope that your stay here will be one to remember, so raise your glasses ... Here's to 'checking out of the Hotel Euthanasia', the right to choose the future you want, and may your final departure be all you hope for." After the toast, Zeca continued, "I can assure you that you have made the right decision and have come to the best place; a place where you will be empowered to make your life's final choice to leave this world. You will take control of your life and do with it what you want. We salute you, we respect you, and we will do all in our power to give you the best experience of your life and of your death.

Your luxury bedrooms all have views of the splendid snowcapped mountains, lakes, and forests of Villadedino. You will shortly be given a tour of this fabulous hotel. The lounges are to your right, along with the bars and dining rooms.

Downstairs, we have the indoor pool and outdoor pools and spa where you can a have a relaxing massage from our Thai masseuses. To your left are the exciting eXi-theme Departure Suites and further on is the viewing area for the crematorium. This is a good point for me to introduce some of our excellent staff. Can I introduce Pope Shamus VI, Swami Riva, and Sexy Suzie Sunfloweroil. They will be pleased to accompany you on a guided tour of the hotel that will orientate you to where everything is."

Zeca was pleased with his performance and 'bonhomie' welcome and turned to Angela, saying, "Is there anything else you would wish to add for the guests, Miss Deff?"

Angela stood up, head and shoulders above Zeca, and, thinking about the manager's previous tale of vineyards, announced to the guests through a clenched smile, in her strangely incongruous and abrupt manner, "There is nothing else I would wish to add to Mr Silva's introductions other than to say that the hotel will now be offering assisted suicide during a full moon."

Chapter 14 Death of a Good Man

The question will remain unanswered, the future bones are undermined

The Song of Villadedino, Saint Dino 240AD

Robin Mitchell, his wife Bethany, and son Ian's route to Villadedino had been a tricky one. Robin probably had one to two years left to live on account of his degenerative Motor Neurone Disease. Bethany and Ian had convinced Robin through a combined and continuous campaign of coercion that it would be better for him if he accepted the release from his, and their, miserable existence by undertaking the process of assisted dying. Subtly and over a period of time, they had worked hard to put pressure on Robin in order to get their hands on the ample bank balance accumulated in his account. Robin was oblivious to their devious deception. At home, they had cultivated a harvest of distress for Robin by sowing the seeds of dependency with constant inferences using such emotive comments as,

'Of course, you're not a burden on us. We are under huge stress, but we just feel so sad that you have to endure all this unnecessary pain and suffering.'

'It would be so hard for us if you were assisted to die, but we know it makes sense for you as you don't have long to go anyway.'

'It would be a mercy that you didn't have to go through this pain anymore.'

'It will hit us hard when we are without you but we recognise that it will be a release for yourself. We will just have to learn to cope without you.'

The coercion eventually paid off and after staring for a week at the front cover of the brochure, helpfully provided by Bethany and Ian, advertising the Hotel Euthanasia, Robin nodded his head and blinked his eyes in affirmation of the only avenue he felt was open to him – assisted dying. Bethany and Ian had won. They looked forward to spending their inheritance ... after all, they deserved it.

Along with the other guests on arrival, they took part in the introduction. There Bethany, due to nerves or resentment, pressure or guilt, drank, knocked back, and replenished glasses of champagne as if they were water. After the general introduction to the group, they were given the formal tour and shown around the facilities by the strange Customer Care Manager, Angela Deff. Angela used her 'unique' customer care skills to engage with the Mitchell family. "Will the cripple leave you sufficient funds to maintain your lifestyle, Mrs Mitchell?" she asked.

"You have taken me by surprise with that question. I am sure Mr Mitchell will have left sufficient funds to help his family, Miss Deff."

"Good, Mrs Mitchell. So how big is your inheritance once he dies?"

"It was £23m but that has gone down to £22.4m in the last fortnight," Bethany said without thinking, surprised by the boldness of the question.

"I am glad you know exactly how much is available,

Mrs Mitchell. So, have you arranged the assisted dying so you can get access to the money for yourself?"

"I don't know what you are insinuating."

"It's not unreasonable that this is a possibility. You are a young, attractive woman. Have you arranged for a fit and healthy replacement for Mr Mitchell?"

"I see what you're doing now, Miss Deff. It's a joke to lighten these very difficult proceedings," and in the spirit of the now perceived but misjudged light repartee and with the effects of the champagne dulling her thinking, Bethany added, "Well if you must know, I've lined up Gorgeous Geoff, my tennis coach," she laughed politely at her joke, that actually revealed her true intentions.

Robin, initially half listening, began to take notice, firstly because of Angela's odd manner, but then to his wife's half-truth revealed in her banter. He had been aware of Bethany increasing the time she spent at the tennis club and that she had been getting lessons that involved her being away for three or four hours at a time.

Could it be? No surely not, he thought to himself, searching desperately for reasons why the idea was outrageous.

Passing by Robin and his family, Rab Lennon nodded a hello in the direction of Robin. Bethany, catching Rab's eye, asked him for his reasons for coming to the hotel, "Are you staying at the hotel for the assisted dying service?"

"Yes, I am," Rab surveyed Robin and directed his question to him, "What about yourself, mate, are you goin' through with it?"

Robin could not answer and Bethany provided the answer on his behalf, "Why yes! My husband is going to be mercifully relieved of the burden on himself and his family."

"Well, my maw and paw also took their own lives and didn't even let me know they were goin' to do it. You just can't trust your family, can you?" he replied, again directing the answer to Robin rather than Bethany.

"What a shame," Bethany continued, "that your family didn't have the good taste to keep you informed."

Robin was considering the phrase about trusting your family, as Rab gave his farewells and moved on. It seemed to have added significance for him and this, combined with the reference to the tennis coach, was pushing his mind into overdrive.

Just at that point, Mark Goodwin approached the Mitchells. "Let me introduce myself. Mark Goodwin, pleased to meet you. I would certainly welcome the opportunity to talk to you if that was okay. I am doing a piece for the Sunday edition of '*The Intellect*'."

Robin could not voice his opposition to this before Bethany, using the opportunity to massage her sense of superiority, had offered, "That would be nice. I always read '*The Intellect*'."

So, the family and Mark drifted off slowly for an interview to one of the many luxurious lounge areas available for the guests. "So, why did you decide to use the assisted dying facility of the Hotel Euthanasia?" Mark asked sitting down and taking out his note pad.

Robin looked to Bethany to provide the response.

"He was in so much pain and discomfort that he just wanted a merciful end. We tried to talk him out of it because we want to have him with us for as long as possible, regardless of his condition," Bethany responded.

Robin was thinking that this was not true, as his family had consistently said that they could not cope under the pressure of looking after him. "Burden," Robin blurted out the single word.

"Did you feel a burden on your family, Robin?" Mark asked, directing his gaze to Robin.

"He wasn't a burden. It was his sole decision to use the services of the Hotel Euthanasia," Bethany lied, as Robin shook his head.

"So, I guess you would have had a lot of discussion before going ahead with it?" Mark continued.

"Yes, we all sat down as a family and arrived at the solution that was best for Robin. It breaks all our hearts to have to see him go, but it is what he wants, so we will just have to go ahead with it. And it will be merciful and painless."

Mark sensed a conflict of interests between Robin and the rest of the family and decided it would be better to bring the interview to an end. "Thank you very much, Robin and Bethany, your story is very interesting." He thought about how he would frame the story of the ... *pressure placed on a person with a long-term condition to end his life for the family's sake rather than his own.* "I wish you all the best. Goodbye."

Bethany thanked Mark, while the effects of the effervescent champagne bubbled thoughts through her brain of the pot of cash and the tennis coach awaiting her after their return from the hotel. *I must give Geoff a call later to line up a 'tennis lesson' as soon as I get back. I could do with some relaxation after this business*, she thought to herself.

*

The day arrived for Robin's demise and Bethany and Ian began to get apprehensive about attending the event with Robin. Eventually, their guilt, combined with their horror of the process of death, resulted in them announcing to Robin that he would have to go through with it without them being present.

"We have hired a nice counsellor for you, Robin, dear, so that you will not be alone. We would prefer not to be there at the end as we don't think we could take it with you … er … dy … ing … passing away in front of us."

The counsellor was in fact Suzie Sunfloweroil, the member of the hotel staff that had been introduced to the guests on arrival and who had one of the combined roles of social worker/sex worker. Suzie, in her white bathrobe, pulled back her long black hair into a ponytail and stroked her olive skin. She was attractive, confident, calm, very skilled, and experienced in supporting the dying with their last moments.

Bethany and Ian wheeled Robin to the eXi-theme Departure Suite and, without entering, handed him over to Suzie, who was waiting outside the door, and smiled sympathetically to Robin as they approached.

"Goodbye, Robin, you were a good husband, I … er … I'm sorry, I … "

"Goodbye, Dad."

With this awkward farewell, Bethany and Ian tried to avert their eyes from Robin and hurriedly made their withdrawal, leaving him to his fate with the capable Suzie. They had packed beforehand and had a hovercab waiting for a quick getaway to take them to the airport and a first class flight, complete with bottle of celebratory champagne, back to Oxford.

"Your wife was a bit uncomfortable with the process, Robin," Suzie said, with a reassuring and engaging tone, "Listen, I want to put your mind at rest. I have been through this many times before and it will be fine. Right now, I'm here for you and we can talk about anything you want to – any doubts you may have, or if there are any other things on your mind."

Robin was relieved to be with someone so understanding. Even though he had only just met Suzie, he felt he could confide in her. "I think they found me a burden in the end," he slowly slurred, struggling with the effort to articulate.

"Can I be direct, Robin? Let me guess, there is a large amount of cash awaiting your wife when she gets back to Olde England, if I am correct. Is that the case?"

Robin nodded, putting the facts together and welcoming Suzie's frankness. He had to acknowledge that he had been in denial about his family, about them seeing him as a burden. As he ran through the discussions his wife and son had had with him over the last few months, it became clearer that they had been grooming him for this eventuality. He thought about the references to Geoff, the tennis coach, Bethany had joked about earlier and the times that Bethany had spent in 'lessons' with him. The callousness of his son Ian and the acquisitiveness of his girlfriend Melanie also came clearer into focus.

"Look, Robin, you don't have to go ahead with this if you don't want to," Suzie offered, applying her best empowerment skills, "We can just carry on talking about this if you want, until you decide what the right course of action is for you."

Robin, with the quiet and patient listening ear of Suzie, reflected on his awful family and the prospect of returning to their reluctant care. *No*, he thought, *I couldn't face that. And all the suffering I have had to endure over the previous months, the loss of dignity in so many ways, and now the probability of more pain and an even more diminished quality of life.*

"No, despite being railroaded into coming here, I'm going to go ahead anyway," he laboriously spluttered out to Suzie.

"Okay, if you are sure. Are there any loose ends or final requests that you would like me to help you with before you go ahead, Robin? I am only too happy to assist you in any way I can."

"There is one thing," Robin struggled to say.

*

Bethany and Ian had a splendid trip back on the plane, where they indulged themselves even more with the finest champagne. After they had calmed down, they reaffirmed their actions to each other, following the discomfort of accompanying Robin to the Hotel Euthanasia. They feigned some mock sentimentality about Robin, telling each other remembered stories from their relationship with a father and husband that helped to assuage any semblance of guilt that may have hung around them like the smell of a corpse. As they stepped out of the stretch limousine and into the house, empty but for them now, they discussed what they would do next.

"I am off to the Porsche Showroom with Melanie to buy that beautiful little bright red motor we saw last week," Ian, now carefree and happy with anticipation, exulted in his new situation, while punching the air.

"Geoff has just texted me. He wants to meet me to commiserate about our loss, so I will just text him back to say I'll see him at the club in an hour. We really should phone the Hotel Euthanasia to see if it all went ahead and we will need to make an appointment with the family lawyer to access that lovely inheritance."

And so, they did. The process had gone smoothly for Robin and he had peacefully passed away as planned using a potion of Pentobarbitone that slowed his respiratory function until his last breath expired. He was then cremated and that was the end of it. Bethany made an appointment to meet with the lawyer the next day, so that she and Ian could conclude the will.

*

"Good day Mrs Mitchell and Ian. Can I order you a coffee?" Herbert Robinson the family lawyer offered, as Bethany and Ian sat down to hear the expected details from the Will.

"I would prefer if you could just get on with it, Herbert. I have an appointment with my tennis coach today and I need to pack for a holiday in the Bahamas – I just booked it last night.

"Okay, Mrs Mitchell, as you wish. Can I, first of all, offer my condolences for your and Ian's loss?"

"Yes, quite. Thank you for that, but please do push on, old chap."

"So, you will want to know the contents of the will and the final estate of your departed husband. There was £22.4 million left by your husband, thanks to the healthy state of his business and the sale of the company at just the right time."

Bethany and Ian leaned forward with greedy anticipation.

"Your husband has left all of the £22.4 million to the 'Motor Neurone Disease Research Fund'. The house was in both your names, so that will remain with you," the lawyer outlined in a dispassionate tone, maintaining a reserved eye contact with Bethany and Ian.

*

Bethany experienced a disconnection between the words that were coming from the lawyer's mouth and her brain. It felt like an out of body displacement, where the meaning of the words from what had become a disembodied voice, jarred with the anticipated understanding that had prepared itself in her head.

Ian was the first to question the sense of the lawyer's statement. "Sorry, I misheard that. Can you say that again?"

"Your father has left all of the £22.4 million to the 'Motor Neuro' … "

The disintegrating Bethany let out an uninhibited high-pitched scream that brought Herbert Robinson's secretary to the door to ask if everything was all right. The lawyer directed her to return to her desk as everything was just fine.

Ian parsed Herbert's statement, "So, you are saying that my father has left all of the money to this charity rather than to his wife and son?"

"Precisely."

Bethany now whimpered like a frightened dog. Ian, bringing some logic to the proceedings, announced, "But this cannot be right. He was meant to leave the money to us," and with the preciseness of firing off the last round of ammunition in defence of his life, Ian expressed his verdict, "He must have been insane if he did that. Isn't there a phrase '*not of sound mind*' or something?"

The nature of the exchange between Ian and Herbert was coming slowly into focus for Bethany now and with the resolve of a mother bear defending her cub, she broke in to support her son and condemn her deceased husband, "Yes, he must have been out of his mind to do this. This is not the action of a right-thinking individual."

At this point, Herbert retrieved the 'Competent Adult Test' results, as planned with Robin and Suzie, his social worker, in their telephone conversation the previous day; he laid these out in front of the two incredulous schemers. "I believe that you were in attendance Mrs Mitchell when Robin was tested by … let me see … "

He lifted his glasses and read from the document, "Yes,

it was Doctor Vernon who indicated that your husband was of sound mind and able to make informed decisions for himself. To avoid doubt, I can tell you that your husband was indeed of sound mind when he made the decision regarding whom to give the money to and that the £22.4 million is now safely lodged, as your husband wished, in the bank account of the 'Motor Neurone Disease Research Fund'. So … ," Herbert Robinson said, rising from his chair and gently ushering Bethany and Ian out of his office, "I understand that you had an appointment that you wanted to get to, Mrs Mitchell. I won't keep you any longer. Thank you for your time and, as I say, I am very sorry for your loss."

Chapter 15 The Best Laid Plans of Men

We meet again truths to impart to dance and then to separate

The Song of Villadedino, Saint Dino 240AD

Half-heartedly, Mark Goodwin reviewed the interview notes for his article, sitting alone with his thoughts at the bar. He became aware of the sound of people entering and turned around, hoping that the company would give him some respite from his grief. Recognising the five plucky partisans from Glasgow from the introductory meeting, he announced, "Hi there guys, what can I get you to drink?"

"Very kind of you, I'll have a beer and that will be the same for Shug and Malky."

"And me too," Rashona prompted.

"I'll have a wee voddy, thanks, Mister," said the grateful Magdalene.

"So, I guess you guys are Scottish and by your accents, I would surmise from Glasgow. Am I right?

"Very good, Sherlock," Rab confirmed.

"I love the Highlands of New Scotland. Such a beautiful and elemental wilderness." Mark resisted the urge to think about Estrela and concentrated his attention on the Scots.

"Never been north of the City of Glasgow myself," added Malky.

"What brings you Scots here to Villadedino?" Mark asked, calculating but not overtly questioning.

"They are gettin' blown up in an incubator," Rashona blurted out without thinking and pointed at the boys.

"I've told you, Rashona, we're being cremated not blown up and it is an incinerator," said Rab quickly trying to recover the situation, "We are all part of a self-help group for people with mental illness."

Rab launched into his pre-prepared justification for the group's visit to the Hotel Euthanasia. "We've been meetin' regularly now for over a year and everythin' was working out quite well for us. We were copin' with our family lives, jobs, and self-harmin' and our attempted suicides were down. We were takin' our medication. It was only after the group received the promotional video from Villadedino in the post about the Hotel Euthanasia explainin' the services it provided that it all started to go downhill. It unsettled us and we started to question everythin' we were doin'. We increasingly felt dissatisfied with the side-effects of the medication; nausea, diarrhoea, always being thirsty, not to mention the constant drowsiness and the effects it had on our sex life."

"Don't forget the weight gains," Rashona added as she had been primed to do by Rab.

"It was a battle to deal with the extremes of, on the one hand, the side effects, or on the other, the depression; so, we decided, after watchin' the video again, enough was enough. We all just felt that our lives were not goin' to get any better and we are in reality, finished. You should see the look of fear on people's faces if you say you are suffering from a mental illness. Society just shuns us. Why should we have to put up with this? So, we decided to support each other all the way and come here to the Hotel Euthanasia and end it all."

"Rashona and I were too scared," Magdalene added, "We still wanted to support the boys with their decision though."

"If I was paranoid, which I am by the way," Rab joked, "I would be wonderin' if the girls just wanted to come here wi' us just to make sure we went through with it, so they could get rid of us once and for all."

"I'll second that," said Malky, "I just think Rashona wants to make sure there are more biscuits for her at the group meetings."

"Anyways, it's just us men that are here for the assisted dyin'. The girls are here to see us off in case we change our minds," Shug added, while wishing that he had just kept quiet.

"It's because they've nothing better to do this week and we also promised them free drinks," added Malky to everyone's amusement.

"So, did you have to get a doctor to sign you all off as competent to make the decision to go through with the assisted suicide?" Mark asked.

"It was easy," Rab replied, "Quite a number of the members of the self-help group are doctors. A depressive lot they are too. Well they couldn't have been more helpful in signin' off our capacity to make an informed decision."

"That was convenient, but you are all very young?" Mark challenged, thinking that there may be a story here. "It's a bit extreme, killing yourself because of a mental illness," he continued.

"It's not a problem, because we're from Glasgow and we're pure dead macho and hard. So, we thought let's do it and so here we are," Malky interjected.

Rab, wanting to maintain the credibility of their justification for coming to the hotel added, "Age is immaterial when you are sufferin' to the point where your life is unsustainable."

"Well, lads, I must say I admire your singlemindedness."

"What do you do yourself? And sorry, I didn't get your name?" enquired Rab to steer the conversation away from his other four compatriots.

"Oh me, Mark Goodwin. I work for '*The Intellect*'."

"Is that in computers?"

"No, journalism."

Malky chipped in, "So, is that about journeys to places?"

"No, newspapers and magazines and online web-blogs."

"Oh, like writin' words and stuff?" Malky asked, warming up his brain now, "Do you get money for that? How much do you get for a word?"

"I suppose the last article was about 2,000 words and I got £10,000 so that works out at £5 per word as a rough guess, but to be honest I never think of it like that."

Malky who was an expert at calculating the odds at the Glasgow betting shops quickly worked out the sums. "So, if I write down ten words you'll give me £50? Sounds easy."

"Not quite as simple as that, my friend."

Rab was concerned that Malky's brain was going into overdrive and at risk of overheating with this conversation with the journalist. "Right!" he said, "It is time for dinner, guys. Let's head up to the dinin' room."

"About time," Rashona agreed, "My stomach thought my mouth had ran away with a ventriloquist's dummy."

"I must say you are all very cool about the whole death thing. Very admirable," said Mark.

"Aye, it's not a problem. Get in there … take the stuff … dead. No more depression, anxiety, or paranoia. Nothin' to it. Happy days! Anyway, nice talking to you and we'll maybe see you around. And thanks for the drinks."

The five, at Rab's request, then headed for the boys' bedroom for some planning before dinner was served, leaving a bemused Mark considering how he might include the idiosyncratic Glasgow approach to mental illness and death in his article. The reason for using assisted suicide because of mental health problems didn't ring true to him, as they all seemed so … if you could call it that … pleasantly unstable. Perhaps death was the only positive prospect they had to look forward to that would relieve them of their depressive state.

The leader, Rab, also seemed an interesting fellow. He was very personable and had a way of engaging that made Mark warm to his genuine personality. He also seemed to hold sway with a natural authority over what appeared to be a motley crew of friends. Mark had to consider that, although he was from the equivalent of another planet, he liked Rab. So, as the five departed, Mark's journalistic intuition was alerting him to the fact that there might be more to their story than they were giving away.

*

"So, let's go through the plan again," said Rab, now sitting in the boys' bedroom, leaning forward conspiringly, and talking in serious hushed tones to the five plotters of mayhem. "Now that we've finally made it to the Hotel Euthanasia, we have to pick up the explosives from our contact Sasha in Figas just outside the border with Villadedino. The rendezvous to pick up the explosives takes place tomorrow night at a farmhouse one mile west of the border, crossin' on the main road from Villadedino to Figas. Once we have the explosives, they will be smuggled into the hotel and we'll keep them in the lassies' handbags. We've booked the eXi-theme Departure Suite for myself, Malky, and Shug to 'kick the bucket'. Malky, you're down to be cremated and myself and Shug will be buried."

"I'd rather be buried," interjected Malky, "And I wouldn't say no to the prostitute social workers' theme as well?" pleaded Malky, reading from a brochure left in the room and remembering fondly the relationships with social workers who had worked with him when he was a young boy.

"Malky, ya numpty, you're not going to be cremated, we're only pretendin' to die, we don't actually die! And you're not here to get your leg over, you stupid eejit," retorted Rab, "No, we stick with the plan and anyway, we have booked confessions from the Pope so that will keep us out of trouble."

They had all been a bit star-struck by the thought of a 'one-to-one' with the Pope, even though they knew he was just an impersonator. "Okay. Concentrate, you lot … so imagine yourselves, all five of us are in the eXi-theme Departure Suite. We've ordered three coffins, one for each of Malky, Shug, and myself. The explosives go in Malky's coffin bound for the crematorium. Malky gets in with Shug in his coffin going for burial. I get into my coffin going for buri … "

"S'fuckin' unfair," said Malky, "Why do I have to share a coffin with Shug and you get one all to yourself?"

"I cannot believe you, Malky. I'm the leader, so I get to decide and besides, we only have enough money for three coffins," Rab was becoming irritated by Malky.

"Well, I'm not fuckin' goin' unless a get a fuckin' coffin to ma fuckin' self," announced the combative Malky.

"I don't mind swappin' places and goin' into the coffin with Shug," declared Magdalene. Magdalene, with her crush on Shug, saw the opportunity she had been waiting for to canoodle with Shug and her imagination was working overtime at the prospect of being intimately entangled in such a small space with him.

"I wouldn't mind going in with Shug either," pleaded Rashona, seeing an opportunity to usurp Magdalene for Shug's affection.

"You're a fat cow and wouldn't fit in the coffin yourself, never mind tryin' to get in one with Shug," said Malky, helpfully telling it like it is and calculating the three-dimensional space available within the coffin which, for her part, Rashona seemed not to appreciate.

"I think I'd rather have Magdalene than Malky or Rashona," affirmed Shug, thinking more of the practicality of the available space and concerned about being flattened by Rashona rather than any amorous liaison.

Malky had to acknowledge to himself that if there were only three coffins, then it was probably best for Magdalene to share with Shug rather than himself. However, he was beginning to regret his stance, as this meant he would have a lesser role. Rashona was seething at the indignity of the insult from Malky. *Imagine calling me 'fat' ... as if? Could they not see I am on a strict diet regime? I hope they hurry up and get this meeting over. I'm starving.*

"Okay," Rab finalised, stamping his authority on the proceedings and successfully focusing the group on the task at hand, "The democratic process has come to pass, comrades. Myself, Shug, and Magdalene go in the coffins. Malky and Rashona, you'll help us into the coffins and then make your way around and help us out of them when they've been transported via the conveyor belt system and have reached the burial holdin' depository chamber."

"While you two are getting' us out of the coffins in the burial holding depository chamber, the one with the explosives will be on its way to the crematorium. Is that a plan or is that not a plan! We're going to blow this place to kingdom come. They think they can tell us when it's time to die; well they've got another thing comin'. We're goin' to show those bastards!" roared Rab.

The others, now in agreement about the plan, and pumped up by Rab's oratory powers, joined in, "Get it right into them!"

"Up your hole with a ten-foot pole!" contributed Malky.

"Time for dinner at last!" a relieved Rashona shouted.

The group were euphoric at the devious masterful arrangement that had been laid out before them, however, they had not accounted for a certain capuchin monkey by the name of Jiki in their ingenious plan.

Chapter 16 Who is in Charge?

The mind directs the hand of action inhabiting the game now twice

The Song of Villadedino, Saint Dino 240AD

Hugh Mann did not know what he would have done if Jiki, his monkey helper, had not dramatically changed his outlook on life. Hugh had suffered a catastrophic spinal cord injury following a car crash twenty-one years ago. He could speak, could still use his hands to operate the computer, but only just, and every other part of his functional ability was gone. Hugh used a wheelchair to get around and needed constant personal care for washing, dressing, and going to the toilet. His dear wife, Hannah, was a great help, but he knew she struggled at times and needed some assistance. When he had been told about the monkey helpers he was too depressed to want to pursue the idea, but after some convincing by Hannah, he had finally given it a try. Since then his mood had rallied and he had become inseparable from Jiki.

Jiki was a beautiful capuchin monkey, who had the intelligent white face of a little old man and the black fur at the top of his head that had given the genus its name. Spaniards, when they had arrived in South America, thought the little black furry cap on the monkeys' heads looked like the cowls of the capuchin order of monks. His arms, legs, and long tail were black, while his throat and chest were the same colour as his white face. Jiki had undergone rigorous training since he was little and been raised to never bite, obey commands, turn on the audio system, and fetch items for his master. Obeying commands is probably not quite accurate because, in Jiki and Hugh's case, it was the monkey that 'called the shots'.

Jiki was a very clever creature and was able to pretend to be doing the bidding of his master, while all the time influencing and directing the requests Hugh thought he was making. This allowed Jiki to get a lot out of the tasks for himself, while, at the same time, making Hugh's life a bit easier.

Jiki had taken quite a bit of time to train Hugh to do his bidding, but after their first two years together, he could get Hugh to do most things he wanted. The trick was looking into Hugh's eyes with an 'imperceptible-to-humans' series of glances at the task or item Jiki wanted to get or do. Hugh would do Jiki's bidding, for example, by instructing Jiki to operate the microwave, turn on the music to dance to Jiki's favourite rock bands, fetch something from the fridge, make a drink, turn on the lamp; all activities that Jiki enjoyed to relieve his boredom, but most of all to give Jiki what he liked most, a raisin!

So, this had been life for the last twenty years with Jiki manipulating Hugh. Somehow, they both got on. Hugh's wife Hannah was very grateful for the support the monkey provided, allowing her some respite from the caring role, which she had been committed to in support of her husband. Jiki was also a very sweet and loving capuchin monkey and would gladly spend time sleeping on Hugh's shoulders or on his lap.

Jiki, being very bright, could understand Hugh's needs and generally, they all bonded into a good relationship.

Hugh had managed his disabilities, thanks to the help he was receiving. The stable arrangement, alas, came to a sorry end. Hugh's wife Hannah had suddenly and unfortunately died last year and he was devastated by his loss to the extent that he was convinced that he couldn't carry on without her. This led to periods of depression and feelings of hopelessness that would have been much worse had it not been for the companionship of Jiki. But still, Hugh considered that he needed to take back some control of his life and so, after some searches on the Internet, he had come across the web site for the Hotel Euthanasia. His initial idea was to find a new caring home for Jiki and then he would make the journey to Villadedino, there ending his life. However, no matter how hard he tried, he could not find anyone to look after Jiki. The advice he received was that Jiki had developed such a long-standing and deep bond with Hugh over the last twenty years that he would not be able to settle with any other person and that the capuchin would likely suffer from separation anxieties and die of a broken heart. So, Hugh had no other option than to consider what he felt was a more humane choice available to him for Jiki. Following lengthy telephone discussions with the hotel about being accompanied in death by his companion Jiki, he was given the reassurance that the hotel could provide the solution to taking control of his and the monkey's destiny. Now, he was here at the Hotel Euthanasia to end what he felt had become his sorry life. Jiki, his best friend, was accompanying him.

Jiki recognised that something had changed; Hugh's mate had disappeared. Jiki thought that perhaps she had found

194

an alpha male from another troop or that she was off looking for fruit, but there it was, she was no longer around. And worse, Hugh had taken Jiki to this other nest, the one they were now in. It was a bit unsettling at first, being cooped up in a cage for the journey, but since they had arrived, he was relieved to be with Hugh and had grown curious about his new surroundings. Fortunately, there appeared to be an endless supply of raisins and fruit and Hugh's mood was the best it had been since his mate had disappeared. They spent their days happily listening to rock music they both enjoyed and which Jiki loved to dance to. Jiki had picked up the moves of the singers from the videos Hugh and he watched and his comical impersonations of rock stars on stage continued to keep Hugh in a happier frame of mind. Jiki was missing his microwave, but there was plenty to do, fetching drinks for Hugh and helping him with snacks and, of course, helping himself to the raisins.

Despite the congenial surroundings and the good nature of his companion, Hugh was still resolved to end his life. Death, he thought, was his choice and it would be a release from the tedious repetitive routine of living. He had had enough. He reasoned that he had had a good life when Hannah, Jiki and himself were together, but he just did not want to receive the support his wife had provided from a never-ending supply of strangers no matter how well trained, kind, and professional they were in their approach. He had tried his best to bestow Jiki on to someone else who might benefit from his companionship and help, but all his efforts to do this had been in vain. He was reconciled to the plan that Jiki join him in the process of assisted dying. So, the day was drawing near for Hugh and the unsuspecting monkey who, despite being extremely clever, did not recognise the fate that awaited him.

Chapter 17 Mutual Disclosures

Truth will heal the heavy heart as dancing seals us to our fate

The Song of Villadedino, Saint Dino 240AD

I still can't believe my mother and father would have gone through with an assisted suicide here at the Hotel Euthanasia, Rab thought to himself. He sat at the hotel bar on his own, having managed to slip away after dinner from his four compatriots for once, and now turned his mind to reflect on the reasons for his involvement in the mission to blow up the hotel. He sat playing a computer game on his phone, that involved leprechauns and little red headed Irishmen battling it out to gain dominance and build villages and castles in Ireland.

So the question kept playing in his head, *why am I doing this when they didn't care for me anyway?*

Meanwhile, a sad Mark Goodwin, who had been thinking about his own recent bereavement, had entered the bar again. Seeing and recognising Rab, the likeable Scot, Mark sat down beside him.

"Can I buy you a drink, wee man?" Rab offered, identifying the journalist, who had bought all the Glasgow group drinks earlier.

"Yes, thanks, a beer would be good. How is the Glasgow party settling in?"

"Just fine," replied Rab, "I left them all in the dinin' room finishin' off their 'Knickerbocker Glories'."

"What is the game you are playing on your phone?"

"Oh, it's just Leprechauns and Ginger Nuts. It's just a bit of fun. I've just had an upgrade on this phone and the characters have really evolved to be quite life-like."

"What about your plans for assisted suicide?" Mark 'clocked' the inconsistency of Rab upgrading the game while planning to die.

"We're organised and just waitin' for the day of reckonin'. How's your article shapin' up?"

"To be honest, I can't get going on it. I have plenty of notes and material but the thing that is really stopping me is that I recently lost someone very dear to me who ended her life here at the Hotel and I just can't stop thinking about her." Mark was not sure why he was unburdening himself to Rab, but he seemed to be someone who was genuinely sympathetic and didn't seem as if he would judge him.

Rab immediately felt empathy for Mark and this, in turn, caused him to respond truthfully, "Funny you should say that, because both my parents came here for assisted suicide, so I suppose we have somethin' in common. I know I said all that stuff about the mental illness support group, but my parents using assisted suicide is the real reason I just joined in with the rest when they decided to come here. We're on our own, we have a similar experience, so I'm lettin' you in on the real reason."

"Both your parents. That must have been hard to take, losing them both at the same time. If you don't mind me asking, how did you cope?"

"Well, it's not been good, really. You see they never even told me they were goin' to do it. I just heard through the Communist Club. They were both red-hot 'commies', by the way, and their death was inadvertently relayed to me by mistake. So, it came as a complete shock that the Communist Party had arranged the whole thing. The Communist Party, would you believe, gave them financial support. Something they justified by saying they were snubbin' the capitalist funeral monopoly. But I know for a fact that it was because my parents were receivin' a pension from the Party and they wanted to get their hands on it. Much cheaper to get rid of them rather than for the Party to pay out on the pension for another twenty years or more. So, you see, I'm a bit aggrieved by the Communist Party for arrangin' this and the Hotel Euthanasia for providin' the service. I ended up leavin' the Communist party and, would you believe it, joinin' the Catholic Church!"

"I don't understand then," questioned Mark, "I can see why you would be angry with the Communist Party and the Hotel, but if you take the church's stand and don't agree with euthanasia, why are you going to go through with the same thing yourself?"

"It's er ... ," Rab was stalling, as he needed to come up with a reasonable answer that justified his stance, "Don't get me wrong, I used to be all for assisted dyin' and in actual fact I supported a group to try and get the law changed in New Scotland. But my parents' suicide taught me that life's a sham. One minute you're here and the next minute you're not. If you're alive, you're alive and if you're dead, you're dead.

What's the point of it all? It really doesn't matter if it's one thing or the other, especially when life has treated you badly like me … they all let me down! My maw and paw and the Communist Party … I had so much to give them all, but I wasn't important to them. So, in the end, it's all the same. If you think about it in a grander sense, the cosmos it's just like this great big thing that's difficult to understand. So, I'm just goin' to 'pop my clogs' and that'll be that."

Mark was taken aback at first, but the more he reflected on his own loss, there was something he interpreted in what Rab was saying that resonated with him. *The state of living or not living was something to think about, along with the illusory nature of the self.* He wondered if he would be as courageous as Rab to just end it. *Perhaps*, he speculated, *Estrela understood this and that was why she had come to the Hotel Euthanasia.* It gave him some comfort to think of Estrela being clear about what she was doing. The ideas Rab had talked about also gave Mark some suggestions for his article. *To see the assisted suicide from the perspective of the people who are left behind. After all*, he reflected, *that was the position he was in as well as Rab.*

"Thanks, Rab, that has given me some ideas for my article. It has also helped me come to terms a bit more with my own loss, although it is very hard. What about the religious requirements, though? How do you reconcile your own philosophy with that of the Church?"

"The Church has given me a focus for my enthusiasm and I'm good at strivin' for a cause, but it's just an institution, just like Communism. Both man-made."

Rab was in full oratory mode now. "The way I see it ... my parents' death made me leave Communism because it didn't treat them well enough. The Party just wanted to get rid of them as an expensive liability. I took up with the Church because there was a big gap in my life. I had the ability and drive to campaign about ideals. It so happened that this death of my parents got me hooked on gettin' revenge against the Hotel Euthanasia. I just thought that maybe I should do somethin' about it."

Mark was not following this and was unclear about Rab's references to 'revenge' and 'doing something about it'. How did this correspond with Rab taking his own life and how was that going to be a punishment for the hotel? The links of all this to the support group for people with mental health problems was now getting beyond him.

"So, I'm on a mission. I intend to do the right thing and in a way, this'll avenge my parents' deaths. When I 'give up the ghost', the Hotel Euthanasia are goin' to know all about it!"

Mark, while admiring Rab's forthright approach to life and death, failed to comprehend how his death would make any impact on the Hotel. *But I can work that one out later*, he thought, pushing it to the back of his mind.

Mark liked Rab's genuine way of expressing himself in a manner that was mostly believable. The causality of Rab's life circumstances and his decision to act on them were honourable and heroic as an example of human self-determination. Perhaps, Rab could be the lead character in his article. This was a good substitute for Estrela, who also had had issues with her biological parents resulting in her suicide. Rab's story was a good way for him to transfer the emotions he was feeling about Estrela into the article.

"Thanks, Rab. I have really appreciated our little discussion tonight. You have no idea how much it has helped me come to terms with my own loss and has given me ideas on how to approach my article. I think I will head to my room now and start getting some thoughts put down on paper."

"No problem, wee man. I'll see you about."

Chapter 18 Bar Stools

And sing another song of life that leads on in time's device

The Song of Villadedino, Saint Dino 240AD

Mark left the bar, passing Malky, Rashona, and Magdalene, singing extracts from one of their favourite hits, on their way to a late evening refreshment.

> *I met Tallulah in a bar room brawl*
> *Her right hook was like a cannonball*
> *We slugged it out, I can't remember it all*
> *But I was love struck when I started to fall*
> *Love struck*
> *Love struck*
> *Love struck by her right hook cannonball.*

At the same time, Shug was making his way to bed, although he couldn't quite make his mind up about 'turning in'. He had got back up twice after deciding to join the other three, but then had returned to bed, when exhaustion had finally decided for him; he was now asleep and blissfully unaware of the other three who were well into the party mode.

Rab, pleased to be relieved of his more serious reflections, joined in as they made their way jovially to the bar, laughing, and enjoying each other's company. "That's just a pure brilliant song, guys," Rab eulogised, cheering up to the rousing geniality created by the singing.

"I totally agree. One of my favourite songs of all time,"

Malky added.

"So, can I get you rock stars a wee drink?" Rab offered, carried away by the bonding through song.

"Sure thing, mate."

"So, how are you all enjoyin' yourselves here? What do you think about this lot that have signed up for the assisted suicide?" Rab asked his drinking buddies.

"If you ask me, they are pure mental," Malky offered.

"But they must be very brave to go through with it. It kind of makes me sad," said Magdalene, "Does no one care for them? If they just took time out to weigh up their decision, maybe they would change their minds and then everythin' would be all right. Someone would love them if only they wouldn't just end their lives." She gave a small sob as a small voice in her head said, '*I care for you mummy.*'

The rest of the group were staring at Magdalene and wondering where all the melancholy had come from.

"Have you seen the spread in the eXi-theme Departure Suites?" Rashona changed the discussion to her favourite subject, "You know, I could die happy after helpin' myself to a banquet like that. Anyway, I suppose some people would be more inclined to accept dying than others. Like me, for instance, I'm naturally big and there is nothin' I can do about it. It's the same with these folk; maybe it is in their genes to want to kill themselves. Maybe it is just like me with … ," she conjured up a chocolate éclair in her mind, " … a chocolate éclair. If it's there, the probability is that I'm goin' to eat it."

"More like a certainty! Well, I just think they are all

cowards," Malky spat out contemptuously, "They are all rollin' in it, too. Rich bastards! Taking the easy road out of an easy life."

"But, surely, they would have to really think about it," Rab reasoned, "And it's not as if they can change their minds once they have done it. Some of them also have serious illnesses and what about if they are in pain and sufferin'. Don't they have the right to choose?" Rab was forgetting that he was no longer an advocate for assisted dying, however, his reason could not be subdued especially after a few beers.

"Not all that fuckin' choosy-floozy stuff again," interrupted Malky, "All that talk the last time nearly had me signin' up to end my life for real. Talk about boring! Did you see the wee monkey? I did like that wee guy that was helpin' the bloke in the wheelchair. It was just like a wee miniature human being with hands and everythin'."

"Maybe the two of you are related," Rashona joked.

"Very funny. You just drive me bananas!" Malky responded.

Bananas, thought Rashona, *I could eat a banana split with cream and syrup right now*.

"What was all that about assisted dyin' in the moonlight by that big blonde. Angela somethin'?" Magdalene queried, "I didn't like her one bit. She looks straight through you and no emotions. She gave me shivers right up my back. A bit like talkin' to a robot." Malky jumped up from his chair and commenced his robotic break dance moves while exhorting in a high pitched mechanical automaton voice, "Get your arses right in here to my eXi-theme Departure Suite and we will set you up with a

205

bucket to kick."

Rashona, inspired by Malky, added in a singsong voice, "If you are feelin' dire, we will help you expire! If you want to chuck it, come in and kick the bucket!"

The group was enjoying the humour and each other's company.

"It's a pity Shug couldn't make it. He would have enjoyed the banter," Rashona said.

"Maybe I should go along and make sure he's tucked in," Magdalene responded.

"You don't want to give him nightmares," Rashona countered, "I think he would prefer me to help him get off to sleep. He has a bit of a soft spot for me."

"Yes, on his backside," Magdalene answered. "I have seen him. He is always lookin' at me. It's me he likes, not you, you fat cow," she raised her voice angrily.

"Now, come on you two, let's not fall out here," Rab pleaded for reason in an effort to cool off the tempers that were flaring up, "We need to concentrate on the task at hand, so let's not get into a fight over who likes who the most. It is gettin' late and we should all probably be in bed anyway."

"There you go encouragin' Magdalene again," Malky joked. This broke the ice as the four friends, Rashona and Magdalene now reconciled, with the additional alcohol fostering good humour. They sat around drinking and telling each other tales till tiredness crept over them, causing them to wish each other a good night, all with their different thoughts of life and death, retiring to their respective bedrooms.

Chapter 19 The Journalist's Investigation Deepens

And finding we've discovered snow forming to a blizzard ice

The Song of Villadedino, Saint Dino 240AD

A sea of faces of the people he had interviewed ebbed and flowed across the mind of Mark Goodwin as he sat in his hotel room drinking a third glass of whisky and staring vacantly into space. A frustration surfaced above the bobbing faces. Mark was annoyed with his own lack of courage at never quite finding the opportunity to ask questions to discover the real reason for his magazine assignment and presence at the hotel in Villadedino. His mind drifted back, pulled by the tide of his emotions towards the last time he had seen Estrela alive.

All had been going so well with the strong loving bond built over the time he and Estrela had been seeing each other. *I knew she was responding to the support I was giving her during our discussions about her early life in the children's homes in Canada.* She seemed genuinely relieved to be discussing how she felt and this had encouraged Mark to take his 'counsellor' role a stage further. There was also, if Mark was to be honest with himself, some niggling professional intrigue about the story of Estrela and how she had developed into the unique person she was now. Mark invoked the unappeasable investigative skills at his disposal and, eager to be gratified, he inevitably set out to identify Estrela's genetic parents believing this would lead to an even deeper connection to the woman he loved.

He traced her history to the children's homes in Canada where she had lived and spoke with the members of staff employed there. When he communicated with them by telephone, they were unwilling to reveal anything about Estrela's records. However, Mark had not become a successful journalist without finding ways around barriers to information. His final call was to the children's home where Estrela had first been admitted. He introduced himself as Doctor Churchill from the esteemed private Churchill Clinic in London. He invented a story about some congenital illness that his patient, Estrela Jones, was suffering from. He said he needed to trace her genetic parents to see if there was a history of the illness in her blood relatives. Convinced by the call, the Unit Manager unearthed the archive records on the computer client system.

"I am sorry, Doctor," she said, "There is no record of who her family was. Yes, I remember this case very well. It was a most unusual and famous episode here in Whitehorse for a time. This was the girl who was found out in the wilds, out past Dawson, and up the Yukon River. When she was found, she was in a poor state. We never did find out who her parents were, poor kid."

Mark, having at last discovered a connection, terminated the call, thanking the Unit Manager profusely for her help, and saying that he was sure they could find a treatment for Estrela's medical condition.

Wow, he had thought to himself, *out in the wilds of the Yukon!* His journalist's mind was working through the algorithms of his mind, putting together the clues to the songs that Estrela wrote and the sense of isolation and loneliness that her voice always invoked. This case was 'famous', so there was likely to be a newspaper story waiting to be discovered. This would help him uncover the facts. His search of '*Girl Found in the Yukon Wilderness*' soon unearthed the story.

'*MYSTERY OF WILD GIRL FOUND IN THE YUKON*'
10th July 2023

A girl who is thought to be around five years of age was discovered yesterday, on her own, in an old broken down shack twenty miles north of Dawson by Dan Quinn and his son Pete Quinn while on a hunting trip in the area.

'We were just tracking game to shoot, when we came across the cabin,' reported Dan, 'At first, we thought it was just a bag of rags on the log outside the cabin and then we saw it move; it was a little girl. We thought she must be there with her family, but we couldn't find anyone ... just the girl with long, dark, matted hair, unwashed, and very thin. She could only say a few words and we had difficulty understanding her. We searched all around the cabin for her parents, but there was no one. We looked inside the cabin and it was a total mess. The girl must have had supplies, as there were empty tins and beer bottles everywhere. But she couldn't tell us anything and we thought we needed to get her back to civilization to get some medical treatment, so we walked out of there back to our SUV and brought her straight down to Dawson.'

The hospital staff said the girl was badly malnourished

and displayed wild animal-like behaviour. Psychiatric staff were brought in to interview the girl they have named Estrela as she was unable to tell anyone what she was called.

Findings to date indicate that Estrela was abandoned at an early age and the hospital staff are calling her a feral child. Her behaviour indicates that she has spent a long time on her own and has been deprived of human interaction, but she has been able to survive by bringing herself up instinctively just like an animal. The poor child displays all the signs of having been deprived of human care and affection for some time; she has difficulty relating to other human beings and does not have any social skills. She speaks a language that no one can understand, except for a few words that can be deciphered, including 'tree' and 'snow'.

Police are on the search for the parents of Estrela, but after a nationwide search there are no missing children that match her description.

Mark reflected on the newspaper article, convinced that the abandoned child was definitely Estrela. He was sure now that he was getting somewhere, as he continued to open another file and check on the next article he had found.

'WHAT EVER HAPPENED TO WILD CHILD ESTRELA?'
21st December 2023

It has been six months since Estrela, the wild child found in an abandoned cabin north of Dawson, was rescued and taken into the care of the Canadian Child Welfare Services. Estrela

Jones (the name given to her by the hospital staff) was found by father and son Dan and Pete Quinn while hunting in the woods. Estrela could hardly speak and had no ability to relate to human beings. So, what has happened to the wild child now?

Estrela was taken to The Pines Children's Home in Whitehorse and we spoke to the Unit Manager about how she was doing.

'At first, Estrela would sit by her window, staring at the trees outside. She ate with her hands and was frightened of people. We could not find a way of communicating with her, until Molly, one of our care workers, was singing to her one day. It was snowing outside and, it was the strangest and most wonderful thing, Estrela started to sing. She only sang a few words that we could recognise, but she seemed to have made up her own language interspersed with words that we could make out. Since then we have introduced more words to her. She does not attend school yet and has a personal tutor. The other strange thing is, now that it has started to snow, she will spend as much time as we will let her outside, dancing around in the trees and the snow, singing her songs. No-one from her family has come forward to claim Estrela and it is still a mystery how she ended up in the shack in the forest.'

So, if you are the parents of Estrela or if you know of any persons in your area that you think had had a child you have not seen in some time, we would like to hear from you. Contact us on 912 900 9000.

And that was that. There were no further articles he

could find about Estrela. Mark wondered how he should go about discussing his recent revelations with her. The findings certainly gave him a greater insight into her nature. Their romance had continued smoothly and very happily thus far and Mark did not want to wreck this in any way. He was already deeply in love with her and knew that he would have to talk with her very sensitively about what he had found out. He decided to play a long game and take Estrela on holiday to the wintry Highlands of New Scotland in January. He thought that if they could spend some intimate time together, maybe the opportunity would present itself to raise the latest revelations with her.

He deliberately rented a wooden cabin for a weekend in quiet countryside in the Cairngorm mountains near Aviemore. They used their time together to go on long walks through the snow along forest paths. Mark discreetly began to introduce leading questions about what she thought of the beautiful wintry conditions.

"This scenery out here is amazing, don't you think? I just love the ancient Scots Pines."

"Oh, yes," replied Estrela, "This is such a beautiful place. It is so peaceful; the cold air kisses your soul and the snow on the trees is just as if heaven has opened up and left a blessing on each and every branch. Do you know that the trees up in the higher altitudes grow much slower than those at the lower part of the mountain? I was told that my new guitar has a spruce top made from trees at the very edge between the forest and the mountain and that its beautiful tone is due to the slow growth and narrowness of the grains that then produce the resonance."

"That is a beautiful thought," Mark replied, hanging on every word that Estrela uttered.

Estrela would touch the snow and the branches and sing with something akin to an elemental connection to her natural surroundings. Mark was entranced by the sound of her hauntingly beautiful voice, although some of the words were strangely unrecognisable to him.

"What is that song you are singing? I don't understand the words. Is that a different language?"

Estrela answered, "It's only a silly children's song with made up words that I used to sing when I was little about the snow and the stillness of my thoughts in connection with the snow and evokes a loneliness and longing when I see it like this."

Mark was beginning to think that this was the opening he had been waiting for, "Did you spend a lot of time playing in the snow when you were a child in Canada?"

There was silence. "You know, don't you?" questioned Estrela after a sudden stop, a long hesitation, and then a hard turn to face Mark.

"Yes, I do, but I am only trying to understand," Mark admitted, feeling both guilty and relieved to have brought the matter out into the open.

"You couldn't just leave it, could you?"

"But darling, I want to know you more," Mark replied, trying to convince Estrela.

"This is all very hard for me to think about. It was a very difficult time for me as a child." Estrela did appreciate Mark's love and concern for her, but she was, once again, overcome by those complex feelings of sadness, longing, and loneliness that she usually always managed to keep locked away from everyone, not least herself   .

Mark, driven insensitively by professional curiosity and wanting to continue, asked, "But how did you get out there to the cabin? Who left you there? I understand that you find this hard, but please try to tell me. There are so many questions that I have to ask, because I want to know everything about you."

"I only have vague memories of a man; I guess he must have been my father. We were together and then he wasn't there one day. I looked for him but he just wasn't there and I didn't understand. It's hard for me to talk about it."

"Can you remember a name, anything about him or your life before the cabin?"

Perhaps it was the setting or the love she felt from Mark, but very strangely, a name suddenly materialized in Estrela's mind, as if the thought had just been plucked out of thin air and had floated like a feather and placed itself in her mind.

"Digby!" she said, "I don't know where that came from, but this name feels as if it is something old and dusty that I used to have a memory of owning."

Estrela was overcome by a wave of exhaustion and suddenly felt disorientated. "I feel so tired, Mark. Please let's go back to the cabin." They walked back to the cabin without any conversation passing between them and, on arrival, Estrela climbed into bed and instantly fell asleep.

Estrela dreamed deep and long of snow and forests of pine. She saw herself as a tiny bird in a silent field of still snow and felt a presence in her dream of rough hands, a feeling of panic … and then there was silence … with flakes of snow starting to fall. The tiny bird was alone, with conflicting feelings of relief, yet loneliness. The bird sat on the branch of a snow-laden tree and sang its song in celebration of the beauty that surrounded it. The images started to shift and disappear as Mark's voice came through Estrela's consciousness.

"You slept through the afternoon, evening, and all night. Here I've made you a cup of coffee."

"Thanks," murmured a drowsy Estrela as she became more awake.

"Mark, I understand that you have wanted to help me, but I just don't want to think about that time of my life anymore. Please don't ask me any more questions and please don't do any more searching for my parents. I am happy with where my life is at the moment. I just can't take any more surprises. So, will you please leave it there and let's move on with our lives."

"Of course, if that's what you want," replied Mark, already swimming towards the hook cast his way by Estrela with the name 'Digby' hanging on it. Tragically, the professional ability (some might call it a compulsion) of Mark the journalist to pursue a story relentlessly, like a tracker on the trail of his quarry, was going to be his undoing.

Chapter 20 Figas Gets 'Eggshited'

To shield the splendid times and deeds that joy entreats us to excite

The Song of Villadedino, Saint Dino 240AD

Sasha turned to his two brothers, Felix and Xavi, and whispered in conspiring tones, "Tonight's the night, boys."

Felix and Xavi looked confused, "But it's still daytime, Sasha."

"No! Later, when it's no longer day and nighttime has arrived and it is this night tonight, then when it is not today but it is tonight tonight, then tonight will be the night."

"Oh," Felix replied, briefly capturing the corner of a sense of what his brother was talking about before it flew off, "So, does that mean today is the day?"

"Never mind!" a frustrated Sasha sighed.

*

The three brothers Sasha, Felix, and Xavi lived in the village of Wod in the country of Figas, two miles from the border with Villadedino, which was why their village priest, Father Marionetta, had contacted them.

"Sasha," he had said, with his distinctive form of speech, "I am sho eggshited, I have received a requesht for an important mission from the Archbishop of Glashgow in New

216

Shcotland. Our cell of Retribution and Inquishition has at last been recognised. It's sho eggshiting. Thish ish a big opportunity, sho … oh eggshiting and if we get thish right, we can really make a name for ourshelves."

The cell of Retribution and Inquisition was entitled the 'Figas United Catholic Knights for the Elimination and Retribution of Sins', the members being blissfully unaware that the acronym spelt out, appropriately in their case, 'FUCKERS'. The cell consisted of the priest Father Marionetta, the three brothers, and a stray dog, who was hopeful, but not that hopeful, that the regular gathering of humans might result in some stray food coming its way.

"Our tashk ish to pash exploshives to a crack Retribution and Inquishition cell from the Metropolish of Glashgow in New Shcotland. They are traveling to Villadedino to blow up the Hotel Euthanashia. Ishn't that sho eggshiting? I am eggshited. Oh, what eggshitement! We have never had shuch eggshitement in Wod shince we were eggshited about the clothes catalogue that was shent to Xavi by mishtake.

"There's only one word I can say to describe how I feel, Father."

"What's that, Sasha?"

"It's so 'eggshiting'!" exploded Sasha, "When is the clothes catalogue arriving?"

"No, the clothes catalogue was shome time ago. Now, our mission ish that we are pashing exploshives to the Glashgow boysh."

"Yes, I've got it now," Sasha acknowledged.

"The Archbishop and I have devised a foolproof plan."

"And where are we going to find the fools to proof it?" asked Sasha.

"Okay, I will keep it shimple. That ish, eggshiting and shimple, but moshtly eggshiting, but shimple too," Father Marionetta continued, "You will rendezvous at the old abandoned farmhoush jusht wesht of the main road in Villadedino, jusht pasht the border. The Glashgow boysh will shpeak to you in code. They will shay, 'July ish like a goat with a lot of grash'. You will anshwer, 'My watch says mid-day' and they will then reshpond with, 'I would mish your applesh for a glash of beer'."

"My watch says midday, my watch says midday, my watch says midday. No problem with that," the 'eggshited' Sasha tested, "But what if it's not midday, Father?"

"Sasha, it doeshn't matter if it ish not midday, but that ish a good point. We will paint your watch fache white and paint on the fache of the watch the hansh at midday. In that way, no one will be confushed."

"Good," a proud Sasha concluded, having been given the recognition he richly deserved for resolving a major flaw in the plan, "I'm so 'eggshited'!" It could be seen that Father Marionetta's 'eggshitement' was infectious.

"Me too!" said the others 'eggshitedly'.

*

The three brothers arrived at the abandoned farmhouse early and, to overcome the boredom, settled down to play a game

218

of cards. Xavi had lifted the bag with the explosives in it as planned; Sasha had painted the face and hands of his watch to ensure it was midday when they met with the Glasgow boys; and Felix put himself in charge of the clothes catalogue, which he had remembered Father Marionetta mentioning but was at a loss as to what part it played in the mission. Father Marionetta had brought the cards and had dealt out a hand to each for a game of poker while they waited for the Glasgow boys.

"Okay, you are allowed to exchange three cardsh each, ladsh."

"I'll give you my three cards for a bottle of beer, then," offered Sasha.

"No, it hash to be for three other cardsh," corrected Father.

"Well, I don't want you to think I'm stupid, Father, but what would be the point of that? You see you have given me five cards, then if I give you three back and you take those three cards and take another three and give me three cards back, then that adds up to six cards."

"Yes," joined in the other two.

"Okay, we will jusht play who can throw a card the furthesht then as ushual," Father Marionetta replied conceding defeat.

*

The Glasgow boys on the way to their rendezvous slipped quietly alongside the farmhouse they had identified as the meeting place for their assignation. Rab, seeing his contact sitting thoughtfully chewing on a piece of grass, approached nonchalantly and conveyed the secret coded password, "July is like a goat with a lot of grass."

The farmer looked up, wondering who these strange people were. Partly deaf, he heard the visitor say, 'Julia is a goat with a fat ass'. This would not have been too great a problem but for the fact that the farmer's wife just happened to be called Julia.

In an angry voice, he responded with, "My word, what did you say?"

Rab, of course heard, something within the famer's accent that was an approximation to, "My watch says midday", and carried on with a confiding wink of his eye, a wide smile and the concluding part of their secret greeting, "I would miss your apples for a glass of beer."

The farmer's hearing was poor and he was perplexed by these strangers insulting his wife. But now he couldn't believe his ears. The man was saying, "I would kiss her nipples for a glass of beer!" He interpreted the accompanying body language as adding further injury to insult. The farmer grabbed the pitchfork lying by his side and proceeded to chase the troublemakers off his farm. Julia, his wife, hearing the commotion and suspecting thieves from Figas, ran out of the farmhouse kitchen to help deal with whatever was going on. Outside, she lifted a bucket of pig shit sitting by the pig sty and launched the contents over the obese Malky, the last and slowest of the retreating 'thieves'.

Running fast to avoid the deadly prongs from the pitchfork, the three swerved and leapt as nimbly as they could.

When they were a safe distance away and were sure the farmer had ceased in his efforts to catch them, they stopped to catch their breath and review their position. Rab looked quizzically at the map to reassess their situation.

"You smell of shit, Malky. That's just pure mingin'. I think I'm goin' to boke!" retched Shug.

"It was that mad woman threw somethin' over me. But I can't smell anythin'."

"Right enough, there's not that much of a difference between that and your normal smell," concluded Shug.

"We should go back and beat the livin' daylights out of that farmer," the angry Malky proposed.

"We are runnin' out of time, so no, Malky, we go on. Keep your anger under control," Rab countered trying to lead the expedition and keep Malky in line at the same time.

"We'll just have to get on with it, smellin' of shit or not," said Rab, "We were supposed to go west of the main road. Let me see."

"Shouldn't you turn the map the right way around," Shug helpfully prompted Rab.

"I was just about to do that!"

So, with the map turned around the proper way, they negotiated the terrain, crossed the main road, and shortly reached the correct farm. The three were relieved to have located the Figas contact, Sasha, who was accompanied by the other three, Xavi, Felix, and Father Marionetta, who had come along to keep Sasha company.

"July is like a goat with a lot of grass," ventured Rab.

"My watch says midday," replied Sasha, holding up his watch for the Glasgow boys to see and thus verifying that it was, in fact, mid-day, even though it wasn't.

"I would miss your apples for a glass of beer," concluded Rab. "Hullo there boys, how is it goin'?" Rab enthused, relieved that the plan was coming together. "Can I introduce Malky, Shug, and myself, Rab."

"One of you smells of pig shit," Sasha clarified for the Glasgow boys just in case they were unaware of the fact.

"Yes, we were attacked by a pure mad farmer and his wife threw shit over Malky," explained Rab, embarrassed, but not half as embarrassed as Malky. "What do we call yourselves, then?"

"Thish ish Sasha, Felix, and Xavi, and my name ish Father Marionetta," the priest introduced, "and we are sho eggshited, sho eggshited, sho eggshited to be part of the plan.

Xavi here hash the exploshives in the bag. We are sho eggshited to be able to pash theshe over to you," said Father Marionetta, nodding to Xavi to pass the bag to the Glasgow boys, which he did.

"Thank you very much for this," said Rab, receiving the bag and opening it to look in. He reached into the bag and extracted, not the explosives, but several strings of very large sausages.

The Wod boys looked at each other. "How did you manage to get our rabbit, pigeon, and dormouse sausages?" questioned Sasha, taken aback by the slight of hand that had produced their supper for the evening from the bag of explosives.

"Xavi, were there two bagsh beshide each other when

you fetched the exploshives?" Father Marionetta asked.

"No, there was only one beside the other one," Xavi replied.

"Could the one beshide the other one, the one you didn't lift, given you lifted the one you did, which is the other bag, the one which Rab now hash in his hand, could thish in fact be the one with the exploshives?" Father Marionetta rationalized.

"Only if it isn't this one," Xavi resolved.

"Xavi, jusht go back to your housh and bring the other bag from there to here, pleashe." Father Marionetta hoped that this would produce a better result than the 'sausages of mass destruction' that Rab held in his hands.

Xavi returned to the brothers' house and, would you believe it, the other bag with the explosives was there where Father Marionetta said it would be. *How could it have gotten here?* thought Xavi, walking around it a few times to check he wasn't seeing things. He lifted it up, as requested by Father Marionetta, and headed back to the rendezvous at the farmhouse.

Things would have gone well but for Xavi feeling tired following the extreme activity of running back and forward between the rendezvous and his home in Wod. As a result, about half a mile from the rendezvous and after a short argument with himself, Xavi placed the bag with the explosives on the ground and sat down on a log for a much-deserved rest and a smoke. He lit the cigarette and with the careless abandon of those who deserve a much-needed rest, closed his eyes, drew the tobacco into his lungs, and flicked the match away. The match, still alight, flew through the air and came to rest, nestling comfortably in the bag full of explosives.

*

"What the fuck was that?" Rab exclaimed on hearing the explosion as the rest of the group were startled by the loud bang. A few theories were posed by members of the company. Was it an attack by the Villadedino secret police ... a car backfiring ... a gas explosion? Before the settled answer emerged out of a smoke of possibilities ... almost in unison they exclaimed, "XAVI!"

The group rushed in the direction of the explosion on the route Xavi would have taken from the brothers' home. There, by a log, was a smouldering circle of destruction. The brothers and Father Marionetta bowed their heads in memory of a noble partisan who had given his life for the cause, as the smell of pig shit mixed with the sulphur of the explosives ensured that the party were reminded of the folly of their first attempt at their noble mission.

*

It was relatively easy to get hold of more explosives, as they were plentiful in Figas, where they were used to blow up fish out of the river by the locals. It should be noted that the fishing rod had yet to be introduced to the natives of Figas. The rendezvous was, therefore, rearranged for the following night and this time there were no exploding Wodsians, angry farmers, or rabbit, pigeon, and dormouse sausages. The exchange went well, with

Rab, Malky, and Shug returning to the hotel carrying a sufficient supply of explosives to achieve their objectives. Despite the loss of Xavi, the remaining confederates of Figas remained positive and wished the Glasgow boys well with their venture. As they disappeared over the brow of the hill on the route back to the Hotel Euthanasia, the Glasgow boys, following the final farewells, continued to hear the Figas FUCKERS discuss their adventure, "Eggshiting, it's sho eggshiting, we are truly truly eggshited about shuch eggshitement."

*

The girls received the explosives, which they kept in their bedroom in their fashionable fake crocodile-skin designer handbags that matched the colour of their six-inch high platform stilettos.

Rab synchronized the timing for the next meeting between the girls and the boys along with the location – 'at the flower bar … See you at 3:45' … which was all very well except that the girls, with ears attuned to hearing locations as drinking venues, interpreted the venue as … , 'Meet by the bar and see you 3 for 5.'

The girls arrived early, at 2:45pm, at the bar, but could not see the others. Thinking that they would be waiting for a few minutes only, they decided that they best not waste any precious time. After surveying the occupants, Magdalene pushed Rashona forward as the emissary of diplomatic alliances to chat up the two older men seated at the bar.

"What kind of drink is that you are drinkin', big man?" Rashona queried of one of the men.

"It looks tempting and thirst quenchin' and I'm soooo thirsty," Magdalene negotiated huskily, leaning forward to adjust the buckle of her platform stiletto, with the top of her loose blouse hanging invitingly with a revealing view of her ample bosom for the nearest gentleman.

"Hey gals, why don't we get you both one of these drinks, then," the nearest guy obliged in a pre-programmed automatic response to the flash of breasts that had worked the female magic for the last six million years.

And so, by 3:45pm, the girls had been drinking amicably with the two old guys for one hour. Rab, Malky, and Shug, in the meantime, were waiting as 'planned' at the far end of the flower bar at the preordained time of 3:45pm. They waited for thirty minutes, but with no sign of the girls.

"Where the fuck are those lassies?" an exasperated Rab exclaimed as he paced backwards and forwards at the flower bar, "Right, Shug, you go and see if you can find them."

Shug headed off in one direction, stopped, thought for a second, then changed course to the opposite route, and then left in search of the girls, while Malky relieved his boredom by sensitively pulling the petals, one by one, off the flowers in the buckets on the stands of the flower stall. It was 5pm by the time Shug, after deciding to search one wing of the hotel and then changing his mind to go to the other wing, saw, or rather heard, Magdalene and Rashona cackling and joking loudly from inside the bar.

" ... an' then, the lassie dropped her chips, that's French fries for you Americans, and that was how he knew that she had had an orgasm," Magdalene laughed uproariously along with the others as she finished off one of her stories from the streets of Glasgow. The girls had now been drinking solidly and with methodical efficiency for the last two hours and fifteen minutes and, with the two older guys, they were in party mode, telling jokes, and laughing boisterously as only those in the bubbles of an alcoholic reverie can do. Rashona had also successfully negotiated with the guys to order some portions of French fries, just to 'keep the primitive wolf from the door'.

"You two, you're pure drunk, so you are. We've been waitin' for ages and Rab is goin' pure mental mad with you," Shug announced as he entered the bar and fixed his eyes on Rashona and Magdalene. He tried to ignore the 'come and get me' eyes that both females were making at him since he announced his presence.

"Naw, not us. Were we Rashona Winterbottom? We were just waitin' for you all and these kind men bought us a wee reshmeshment. Is that not right, Hank?"

"Just shut your 'geggies' and move your drunkin' arses," the worried Shug demanded as he herded the two inebriated girls out of the bar, while they, with the etiquette of a finishing school, were falling off their stilettos and tugging down their mini skirts riding up their thighs, as the fond farewells tripped off the tongues of their drinking buddies.

Arriving at the flower stall, Rab was beyond furious with the two inebriates as they caroused their insincere apologies, while the tears of previous laughter and present contrition contrived two rivers of black mascara to wash down each of their cheeks.

"I cannae believe it. We've got all the way here and you two get totally wasted on the drink!"

"We're dead sorry, Rab. Honest. We were sittin' quiet as mice and waitin' for you all, so we were. Weren't we, Rashona? Quiet as mice and the gentlemen were so kind when they saw us, quiet as mice. We were so pleased to see Shug. I could have kissed him!"

"Me too and I could just have dipped him in a nice avocado sauce and eaten him up for tea," Rashona blurted out, mixing her emotions of passion and consumption into a smorgasbord of fondness, while her compatriots tried to put all thoughts of Rashona's cannibalistic imagery out of their minds.

"We will just have to forget it," Rab said, sensing no benefit from any further dialogue and moving on, "Just give us the explosives and we'll go ahead with the plan."

Rashona and Magdalene felt for the bags, that should have been hanging from their shoulders, looked at their empty hands, and then at each other. "We haven't got them!"

"Oh no, I had a king size 'Chocowhale' bar in my handbag," panicked Rashona.

"What! For fucksake, I cannae believe it!" said Rab, with a red mist starting to descend around his head. Realising that the explosives had been left in the bar, he sprinted away from the flower stand, followed urgently in his wake by Malky and Shug and with Magdalene and Rashona sobbing, falling off their stilettos, tugging down miniskirts, with cheeks and now necks and shoulders streaked with mascara.

An old couple, coming from the opposite direction, were only moderately aware of a group of people rushing off as they approached the flower bar to select their favourite blooms in preparation for their demise. As they stood in front of the disassembled floral displays, they wondered what disease had befallen the poor flowers that had lost every single one of their petals.

"Hey, Hank, those Scattish chicks have left their purses," one of the Americans, Billy Bob, told his compatriot as he reached for one of the fake fashionable items that lay abandoned at the foot of the bar stool that had so recently been occupied by the gregarious Magdalene.

"We'll need to get them back to them. Are their room keys with their room numbers in there? Have a look," Hank pointed at the handbag. Billy Bob fiddled with the clasp at the top of the bag and opened it up, peering down into the hidden subterranean depths of Magdalene's handbag. He couldn't see any hotel room keys through his whisky soaked eyes.

"Here, give it to me," Hank grabbed the bag out of Billy Bob's hands and emptied the contents onto the surface of the bar. "What are these?" he said grabbing the explosives, "Do these look like sticks of dynamite to you, Billy Bob?"

The Glaswegian five rushed into the bar, at this point out of breath and with Rab in the lead. Seeing the scene before him, he shouted out, "We'll just take the lassies' handbags, guys. Nothing for you to see here."

"Hold on, fella, what are these here? They look mighty like sticks of dynamite to me," challenged Hank.

"That's just pure dead embarrasin'," Magdalene rebutted, "It's just a pure big riddy you seein' my tampon feminine care products, so they are." And, as she gathered the contents back into her handbag, completed her quick thinking to rescue the situation with the parting shot of, "And them bein' extra-large size as well!"

The five exited the bar quickly, leaving the two gentlemen considerably confused, drunk, and with a greatly enhanced education concerning matters of the feminine care department.

Chapter 21 Cheeky Jiki's Fear of Needles

But fear can take the once sweet song and scatter in a paradigm

The Song of Villadedino, Saint Dino 240AD

"It's time to start to make our way to the eXi-theme Departure Suite, Jiki," Hugh Mann addressed his capuchin monkey helper on the day he considered had arrived rather quickly for the demise of himself and Jiki. Hugh had booked one of the eXi-theme Departure Suites. He had given the arrangements a great deal of thought. His death would be straightforward. He didn't want any of the more exotic themes, given his disabilities and simple tastes. He had asked the hotel technicians to use the maXiviewalls to project images of a calm forest setting with the gentle calls of birds and rustling of leaves. He thought this would be a sensitive setting for Jiki. He would just have a final chat with Jiki, give him his deadly drink, and then he himself would receive a lethal injection from one of the hotel's physicians. He had considered the range of options available from poison to gas and settled on the needle to celebrate the last injection he would ever receive. He would think about Hannah and hope he would meet her on the 'other side'. The plan was for both him and Jiki, his friend, to be cremated. However, it did not quite work out that way.

It started off fine – Hugh and Jiki made their way to the room in the eXi-theme Departure Suite. They made themselves comfortable. The images of the forest were projected as had been requested, calming and green with the faintest of sounds of birds whistling in the distance. Jiki looked happy and relaxed in this environment and had his favourite stuffed toy panda for company. Hugh was quite nervous with this major step into the unknown but was also content that he had the courage to carry it out and with the plans he had arranged.

"Listen to that beautiful bird call. You know, Jiki, you have been my best friend all these years and I don't know what I would have done if it hadn't been for you, particularly after Hannah passed away. The three of us got on together so well, with Hannah making all the food and keeping the house and you making me snacks and getting things for me under my supervision, of course," Hugh said in warm self-congratulatory tones as befits what he assumed to be the superior primate in the relationship. He looked into Jiki's eyes.

Jiki responded by returning his gaze, looking at Hugh with his deep black eyes while thinking to himself … *raisin!*

"Really, my little friend, you have been my constant companion, a true friend and you have done all I ever asked of you. You were almost an extension of my mind. All I had to say was the word 'microwave' and you would be jumping up alert, running to the cupboard to fetch a snack for me, and heating it up in the microwave.

Jiki, having heard the word 'microwave', started to get excited about one of his favourite tasks and looked around for the cupboard with the big monkey's food in it and also for a microwave. Seeing nothing, he thought to himself, *the big monkey has really lost the place since his mate disappeared. Any primate with half a brain can see there is no microwave here.*

"I am truly sorry to end it this way, but I cannot think of another solution. It is just a pity that I could not find anyone to give you a home," Hugh pined as he remembered the endless searches for someone who would give Jiki a good place to reside after he had gone. It had always ended in failure. He also remembered with distaste the 'close call' with the offer from the owner of a petting zoo. Hugh had only found out at the last minute that the owner intended to extract all of Jiki's teeth. Luckily for Jiki, he was saved from that particular fate.

"I know how much you look up to me with my superior human brain and intellect, something a poor creature like you could never hope to understand," said Hugh, who had obviously not figured out who was in charge in this relationship.

Meanwhile, Jiki, who had heard it all before, *blah ... blah ... blah ... blah*, was getting decidedly bored with the indulgent tone of voice that he had heard so often before and intervened in Hugh's discourse to use his rapid glance technique to get the big monkey to give him a raisin.

"Look at you ... you cute little creature. Hey, you know what! Why don't you have a raisin?" Hugh felt that pleasurable sense of superiority that came from being considerate and altruistic in initiating the bestowing of a treat to his little helper.

The entrance of the doctor, in his white coat and carrying a metal tray, broke the fuzzy feeling of supremacy in which Hugh was immersed. Hugh and Jiki watched as the doctor smiled reassuringly at them, placed the tray on the table, and removed the cloth to reveal the contents of the tray.

Instantly, Jiki froze. He had been a bit anxious about the white coat, but what he saw on the tray really made the hairs on his back and tail stand on end and his eyes open wide. On the tray were two items. One was a baby cup with liquid in it (the drink that Hugh had arranged that would end Jiki's life). This item was not the one causing the concern for Jiki and the catalyst for his anxiety. The thing that had made his heart beat faster was something that was the precursor to more chilling undertakings. It was the syringe with the preparation that would terminate Hugh's existence that sparked such fear in Jiki. He had always been afraid of needles since the visit to the vet as a young capuchin monkey, where he had received an injection from a needle, similar to the one on display, which had knocked him out. When he awoke, there was an intense pain in his groin, but worse, there was something, or rather two things, missing. Jiki associated his pain and loss with the needle. So, it was no wonder that the sight of a needle triggered such terror in the capuchin.

Hugh wasn't quite sure what happened next. He was not fully aware of Jiki looking nervously at the doctor carrying the tray and becoming physically agitated. Hugh was reminding Jiki about some of the adventures they had got up to as the doctor arranged and rearranged the contents of the tray on the stainless-steel table …

"Jiki, do you remember the time I asked you to put those grapes in the microwave when we ran out of raisins? We can laugh about it now but at the time … "

Before Hugh could finish his sentence, Jiki suddenly screamed, jumped up two feet in the air, somersaulted over

Hugh's head by grabbing on to his nose, opened the door, and was out of the room before you could say 'cheeky monkey'.

Chapter 22 Perfection of Harmony

Until the harmony of snow once more finds perfection in a perfect form

The Song of Villadedino, Saint Dino 240AD

Mark, like any addict, could not resist the temptation to feed his professional journalistic habit. The research always gave him an initial buzz of anticipation as a precursor to the stronger narcotic contained in the natural high that followed any revelations from his investigations. So he surreptitiously delved into the name Estrela had told him on their trip to the Highlands of New Scotland ... 'Digby'.

He worked his way through details of the population in the Yukon and surrounding British Columbia and Northern Territories, refining to the likely age group of people called 'Digby', who would have had a five-year-old daughter in 2023. The name 'Digby' was seldom used and the likely possibilities were reduced to twenty-two people. He traced the addresses of the twenty-two and eliminated those that had died before 2018. He then began to telephone and email the nineteen likely candidates he thought could be Estrela's father. After talking to eighteen of them and, following an analysis of the communication eliminating them, he was left with one last possible prospect, Jed Digby, a resident of Kent Maximum Security Penitentiary in Kent, British Columbia. Mark checked out his history, revealing that Jed Digby had been locked up for the last thirteen years for the murder of five prostitutes in Western Canada. Mark contacted the governor of the prison and arranged a telephone call to Jed Digby as he prepared for the effect of the really 'hard stuff' of purer quality to course through his brain.

"They tried to pin another five murders on me," Digby drawled, "but they ain't never gonna pin them on me."

Mark got to the point of his telephone call. "Look, Mr Digby, I have no interest in what you have or haven't done. I just want to ask you one question. Did you leave a little girl in a cabin in the woods up north of Dawson?"

"Why should I tell you anything," Digby spat out in an irritated tone, "What's it to you, anyways?"

"Never mind why I am interested, but if you can tell me the truth, there will be a weekly supply of cigarettes coming to you from me for the next year. Given you have another twenty-five years to serve, I think that would make life a little easier for you. So, what do you say?"

"Make it two years and we have a deal, bud."

"Alright, you have a deal, Mr Digby."

"Yeah, the kid is my daughter; spoiled little brat … always wantin' food and attention. I never had no time for the kid since her hooker mother ran off with her new pimp. The kid was lucky I didn't cut her throat and leave her in a hole in the forest."

"Okay, I need a bit more proof. How can you prove that you left the little girl there?"

"Well, who else would know that there were two hundred cans of 'Sea King, Best Pacific Salmon' at the cabin along with ten crates of beer? So, check out the facts, man. Also, you can look up that whore of a mother, she'll tell you. Annie Digby, that's her name, lives somewhere in Whitehorse, I heard."

"Okay, I'll check it out and if she comes through, then there will be a two-year supply of cigarettes on its way to you, Mr Digby. By the way, what was your daughter called?"

"The little brat was called Annie, just like her mother."

*

Mark did track down and spoke by telephone with Annie Digby, the biological mother of Estrela, and she was in a poor state, injecting drugs, and living hand to mouth in Whitehorse. She said she had a daughter called Annie once but, "That serial killer of a husband must have murdered her because she had not seen her since she was a baby." The local police records also corroborated the factual accuracy of the contents of the cabin. Mark had identified Estrela's genetic parents, but how was he going to break it to her that her father was a serial killer and her mother was a drug-addicted prostitute?

Mark did not have to figure that out, due to bad luck on his part and Estrela's search for a hat stored in the furthest corners of their closet. She had stood on the chair and had the hat from the top shelf in her hands when she noticed the folder with 'ESTRELA' written on it. Curiosity did the rest.

Mark had arrived home to find her sitting on the bedroom floor, where she had been for the last two hours with the documents and details scattered around her. She could not look at him as he came into the bedroom and he knew instantly what had happened.

The waves of emotions that struck Estrela like hammer blows fazed and disorientated her. *What was she reading? Was this about some other person?* She threw the materials away and then immediately gathered them together again, perversely compelled to know more. The names seemed to slot like red-hot pokers into the freezer of her memory. *Digby – Jed Digby – Annie Digby – Annie.* The reality moistened her eyes. *Annie – that was who she was, that was her name.* It was hard for her to accept. *No, I'm Estrela, I'm not that person*, she thought, while admitting to herself at the same time that she could not deny it. The memories started flooding through as the damn burst … feelings of being small and alone… crawling through the detritus of a chaotic life looking for bits of pizza and other scraps of food … abandoned to all hope.

Words formed silently and involuntarily in her mouth, "I'm hungry … I'm hungry … always hungry … " Then there was no mummy. "Where are you, mummy? Where have you gone? Come back, mummy!"

The efforts to get her father to speak to her came flooding back and the sense of failure when he would only shout some obscenity at her or would ignore her as if she did not exist.

"You little brat!" came to her memory. Then, there was the car journey … traveling through highways of snow… endless unbroken views of snow … endless fields of snow … finally to a still forest of snow. Alone with the man in the snow … then alone … hungry … struggling to get food out of tins … alone in the snow … the cold … the cold long nights … the fear … the lonely fear … and then … the peace.

Other words were appearing before Estrela's eyes. Words that she understood the meaning of but could not comprehend why they were there appearing in her life. *Serial killer – Prostitute – Drug addict.*

In anger, she shouted, "Who are these people and why are they in my life? This is not me! This is not me." Freakish insights were attacking her like small evil bats trying to get inside her head. She felt like she was in a dream and was desperate to wake up. Estrela realised she had been sitting on the floor for two hours and was drained of any feeling. However, new emotions were beginning to stir within her. She started to feel dirty by association and by the unacceptable but inevitable reality that she was the child of two defective adults, albeit adults with arrested development, who were evil in their thoughts, attitudes, and actions. They had treated her with indifference, neglected her, malnourished her, and deprived her of love. Is that why she found difficulty in loving herself? The self-hatred grew wings and rose up inside her being.

She was only vaguely aware that Mark was kneeling at her side. "I didn't know how to tell you. Estrela, believe me, it wasn't meant to be like this."

"I warned you to stop. I didn't … don't want this."

"I'm sorry, please forgive me."

"It's too late. The damage is done," Estrela's shoulders heaved as she burst into tears.

"I was only trying to help, Estrela."

"Why couldn't you just let it lie?"

"Can we just talk about it," Mark pleaded, realising too late that his words were at best ill-advised and at worst his deeds had been destructive.

"No! No!" and with this, Estrela rose and staggered sobbing into her bed, where she stayed for four days sleeping or staring into the distance. All offers of food or contriteness from the desperate Mark were ignored and rejected.

It was on the fourth day, as Mark rushed back anxiously from an unavoidable assignment, that he discovered the bed empty and Estrela gone. There was no note and her mobile phone was on the bedside table uncharged. Mark informed the police that Estrela was missing. Three weeks later, having heard nothing constructive from the police and having exhausted all his professional connections to find her, the breaking news on his maXiviewalls announced: *'SINGING SENSATION ESTRELA PURE IN ASSISTED SUICIDE AT HOTEL EUTHANASIA'*

*

After some negotiating with his boss and finally convincing him of the value of an assignment to examine the assisted dying industry, Mark set off for Villadedino to the Hotel Euthanasia, to undertake the investigative piece that was a façade for something else. His real reason was because he could not come to terms with the loss of Estrela and his guilt was tearing him apart. He wanted to find out how she died and if there had been any sliver of forgiveness that he could take to assuage the guilt he felt for provoking her actions. He missed her so much and his constant feelings of culpability for her decision to take her own life had to find some release.

At first, when Mark arrived at the hotel, Zeca had been reluctant to talk about any individual assisted suicide, but with skill, Mark had encouraged more and more from him about Estrela.

"Zeca, there have been some quite high profile assisted suicides, that must raise the prominence of the hotel and make the process more acceptable."

"Yes, this is true. Acceptability is a key issue for this industry and when a well-known person partakes of our services, then this does send a message to people that, if they can do it, then so can I."

"There was a recent one that I think has really encouraged people to arrange assisted suicide. Estrela Pure. She is a good example, don't you think?"

"Why yes, that would have been a good example, but I am under a code of confidentiality with this and Estrela's case was rather unique."

"Oh, why was that, Zeca?"

"You are a clever man, Mr Goodwin, but so also am I and I can see when you are trying to extract a confidentiality from me concerning Miss Pure. The Internet is a wonderful thing, don't you think, and hotel managers as well as journalists can also do their research. So, I am afraid I am under complete confidentiality regarding any information about your girlfriend."

Mark realised that the game was up and there was no further benefit to be had in trying to extract information about Estrela from Zeca. Perhaps one last try with Angela Deff might be more fruitful if he handled it carefully.

*

Angela Deff had just visited the manager's office to deliver her seventh revised draft of her planned programme of customer care duties for the forthcoming six months. Zeca received it with grace just as he had done with all the other drafts that Angela had decided, unsolicited, to give him.

"Angela, thank you for your report, which reminds me of a story from my homeland." Angela sat half listening to Zeca and half going over the list of her planned customer care programme.

"There was once a beautiful young woman called Inez, who lived in the town of Evora. Now Inez had an admirer, young Fernão, who dearly loved the girl and wanted to be her suitor. So, Fernão, in order to win the object of his heart's desire, would bring her gifts. Devotedly, he brought her the gifts wrapped in beautiful packages. The first one he brought her, she opened to find a fishing net. '*Thank you,*' she said, but Inez did not like fishing and so it was of no real interest to her. Next, he brought a package and Inez opened this to find a paintbrush. '*Thank you,*' she said again, even though she did not paint. On the next occasion, Fernão brought her a package and she opened it carefully and found a book. '*Thank you,*' she said one more time, but Inez did not like to read and preferred other activities, like going for a walk. Fernão, bolstered by the gratitude that Inez had graciously bestowed on him, finally worked up the courage to ask her to marry him. '*Dear Inez, I love you and adore you. You are everything I could want. Would you please do me the honour of becoming my wife?*' Inez immediately said, '*Yes,*' and they both were married and lived a happy life. When they were old and all their children had grown up, Inez, after a long illness, was on her deathbed. It was very sad. Fernão asked Inez, '*When you agreed to marry me those many years ago, was it the presents that made your mind up?*'

'*No*', replied Inez with the honesty of an old woman on her deathbed, '*Each of the presents you gave me did not really interest me.*'

'*Well, why did you agree, then, as I thought you seemed so happy to receive the presents,*' Fernão continued slightly surprised   .

'*It was you I liked, Fernão, and the best present you could have given me was yourself.*'

The next day, Fernão went out and bought a present, which he presented to his dying wife. She took a small box from the bag and opened it to reveal a locket with the words 'I love you' inscribed on the inside. Inez wept happy tears and just before she passed away, she said to Fernão, '*I love this present and I love you too.*'

"So, Angela, what was the meaning behind this story?" Zeca asked.

"It is simple," Angela proposed, "The man was wasting

his time buying a present for his wife as she was obviously going to die and wouldn't be able to wear the locket."

"Okay, Angela," said Zeca with a great deal of exasperation in his voice due to Angela's continued lack of any moral discernment as to the true nature of his tales. "We can talk about this one later," he said as Angela left the office to continue her programme of work.

"Hi, Angela, good to see you!" Mark greeted the Customer Care Manager as he accidently on purpose bumped into her on her way from Zeca's office.

"I am pleased to see you too, journalist, but I am also pleased to be getting on with my job."

"Sorry, Angela, I didn't mean to interrupt you in your work, but I just wondered if you had seen and heard this video of one of your recent guests? It will only take a minute to listen to it."

"I can displace one minute of my programme for the purpose of offering customer care to you, journalist, as I recognise this is in my job description. But only one minute, then I must continue with my programme of work."

Touching the controls on his mobile phone, Mark started the video of Estrela Pure singing one of her famous songs, 'Small Bird Sings of Snow'. Angela watched the video with what she hoped was a suitably interested expression, while constantly glancing at her watch. After one minute and the song still playing, she announced, "The minute has ended, thank you for showing me the video. I recognise Miss Pure. The song is good, like the one she recorded while here at the hotel."

"Sorry? What did you say?" the surprised Mark

responded, clutching on to Angela's words '*recorded-while-at-hotel*' before they fell to the floor and melted away like flakes of snow.

Angela was anxious to get on with her programme of work and she had already made excellent conversation with the journalist meeting his request to watch the video for one minute. "Good day, journalist. Have a good stay." And with this, Angela made off for the next item on her daily programme, which in this case was to sharpen her pencils in preparation for the meeting with the new guests that day.

Mark was left paralysed, dumbstruck, and wrong footed, both by Angela's manner and her revelation. Before he could assimilate what she had said, she was gone and he scrabbled through her words before they evaporated before him. *So, there is another video of Estrela*, he thought to himself, *how can I get my hands on it and I wonder what it is about? It was a song, which is good. That was what Angela said. Estrela doesn't write a song unless she has something important she wants to express. I need to get my hands on this video.*

*

Later in the day, Angela was aware of the journalist again. He was standing outside her office, hovering in the hallway, as she left, locking the door, and making her way to meet the new guests in the reception room. *I hope he is not going to interrupt me again*, she anticipated as she hurried past him looking at her watch. She understood this was a signal used

246

to communicate that she was in a hurry. Mark caught up with her and walked alongside her.

"Angela, I can see you are on your way somewhere. I am glad to see that you are keeping to a precise work schedule and that you will need to arrive at your meeting in time. A good way of saving time would be for you to give me the key to your office, so that I can watch the video you have of Miss Pure."

The conflict of ideas pressed on Angela's brain like a vice requiring a resolution to be squeezed from it. *The journalist is asking for my key; I also need to get to the meeting on time. He is replicating the thoughts I have about being on time, which is good. He wants to see the video of Miss Pure and he showed me his video, so I think it might be the right behaviour to reciprocate in the same manner. Yes, that's what a good Customer Care Manager would do.* With this rationalisation, she handed Mark the key to her office, saying, "The video is in the top right hand drawer of my desk, journalist. Please leave the key at the reception when you are finished. Good day," and continued on her way with some comfort that she had not wasted any time and she had also satisfied a customer.

Mark wasted no time in returning to Angela's office, extracting the video from the drawer, and sitting back to watch it play on her maXiviewall. There she was, Estrela, looking much better than he had last seen her on that fateful day he left the apartment for work, the last time he saw her alive. At the start of the video, she smiled, pushed her hair behind her ear, looked directly towards the camera, and started to sing the most beautiful song:

I bear no responsibility for my making,
For the liberties and taking
Summer's been good but this tree needs renewing
By the snowline for fine tuning
In peace and perfect harmony

This small bird returns to the snowline,
Where the hardwoods grow along the outline
Traced slower than slow to redefine,
The perfection of harmony

On the snowline I am the cold point
My love is the warm counterpoint
But the circles of our life conjoined
One tighter than the next adjoined
Are hard and pure in harmony

This small bird sings in the snowline,
Where the hardwoods grow along the outline
Traced slower than slow to redefine,
The perfection of harmony

On the snowline, mark my drift,
Where the warmth permits the cold his gift
A constant separation and harmony shift
Snow and small bird fly so swift
To sing in perfect harmony

My love will find me on the snowline,
Where the hardwoods grow along the outline
Traced slower than slow to redefine,
The perfection of harmony

Mark replayed the video again and again, watching each small movement and listening to every intonation in Estrela's voice as she poured out her heart and emotions. He recorded the song on his mobile phone at the sixth listening. He had been transported he knew not where by the singing of Estrela.

Such a beautiful song, he thought to himself. *So, this was her final song before her death. The snowline must be the boundary between life and death and she saw herself as a small bird flying across to the snow side of the snowline. The lyrical and allegorical resonance between Estrela and the beauty within the poem echoed from the idea of the tight even grain in the wood, narrower together and lighter because of the slow growing season at the snowline altitudes. The lyrics spoke of the relationship between the narrowness of the grains, the drying of the wood by air at the highest altitudes, and the beautiful tone that this wood will render when fashioned into the finest violin or guitar. Did she see herself perfected through a similar transformation in death? The whole song evokes the perfection of harmony; so sad, so poignant, and such a waste.*

Mark returned to his room to contemplate his own very empty existence and feel the sharp stabs of guilt swelling up again in his chest. *What must I do next to resolve this pain?* he wondered with a sadness akin to despair, as tears flowed freely

Chapter 23 Chaos in the eXi-theme Departure Suites

Chaos still confuses and compels the patterns of the child unborn

The Song of Villadedino, Saint Dino 240AD

'*I hate America*', His Eminence, Star of the Heavens, General Mustapha Sultana said to himself as he entered his eXi-theme Departure Suite. He had a lot to hate them for as he reflected – things had been going so well in Kushara, his North African country where there was no political opposition … the fact they had all been jailed or died unexpectedly was neither here nor there.

The populace loved him like a deity, at least that part of the population who were related to him; the ones from his hometown he had appointed to good government jobs.

If it hadn't been for those infidel Americans and their CIA, stoking discontent among the population, the rebellion would not have started. Okay, there were bread shortages; no jobs; schools were a joke; the university had closed and the TV was, I suppose, rubbish, but he had taken on the most noblest of ventures, namely the responsibility for his country. It was he, after all, who had established law and order. Crime was down, there were excellent roads between the oil fields and the port; the press was only writing responsible articles about himself; he had commissioned art works and statues in his honour; he had reduced the power of those stupid imams. The people should have been grateful instead of hounding him out of the country the way they did. Getting out on the last plane before the airport was taken over by those scoundrel rebels was a stroke of luck. It was a pity my family and relatives had to stay behind and face the humiliation of trial and goodness knows what else in those kangaroo courts.

"Well, I will be declared a hero when the world finds out I died for my country," he said out loud. It was the honourable thing to do. He had only been able to get out of the country with as many crisp one hundred dollar bills as he could stuff down his underwear and in the pockets of his smart army uniform; only enough money to pay for his honourable death at the Hotel Euthanasia.

And what a death I've planned. I will die burning the Stars and Stripes and when the video of my martyrdom is circulated, I will truly be seen for what I am ... a hero, he thought as he consoled himself. *Death is so unrefined, but paradise will be worth it.*

He had wanted to make a lasting impression. It was clear to him that the momentous event should be captured on professional video footage and so he had gone in search of a suitably qualified filmmaker in Villadedino. However, at short notice, there was only one company available for hire to do this. *But still, because of my greatness and elevated status, the 'Luvvy Duvvy Wedding Video Company' will be good enough for my purpose*, he thought.

"So, here I am, Generale," proclaimed Fabio, the

cameraman and owner, or rather the sole personnel of the 'Luvvy Duvvy Wedding Video Company'. The General thought there was something a bit strange about Fabio, but he couldn't quite put his finger on it. He displayed unusual mannerisms and talked in a high-pitched voice, calling him 'dear' and 'darling' instead of 'Sir' with every sentence, something the General was not used to where he came from. Fabio was, of course, flamboyantly unaware of the consternation his salutations were having on the General.

Fabio looked at the General in his full uniform, military cap, and over fifty medals hanging proudly like garish tinsel from a Christmas tree. "Nice Michael Jackson outfit, by the way, and I just love your gay pride rainbow badge. If I can just set up a few scenarios, Generale, darling," Fabio instructed the General, "First, if I can film you arriving at the room." The General complied and went back out into the hallway as Fabio filmed what in the General's mind would be a grand and princely entrance.

"Now, can we film you, darling, with the American flag and then without it," Fabio continued and so it went on for the next half hour, with the General in a variety of poses with the flag, saluting to the camera while holding the flag, shouting at the flag, proclaiming his greatness and declaring his love for his country, for his family and his hero Abraham Lincoln. It was lost on the General that Abraham Lincoln, as well as being a great leader and politician and as well as freeing the black African slaves in the Confederate South, was also a great American. But this was just a minor point.

"We will finish, Generale, dear, with you lighting the flag, of course being careful about the Health and Safety Regulations for the hotel." Fabio had recently attended a Health and Safety Regulations course provided by the Villadedino Small Businessmen's Support Service, that is, where the businesses were small, not the men who operated the businesses. "And then, finally, Generale, with you taking your lethal dose and climbing into the coffin. I would like to get your eyes as they close for the last time, Generale, dear."

"Excellent," the General replied, although for the first time, and with some trepidation, he began to more fully comprehend the permanency of what he was about to do in his final act. As he readied himself, he had an empty stomach to help absorption of the pentobarbital mixed with orange juice to mask the bitter taste of the medication. During the proceedings, some niggling desires for self-preservation were starting to surface … *Was he the great man he proclaimed himself to be? Of course he was*, he thought. Then, as his life began to flash before him, he recalled the shame of the bedwetting and his mother's slaps to the head for being such a dirty, stinky little boy. His cheeks flushed at the shameful memories he retained from the nickname '*stinky*' given to him as a child. *Still, he had come this far*, he thought, *there is no way back* … and he wasn't going to spend his time in poverty or, worse, prison, for supposed crimes that he believed he had never committed. He knew the squalor of the prisons in Kushara. So, he did the only thing he could and lit the Stars and Stripes, letting the flag burn out in the Health and Safety Regulation supplied fireproof bucket, took the poison, and climbed into the coffin with all the dignity he could muster. As his mind started to drift into the haze of death, he became aware of the trickle of wetness as it passed down his groin and spread below his buttocks, up his back, and down his legs. His last sense was the smell of urine as he grimaced and then, in a drug-induced state, he involuntary shouted out his final words in Arabic, "Samihini ya ommi, ana lam aksoud an obalila sirwali."

Mustapha was thankfully as unaware as a dead person could be of Fabio's best job of editing the video, using the skills and experience that he had at his well-manicured fingertips. Fabio's fingertips, in this case, unfortunately consisted of a library of songs suitable for weddings and the standard 'set piece' scene arrangements he was familiar with for a wedding ceremony. And so it was that there was much consternation in the Arab world when, after his death, the video was released onto the World Wide Web as the General had requested. The video lasted approximately two minutes; opened with the General walking up the corridor splendidly and entering the room, grandly turning the handle of the door to the tune of '*You Look Wonderful Tonight*'; followed by much posing, grinning, and erroneous saluting with the American flag to the tune of '*I Love You Just the Way You Are*'; then some solemn shouting at the flag combined with the chorus from '*My First, My Last, My Everything*'.

And, even more unfortunately for the General, Fabio had forgotten to press the record button on his camera in his excitement about Health and Safety for the scene of the burning

254

of the flag, resulting in this part of the General's vision failing to materialise. So, the final scene of the video comprised of what Fabio thought to be a heartfelt and sincere Arabic oath, but in fact, as every Arab who watched the video knew, was the General shouting as he passed away, '*Sorry Mummy, I didn't mean to wet my pants*', which was then elevated to another level of absurdity when combined with Fabio's choice of a musical medley of '*Goodnight Sweetheart, It's Time to Go*' and his own favourite; the gay anthem '*I Am, What I Am*'.

*

"Stop barking, Tyson, you little shit," yelled Mrs Merger, the seven times married widow, at her diminutive Yorkshire Terrier in his little tartan doggy coat, while they were sitting in her eXi-theme suite awaiting the start of her assisted suicide programme, "Just behave, I don't know what has got into you."

"As for you lot, you can just stop making those rude gestures at me," she shouted at the seven apparitions of her seven late husbands that sat around the room varying their entertainment between giving Mrs Merger the finger and shouting out abuse, 'You syphilitic old cow'; 'Why don't you hurry up and kick the bucket so we can really get our own back on you'.

She was also aware that the haunting spectres were forever giving her final husband, Harold, congratulatory slaps on his ghostly back while telling him that they appreciated how he had conned her into marrying him when he didn't have any money. The point was that they, having all been duped by Mrs

Merger, were glad that she had received her just deserts from Harold and they weren't going to let her forget it. *How unjust for them to gang up on me this way*, she thought despondently, feeling very sorry for herself. She was reassured, however, she was doing the right thing by using the savings that she had kept back from her richer husbands' fortunes to end her life. *I can't stand it anymore; I need to escape those spiteful spirits.*

The ghosts had also been party in the past to winding up Tyson the Yorkshire terrier by making scratching noises on the wall and ringing the front door bell, all of which sent Tyson into spasms of barking and chasing around the house like a demented hairball. On this occasion, however, they did not have to do much to upset the small dog … only waft the smoke of the burning flag set alight by the General in the eXi-theme Departure Suite next door through to the one occupied by Mrs Merger.

Tyson continued to bark. *Smoke smell, smoke smell*, he thought to his canine self, *Danger! Danger! Must get away, escape, escape! Get out, get out!* Mrs Merger's suite, located next to the one occupied by General Mustapha Sultana, was in sufficient proximity for the dead ghosts of Mrs Merger's former husbands to be able to stimulate Tyson's doggy senses to pick up the tell-tale smell of smoke. The dog made for the slightly ajar door leading to the hall and fled from the smell that was invading his senses. The combination of the rooms, with the smell of cadavers along with the smoke, not to mention those seven wraiths that accompanied his owner and himself wherever they went, was just too much for poor Tyson and all these sensations were combining to signal *DANGER!* So, these overriding instincts led him to ignore the prattling of his mistress, Mrs Merger, now standing in the middle of the eXi-theme Departure Suite, surrounded by her seven abusive apparitions, awaiting her planned death, and wondering what had got into silly Tyson.

"This is really such a bother, I will have to put off my death for another half an hour until someone fetches Tyson," moaned Mrs Merger in her high whiny voice. She turned to the technician and requested he rewind to the beginning of her chosen final theme, which consisted of a chronological sequence of videos of all her seven wedding ceremonies to each of her seven husbands, interspersed with a slide at the end of each ceremony of the amount she had inherited following the death of each husband. 'Why don't you just do it without the dog, you stupid old bat,' the dead husbands shouted to her, 'It's not as if you're getting any younger!'

*

Jiki the capuchin monkey helper was in panic mode. He could hear a dog barking somewhere in his consciousness, but his only thought was to get as far away from that needle as he possibly could. He was using all his agility to jump from chair to velvet curtains, to sideboard, to wall light to make his way down the corridor and away from the eXi-theme Departure Suite with the dreaded needle. Jiki did not like needles after that bad experience he had had at the vets. It was when he saw the small dog running that Jiki saw an opportunity to hasten his flight and so grabbed onto his tartan coat and hitched a ride on Tyson's back. Now both of them were racing fast down the corridor with Tyson continuing to bark at the top of his voice. People were opening doors and coming out of their rooms to see what the commotion was all about.

*

For the sake of authenticity and avoiding suspicion and also, to be honest, as a guilty pleasure, Rab and his group had decided to take the 'Ultimate Catholic Death Experience' as the theme option for their fake deaths. This 'experience' involved Shamus McNamara, an ex-priest from Donegal, dressing up as the Pope, coming into the eXi-theme Departure Suite, and hearing the participants' last confessions. The heroic members of the Glasgow Catholic United Network for the Transgression of Sins were now ensconced in their eXi-theme Departure Suite. Next to this suite was a dressing room, where Shamus McNamara fitted himself out in the fine authentic vestments of the Papal regalia. He had two sets of vestments at his disposal. Included in Shamus's paraphernalia were the Pope's crown, in case the person to die was wealthy; a couple of mitres, one in white and another a jaunty off-yellow one; not forgetting the bling of the gold ring; a couple of staffs, one topped with a crucifix, the other shaped like a shepherd's crook; an all-white combination and separate yellow combination of chasuble, pallium cloak, fanon shawl decorated with crosses, maniple, falda, alb, and mantum. The whole shebang! The incongruity of this collection of liturgical attire was that Pope Hilarius II had abolished all papal paraphernalia in 2023, adorning himself in the less discriminatory garb of a plain sweatshirt and white jeans. But with the ascendency of Pope Leo Sixtus I in 2032, the Papal vestments were now reinstated, invoking the past opulence and glory of the Vatican. It was safe to say that Shamus had enough vestments to dress a couple of Popes. And so it was that the Pope impersonator checked himself in the mirror one last time, blessed himself, *well, he was the Pope after all*, and left the room for his next gig. He never got there.

*

Okay, I fit all the criteria for a psychopath and okay, I suppose I am one, but I like to think of myself as just a more evolved human being than the rest of the rag tags out there. John LeMaistre was in deep reflection before the final loaded dice was to be thrown, if you can call the processes of his brain something that resembled normal human thought, given his sociopathic predispositions. LeMaistre computed more than reflected. He counted this as one of the things that made him superior to other people. He had built up a nationwide financial empire. *I like to keep busy*, he thought to himself. And he had, in his own opinion, been incredibly successful. Okay, he had had to make difficult business decisions and some of the small companies and their pension pots he had acquired felt cheated after the takeovers. *I wonder why?* he smirked to himself.

He had the ability, *yes, another*, toting up his score of qualities, *the ability not to feel guilty or have any remorse like* these weaklings who ran their businesses badly. Not for me the possibility of entertaining any regrets for the harsh but necessary decisions impacting on the lives of others. Perhaps my greatest ability is my charismatic personality along with my insight into how the idiots that I do business with are feeling. Yes, he thought, a psychopath who could sense emotions, ah, but all the better to manipulate them. Once I sense someone's weakness, I have the precision of a predator. Straight for the throat, rip it out, stamp them into the dirt, and feed from the satisfaction in having power over those weaklings. I remember when I was young that I was first able to connect with my power. Dear sad mother, she was easy and barely worth the effort. She was only too willing to do my will. How can I say it, small pets mysteriously disappearing, me in fake tears to those stupid parents to get me a new one, and then the control would begin again.

I started off with mice, staking them out in the sun and cutting out their tiny organs. I advanced to cats and then dogs. Yes, it brings back memories of a fine development, honing my incisive skills literally to the bone. There were the troubles, though, of my teenage years; I suppose you have to calibrate your instincts to be ready for greater challenges ahead. The crimes I was caught for – well they were hardly worth mentioning in comparison to those I got away with. I had it all, money, charm, and the girls just loved me. In return, I fucked them all, took what I wanted, and, most gratifyingly, I left them with broken hearts. They were never the same once they associated with the great John LeMaistre. It gave me a real sense of achievement to see them broken, even admitted to institutions to recover their mental faculties. If they suffered, so what, I didn't give a fuck. My parents never did figure out what the scoreboard on my wall was all about.

So why am I here? John rehearsed with himself, *I have done it all, but now I am bored, impatient with the routine. I have moved from business to business, successful each time, but I can't be bothered with this life; life is too much of a long-term project, if I say so. And with those stupid national regulators and fraud people crawling all over the business, I suppose it was risky, but I couldn't even be bothered covering my tracks properly. Yes, but risk is good. If I have any problems, it isn't really my fault, it's the fault of those incompetent regulatory bastards that inspect me if they can't see what good business is. The whores that I married, well they deserved all they got after the businesses went under, attempted suicide, domestic violence my arse, more like attention seeking self-pity, if you ask me.*

But the authorities, do they think they could control me? No way! I decide what and when events happen. They thought they were going to lock me away in a prison cell. Well, not for me. I am an indomitable force and I have taken control again. Again, I say. I am booked in for the exit here and, in a way, I can't wait ... there goes the impatience again! I can't wait to get one over on them all. And these saps that have booked into the Hotel Euthanasia, they are so easy to manipulate. I suppose I could delay the end for a little while and give in to the temptation to go after a final bit of fun with them before I remove my life from this game. Always on the lookout, eh!

John LeMaistre commended his own guile and his

notion of superiority over the rest of humanity. "What's the commotion outside," he said out loud as he opened the door that led out of his eXi-theme Departure Suite in time to see the what looked like the Pope running down the corridor chased by a barking snapping dog with a monkey riding on its back!

*

John LeMaistre did not have the most superior brain known to mankind (in his estimation) without the ability to use it. He was able to assess the situation, analyse the possibilities, and come up with an instant and cunning plan to make the best of the opportunity that had landed in his lap. It had the potential, after all, to be his last escapade in the art of control before he ended his monumental and illustrious life. He saw the door open into the changing room and the appointments calendar on the table with the time of the next confessionals. Before you could say 'watch out for the psychopath', John was there, dressed in the Pope outfit and knocking with his long wooden staff at the door of the eXi-theme Departure Suite occupied by the five Glaswegians, who were waiting for the Pope's next confessional.

"Hello, Your Highne ... Your Eminence, please come in. We're lookin' forward to this, Holy Father," Rab spoke reverentially, bound into automatic responses from his years of indoctrination at Catholic schools in Glasgow.

"I will just sit in the confessional, my child," proclaimed Pope John LeMaistre, struggling with the effort of deciphering Rab's dialect but thinking to himself, *this should be fun.*

Pope John LeMaistre opened the door and entered the traditionally constructed confessional booth located in one corner of the eXi-theme Departure Suite. It was designed with two compartments separated by a wooden wall containing a lattice grill with red velvet curtains, through which the person seeking penance whispers their sins to the priest/pope hearing the confession. The penitent kneels while the Pope sits. The compartments are barely lit by two small lights that emphasise the sombre nature of the confessional.

Shug was first to enter and knelt down, "Bless me, Pope, it's been one week since my last confession."

"Tell me your sins, my son."

"Okay, Holy Father, I've been very lazy, sleepin' in most mornin's, and generally lazin' about all day watchin' TV."

"Ah, the sin of sloth?" Pope LeMaistre deduced from the accent.

"That's correct, Holy Father"

"Tell me, when you are sleeping, can you force yourself to wake up?"

"No, Holy Father."

"Ah, so it is not a voluntary sin, my son. To be a sin, the act needs to be voluntarily performed. I conclude then that you have not committed any sin, my son. But I think you are over tired and could need some help with this. Here, take these pills that will give you extra energy." And so doing, Pope John LeMaistre passed three Viagra tablets to Shug through the gap at the bottom of the lattice in the window. "Take these now, my son, and you will find that your tiredness will soon disappear to be replaced with a new, shall we say, vigour. Now say three '*Hail Marys*' and a '*Glory Be to the Father*'."

Shug gulped down the pills automatically, carried away by the charisma of the Pope, and before he could think through clearly about what had actually happened. The facts were that the Pope was, of course, an imposter, substituting for a fake, and even if either pretender had been the Pope, it would certainly be unusual for him or any priest to administer pills during confession. "Ach! To heck with it!" he reasoned, having swallowed the pills, "What harm could come of it? They are probably fake pills in any case."

"That Pope is some guy,' exclaimed Shug to the others when he exited the confessional, "I know he is just an impersonator, but I reckon he would give the real Pope a run for his money. Right, who is next?"

Magdalene opened the door, entered the confessional, and knelt down nervously. "Bless me, Popieness, for I have sinned, it is sex weeks, sorry, six weeks since my last confession.

"Are you the cute, pretty one?" asked the Pope.

"Yes," was the instant reply from Magdalene, who took for granted that, of course, she was the beauty in the group. After all, she had a curvaceous figure, silky hair, and, unlike Rashona, she wasn't cross eyed and still had all her teeth.

"Excellent," the Pope responded, "if it has only been six weeks since your last confession, I can't think that such a beautiful heavenly creature as you could possibly have committed a sin."

"Well, father, Popieness ... sorry, Pope, the reason for goin' to confession every sex, sorry, six weeks is that I keep committin' the same sin."

"What might that be, my sweetness and light?"

"I have these bad thoughts."

"Tell me more."

"I don't like to say, Your Popieness."

"Oh, come now, my dear, sweet child, you need to tell me if you want your sins removed and the slate wiped clean."

"Oh, I suppose so," Magdalene, just like Shug, had been sucked into the enactment. Over the years, she had also had plenty of indoctrination into accepting her own guilt and self-loathing. This was more than enough to ensure that she would respond to the urge to reveal all to someone who was not the Pope, not even a priest! "I keep gettin' these desires, Your Popieness. There's someone that I really fancy and I've got these emotions and fantasies of a ... sexual nature. I don't know what to do about it and they keep appearin' when I least expect them in my mind, when I'm shoppin', in the chapel, in the park, in the confessional even. I'm so sinful."

"My sweet thing, these are natural feelings and certainly not sins. I would recommend that you have sexual intercourse with the object of your fantasies as quickly as you can. And you should not feel guilty about it. In fact, the guilt itself is a sin.

Right, that's you done," the Pope concluded, sniggering to himself. "Say three '*Hail Marys*' and a '*Glory Be to the*

Father'. Send in the next one, please."

The others could see a glow in Magdalene's cheeks as she withdrew from the confessional and thought to themselves, *this Pope is good.*

"Me next," shouted Rashona, entering the confessional with Rab prodding her in the shoulder and reminding her not to give the show away.

"Are you the ugl … sorry, the other one?" whispered Pope John.

"I am Rashona. Bless me, Pope, it's been six weeks since my last confession and I've committed the sin of envy. I'm jealous of Magdalene. All the men love her and treat her well and they just ignore me. I wish Magdalene was not so beautiful but I know that's a sin. What should I do?"

"Well, I am surprised about that. The first man who confessed to me today said that he was infatuated by someone called Rashona, so that must be you. There is a test that the women use in Africa to find out from a man if they have any feelings of tenderness for them and I suggest that you try this yourself with this young fellow. What you must do is look into his eyes and say '*My love for you is stronger than an elephant's trunk and bigger than an elephant's ears'*. Then pull his nose first and then his ears. If he has been immediately stimulated by your exhortation, then he is truly in love with you and has only been too embarrassed to reveal his true feelings about you."

Rashona was enraptured with the idea of the test. While a bit risky, she felt getting her hands on Shug was legitimate, given the Pope had sanctioned it himself. What had she got to lose? "Thank you, Pope, I will try this."

"No problem, say three '*Hail Mary*s' and a '*Glory Be to the Father*'." And with this, Rashona, a little hungry but excited about the prospect of the test, left the confessional.

Next to enter the confessional was Malky, who had been impressed by the other three's reactions to the confession and was predisposed to give it a good try. "I've got a problem with disobedience, Pope. I cannot take orders too well and am inclined to argue. Oh, and by the way, it's been a long time since my last compression."

"You are a hero, my man, who will stand up for truth. And didn't our good Lord say, 'I am the way, the truth and the light'? It does not mean that you are wrong when you don't give in to lies and wrongdoing. You stand up for righteousness and if what you are asked to do is wrong, then morally you have to disobey. In fact, I demand that you take it one step further and the person who is transgressing against the moral imperative should be made to pay with a swift hook to the nose. Only this will bring them back to a humble and true road to salvation."

"That's exactly what I think, Pope. I won't let you down." Malky was getting pumped up with moral righteousness and ready to do the Lord's work. He, like the others, had been totally taken in by Pope John LeMaistre.

"Three '*Hail Mary*s' and a '*Glory Be to the Father*'."

Last in was Rab. As the leader, he had given his team the chance to go in first, but now it was his turn. He had been impressed by how filled with enthusiasm the other four had been and was interested in what this fake Pope was going to provide for him.

"Comrade, it has been four weeks since my last confession."

"Go on, my son."

"I have sinned, comrade; I have been short and impatient with my brothers and sisters. I'm ashamed to say that I've contrived to stoop to methods of shoutin' and I've been really frustrated with my team. I've seen the expressions on the faces of my fellow compatriots and what you have done for them. I can only hope for the same forgiveness that you've blessed them with." Rab bowed his head and waited for the response.

"Was God not angry at the transgressions of the Israelites in the stories of the Old Testament? Were not his people fearful of this God, a vengeful God and an angry God? Wasn't Jesus angry when he chased the money-makers out of the temple? My son, you are only doing the will of your maker. I urge you to be angrier with them. If they are disobedient, you must beat them within an inch of their lives, make them humble in the eyes of their Lord. Now go forth and dispense righteous justice to save their mortal souls. And, by the way, say three '*Hail Marys*' and a '*Glory be to the Father*'."

At this, the Pope left the confessional, blessing the penitents on his way out of the room. After closing the door, he waited outside with his ear pressed to it, listening to hear the outcome of his cunning manipulations.

*

268

Rashona had ushered Shug to one side of the room, away from the other three Glaswegians cornering him to ensure he did not escape. Shug was feeling a bit strange, starting to attribute the feeling to the blue pills the Pope had given him, and hoping it wasn't going to make him sick. He was also wondering what had got into Rashona and why she was so anxious to speak to him. *She seemed a bit weird.* Rashona looked Shug straight in the eye, trying to remember the phrase that the Pope said would tell her if Shug had the same feeling as she did. It also helped that she was unaware of the inappropriateness of her actions.

"Right," she thought she had it, "Shug, my love is longer than an elephant's trunk and bigger than an elephant's ears."

"What the fuck! What's got over you, Rashona?" Shug exclaimed, just before he felt her pull his nose and then his ears and, what's more, he suddenly realised he had the most enormous erection he had ever experienced. "What the fuck!" he cried out, along with thinking, *Where did that come from?!*

Rashona looked down and shouted, "You love me. I always knew you did." She did not see Magdalene coming across the room to see what the commotion was and thwack! Magdalene slapped Rashona hard across the face.

"Ya fuckin' whore, what do you think you are doin'?"

*

Pope John LeMaistre, listening outside the door, started to laugh.

Rab was half aware of Rashona and Shug talking in the corner as he approached Malky to reinforce his assigned role in the plan, saying, "You'll need to make sure you're at the burial room on time to get us out of the coffins."

"No, I don't."

"What do you mean? Yes! You do! I'm tellin' you, you will."

"No, you're not. Don't boss me about."

"I bloody well will boss you about, you big stupid 'dumplin'."

"No, you won't, you 'glaikit tumshy'."

"Right, that's it."

"No, it isn't."

"Aye, it is," and at this point, remembering what the Pope had told him, Malky punched Rab right on the nose, resulting in blood spurting out in all directions.

Rab, also remembering what the Pope had told him, grabbed the first thing he could, which happened to be a serving spoon and a French baguette that had been laid out on a table in the centre of the room, finger buffet style, for their final supper. Rab used both implements to batter Malky into submission while he continued bleeding.

Rashona and Magdalene, who had grabbed each other's hair and were locked in a tussle, stopped to look up at the sight of Rab thumping Malky with what was now a quarter piece of baguette and a long metal spoon. At the same time,

Rab was shouting at the top of his voice, "Your God is a fuckin' vengeful God, ya big stupit bastart."

*

Pope John LeMaistre was almost wetting himself with laughter now outside the door, when he suddenly felt a sharp pain to the top of his head and his muscles seizing up beyond his control. With a strange sensation he seemed, suddenly, to be on the outside of his body watching himself fall slowly to the ground. Lying in a heap on the carpet, his mind refocused; he was now more conscious than he had ever been. *Why could he not get up? Why could he not move his legs?* A small barking dog with a monkey riding on its back ran past his line of sight as he lay on the floor. *Why could he not roll over to continue to see where the dog and monkey were going?*

What had happened to John LeMaistre? And what was to become of him in the future? Well, the fact was that he had experienced a brain stem stroke, resulting in a condition known as 'locked-in syndrome'. This was probably the worst condition for a psychopath to acquire. He was totally paralyzed, could not speak, could not move his muscles, but could think clearly. He had also become totally and irretrievably dependent. While his brain was fully functional and lucid, his only physical ability was to be able to see and hear, along with some small ability to move his eyes. If this was not bad enough, he was admitted forthwith to a local hospital in Villadedino. Two weeks later, he was flown to a hospital near his home in Los Angeles and ensconced there in a long-term ward. His controlled plan for death at the Villadedino hotel did not take place.

From bad to worse, he discovered that one of his ex-wives, who just happened to be a professionally qualified occupational therapist at the self-same hospital, was responsible for his care. What fun they had, as he tried to spell out his wishes by blinking his eyes to select letters on the alphabet board. He would be trying to say, I--w-o-u-l-d—l-i-k-e—a—d-r-i-n-k, and his former wife would helpfully interpret this as I--w-o-u-l-d—l-i-k-e—a-n—e-n-e-m-a!

John went on to live for the next twenty years, thus experiencing the indignity of 205 resuscitations, 7,300 bed baths, 21,900 force-fed meals, and, thanks to the commitment of the occupational therapist who had dedicated her life to his care, 1,322 enemas. Every minute of every day he suffered the frustration of not being able to figure out what the dog with the monkey riding on its back had been up to.

*

Meanwhile, back to the fearless five, 'locked', in another sense, into a battle of blood, baguettes, tears, and snotters. A knock came to the door and the resident doctor, carrying the preparations that would end three of their lives, let himself in. This seemed to have a calming effect, particularly when they saw the Pope, being attended now, lying just outside the door, prostate on the ground, with a thin white foam of saliva dribbling out of his mouth.

"I think we need to pull ourselves together, comrades,"

Rab suggested to the other four while mopping up the blood from his nose with the tablecloth. This seemed to snap them out of the spell in which the Pope had trapped them and thus Rab galvanised his compatriots into action as they all started to recall the momentous assignment awaiting them.

*

In the meantime, Tyson and Jiki were rampant across the hotel, causing havoc wherever they went. Tyson would snap at the ankles of anyone they met in the corridors while Jiki would screech at the top of his voice. They hurtled down a corridor and came to a dead end beside a glass door. Jiki looked through the glass door and was excited by what he saw. It was no problem for him to open the door. To Jiki it seemed like heaven; a room full of microwaves, his favourite toy apart from his stuffed panda. He did like to press the buttons and turn the switches on microwaves.

They had entered into the logistics control room of the Hotel's main function; the automated operation for the one-mile of conveyor belts that took the dearly departed to their resting place after their final moments. The control room was unoccupied, as the switches, nobs, and buttons once set meant that the operation was mostly automated. Each cadaver was lifted and loaded into a coffin that was then screwed shut and systematically carried via a tributary conveyor belt to join one of two main conveyor belts: one to the crematorium and the other to the depository burial chamber warehouse to await transportation by the grave digger crew to the cemetery for internment.

273

Residents at the hotel signed up for their choice, cremation or burial. The '*coffin you go off in*' (another of the manager Zeca Silva's aphorisms) had an electronic tag that was scanned as the coffin made its way along the conveyor belt. These electronic tags provided the signals that then directed the coffin to either of two options: green for burial or red for crematorium. This signal was operated by two different switches in the control room that could be turned to each of the two final destinations: crematorium or cemetery. Normally, the green switch was set to cemetery and the red switch to crematorium. Unsurprisingly, however, nobody had taken account of a capuchin monkey with skilful manual dexterity and a fetish for microwaves, gadgets, buttons, nobs, and switches.

Jiki, jumping from Tyson's back, looked around the room for some food to put in the microwave, but there was none to be found. He then turned his attention to the buttons and switches, which he excitedly turned and pushed. For a few minutes, forgetting where he was and being simply focused on his favourite activity, his tiny hands turned, pressed, flipped back and forward anything he could, with the total absorption of an absent-minded professor intent on setting his controls for a groundbreaking experiment. Randomly, he came to the green switch that was set to cemetery and the red switch that was set to crematorium and turned each of them so that all coffins with a green signal would now be directed to crematorium, while those with the red signal would in turn be sent to the burial holding depository chamber. This was not much of a problem for a dead person other than it would not be quite their selected choice of terminus. However, this change certainly would be problematic if you just happened to be a Glasgow Catholic terrorist whose means of escape, after depositing a bomb, depended on being routed to departure via the burial holding depository chamber.

*

Now, after breaking the spell cast on them by the evil LeMaistre, the five intrepid Glasgow Catholic terrorists pulled themselves together like a drunken conga line in preparation for their daring actions. Rab was helped by Malky to stem the final flow of blood from his nose; Magdalene and Rashona fixed each other's hair and wiped the streaked mascara and snotters from their cheeks. But, while the others heightened emotional crisis had returned to normal, Shug's physiology was still a humble subject to the rule of the Viagra medication still in his system. So, Shug was trying to talk to the others while facing the wall and pretending to sort out some cups, in order to hide the evidence of a monumental extension to his anatomy that was doing its best to stretch the material of his distressed jeans to breaking point.

The doctor had now left after depositing the suicide potions with the girls whom, he supposed, were going to be responsible for administering them to the boys and assisting them into their coffins.

The group was ready to carry out their plan. Firstly, they disposed of the poison by pouring it into a pot plant innocently cowering at the corner of the room. They then turned to face the sliding doors and opened these to reveal the conveyor belt on which lay the three intimidating coffins ordered by the group.

The explosives that had been concealed in the girls' handbags were now removed and placed ready to arm. Attaching the timer to the fuses, they placed the now live explosives inside the coffin with the red electronic tag that designated it would be destined for the crematorium. Rab then climbed into a coffin marked with the green electronic tag, identifying it as the one to go to the burial holding depository chamber. Avoiding the embarrassment of his troublesome appendage, Shug quickly followed into the other green-tagged coffin. Finally, Malky and Rashona helped Magdalene into this same coffin occupied by Shug. After fixing the lids of their compatriots' two coffins, Malky and Rashona wrote the initials of the Catholic United Network for the Transgression of Sins on each of them. They had all agreed that the use of a white marker would make it easy to identify the two coffins when they appeared at the other end in the burial depositary chamber.

"Wish us luck," shouted Rab from within his now sealed coffin, "and we'll see you in ten minutes in the burial holdin' depository chamber."

"It's a bit of a tight squeeze in here," shouted the excited Magdalene, "but I'm sure we'll come good in the end."

Shug was thinking that it was an unfortunate choice of phrase that Magdalene had used as he shouted and immediately regretted, "Touch wood!"

Malky had set the timer on the explosives for thirty minutes, as he had been instructed, which would be enough time for them to get to the burial holding depository chamber, evacuate from the coffins, and then make their getaway from the hotel before the bomb exploded. They had seen the itinerary for the day. Three assisted suicides scheduled ahead of them and these coffins would be in front of the coffin with the explosives heading for the crematorium. Each cremation took about ten minutes.

They had no idea that they would be following these three coffins towards the crematorium. They were also still completely unaware that a capuchin primate had inopportunely spent time monkeying around with the dials of the control panel.

Chapter 24 The Catholic United Network for Transgression of Sins (on Fire)

A carbon eager for the stars when sun demands the child's return

The Song of Villadedino, Saint Dino 240AD

The conveyor belt started to move slowly, carrying the two coffins with the three Catholic revolutionaries. Rab shouted, "Can you hear me, you two?"

Shug and Magdalene responded in unison, "Yes!"

"It should only take us about fifteen minutes to reach the burial depository chamber and then Malky and Rashona can get us out." Rab heard no answer from the other coffin and interpreted that everything was alright.

In the other coffin, meanwhile, Magdalene was starting to realise that it wasn't a screwdriver that Shug had brought, but rather a tool of another type. She was overjoyed with their opportune confinement. Here she was in a tight space, okay, it was a coffin (a bit depraved), but, nevertheless, a tight space with the object of her desire. Not only were they in a constricted environment, but also Shug was indicating, in no uncertain terms, that he was excited to be there with her.

"I have always dreamed of this, Shug," she cooed as she put her arm around his back and pulled him closer to her.

Shug, who had been extremely embarrassed by his predicament, momentarily had the fleeting thought that he would have been monumentally more embarrassed had he been in the coffin with Malky who, on account of wanting a coffin to himself, had, thankfully, refused. He was now warming, literally, to his position and more positively reconsidered his standpoint, "Magdalene, there is no one I would rather be stuck in a coffin with than you."

"Why, you're quite stimulated, Shug, is this the effect I have on you?"

Shug whispered, "We probably have about twelve minutes before we reach the burial depository chamber for me to show you what effect you have on me." With that, the two companions adjusted what items of clothing they could and enflamed each other with an ardour and passion that was intensifying by the second.

"I have to say, I'm getting quite excited now," shouted Rab to the other two. He thought he heard some acknowledgement of, "YES!" emanating from the other coffin. "We're goin' to show these bastards!" Again, screams of, "YES!" resounded from the others. "Where do you two reckon we are now?" questioned Rab.

"Up a bit, yes! Just there!" was the response he heard.

"Yes, that's what I thought too," Rab answered. Then, in a spontaneous invocation of joy, and in response to the positive sounds he heard coming from the other coffin, the elated Rab belted out the group's favourite hymn:

> *'The sun is shining brightly*
> *The trees are clothed with green*
> *The beauteous bloom of flowers*

On every side is seen
The fields are gold and emerald
And all the world is gay
For 'tis the month of Mary
The lovely month of May'

He was on a high now and the enthusiastic response he was receiving from his colleagues, banging on their coffin in time to his song and impregnating his stanzas with encouraging calls of, "YES! YES! GO ON! GO ON!" only inspired him to sing with more abandon at the top of his voice, a second verse, and then to repeat the song all over again. A warm glow wrapped around Rab like a fur-lined duffle coat as the admiration of his team climaxed with one last almighty shout of ecstatic approval issuing from the other coffin.

It was quiet now and he was aware the conveyor belt had stopped moving; perhaps they had reached their destination. However, he realised that the coffin couldn't possibly have arrived there so quickly. Perception of time when you are ensconced inside a coffin can be a little skewed, it occurred to him. He could hear the roar of something that was swooshing out… *no, it couldn't be,* but the smell of something burning was causing him to reassess his situation. He became more than a little uncomfortable that it was very like the smell of bacon; and the roar he was hearing did sound like a jet of … of … of … he couldn't seek solace in the denial of the realisation any more. *Oh, my God!* he his mind began to scream at him. *They were on the conveyor belt heading for the wrong destination, in coffins that were screwed down tight, with no way of opening them from the inside, and destined for the crematorium!*

*

Malky and Rashona reached the burial depository chamber in good time; Rashona for once resisting the impulse to stop for a snack along the way. The warehouse space opened out through a large hanger door to the road that led a short distance to the graveyard. They had timed it so that the rescue of their colleagues coincided with the gravediggers' lunchtime. The hanger door was open to the road, offering them easy access and the place was empty. The conveyor belt was continuing to roll, automatically delivering the coffins to the mechanism that then unloaded and stacked them ready for transportation to the cemetery. They checked that no-one was around, then waited expectantly for the two coffins with the white ink-marked handwritten initials of the Catholic United Network for the Transgression of Sins scrawled on them. None arrived. They endured the wait for the anticipated arrivals, thinking that in their excitement they had perhaps reached the burial depository quicker than they had rehearsed. But still no coffins with the white initials appeared.

"Perhaps we better look through the coffins that are here in case they've already arrived," Rashona sensibly suggested. They checked through the coffins that had been unloaded and mechanically stacked in the depository, but still no Rab, Shug, or Magdalene.

"Hey, I thought all the coffins with the red electronic

281

tags were supposed to go to the crematorium," shouted Rashona to Malky as it started to dawn on her, like a fridge door opening on a midnight feast, what might have gone wrong.

"Fucksake! What are we goin' to do now?" Malky muttered as he also realised that all the coffins, since they had arrived, all had red tags, "Rab must have misunderstood the system and now they'll be heading for barbecuin' in the aquarium." In a moment of clarity, for once in his life, the cogs of Malky's brain all clicked into the correct place as he made the right decision. He grabbed Rashona by the arm before she could think of her next snack and started to run, dragging her by his side to the manager's office.

*

"We're startin' to move again," exclaimed the traumatized Rab, "I'm sorry to tell you both that this isn't workin' out quite as we'd planned."

"What do you mean?" Magdalene answered, calmer now after her experience with Shug had dissipated and sensing a mounting panic in Rab's voice that was beginning to worry her.

"The system for the coffins must have changed. I can feel the heat of the crematorium flames and I don't want to admit this, but we're on the wrong track. I think we're goin' to end up gettin' burned." He started kicking at the lid, but it was clamped solid and there was no way out. Magdalene and Shug also started pushing at the lid, but they too were fastened down tight and they knew from their recent activities that there was little room to manoeuvre.

It was getting hotter and the three Catholic guerrillas were sweating profusely. "I can't stand this heat anymore," Rab shouted to his colleagues while trying to remove as much clothing as he could in the tight space. Shug and Magdalene, who had already had one rehearsal of removing parts of their clothing, helped each other out of the rest and still the coffins and their live human contents continued to get hotter and hotter.

Rab came upon his mobile phone in his trouser pocket as he was removing them. Grasping at a solution, he scrolled through the list in his contacts to find Archbishop Romario's number. He pressed dial. Philomena O'Shaughnessy, the eighty-seven-year-old Irish house keeper at Archbishop Romario's residence, was napping, as she often did, to ease the pain in her back resulting from sixty-seven years of service to the catalogue of Archbishops she had looked after. She roused herself and made her way to the vintage telephone that had been installed in the 1960s.

"Hello there! Archbishop Romario's residence."

"Philomena, it's me, Rab Lennon, I need to speak to the Archbishop urgently".

"The Archbishop is eating his lunch, Mr Lemon. Can you call back later?"

"Fu ... Philomena, this is life and death," pleaded the exasperated Rab.

"Well, to be sure, can you tell me what it's about and I will see if the Archbishop will speak to you, Mr Lemon?"

"Fu ... Philomena, I'm in a coffin, I'm heading to be

burned to death if I don't get out of here. Can you please get the Archbishop, now!"

"Oh, come on now, Mr Lemon, no need to shout, to be sure, I'll go and ask the Archbishop if he will come to the phone."

Philomena O'Shaughnessy put the receiver on the table, thought about it for a second, and then took her polishing cloth out of her apron pocket and gave the phone a little wipe, turned and proceeded as fast as her eighty-seven-year-old legs could take her – that is at a snail's pace – through the hall and kitchen. In the conservatory, the Archbishop was having his lunch of cold beef and mustard sandwiches while reading one of his favourite pulp fiction detective novels, '*Gus Gunner Goes Gunning for Gold*'. He looked up as Philomena slowly crossed the floor.

"There's a Mr Lemon on the phone and he says it is urgent that he speak to you. I told him you were at your luncheon, but he was insistent, to be sure."

"I don't know any Mr Lemon. What did he say it was about?"

"He said something about coughing and that he was burning up. I think the poor man was a bit feverish, to be sure."

"What does he think I can do for him? I am not a doctor. Tell him he should phone a doctor and that he certainly must be in a fever if he has resorted to phone an Archbishop about his condition."

Philomena turned around and made her way back to the kitchen, pausing to wipe the surfaces down and tidy away a few pieces of crockery that had dried in the draining tray. She eventually reached the phone and lifted the receiver to speak to Mr Lemon.

"Hello Mr Lemon, the Archbishop said that you should call a doctor. He is very sorry that you are burning up, to be sure, but there is nothing he can do about this. I would recommend some paracetamol with olive oil and honey, with a wee bit of whisky. This always works for me, sure it does."

While Rab was trying to figure out why he was being told about taking this homely course of treatment as a cure for incineration, he heard Philomena bid him a farewell and the long tone after the phone was hung up on the other side. He felt the heat intensify, as the coffin with its contents, which he thought was just ahead of his own, began to be reduced to ashes.

"We're goin' to burn to death," Magdalene, now in a state of shock, sobbed against Shug's shoulder, "This is a punishment for our sin. It's punishment for all my sins. '*Don't worry, mummy, I'm waiting for you,*' she heard a small voice say in her head. "We should never have shagged, Shug," extoled Magdalene, whimpering now, her shoulders heaving, and, in between tears, mumbling variations on, "Shag, Shug … don't waaah, Shug … shag, I don't waaah wanna die, Shug."

Shug was also in a state of panic, but tried to comfort Magdalene. This was difficult, as the effects of the three Viagra pills had still not worn off and his indiscretion was interjecting on his efforts at consolation.

"What do you think you're doin', Shug? This is not the time for shagging, Shug. I don't waaah wanna shag, Shug … don't waaah wanna die, Shug … shag, Shug, don't … waaah!"

Malky and Rashona, out of breath and panting, reached the manager's office, where Zeca Silva was putting the finishing touches to what he just knew would be another hit to add to his litany of famous aphorisms. '*The Hotel Euthanasia, where dining and dying will be to your taste*'. His self-absorption was disturbed by his door bursting open and two wide-eyed individuals shrieking. He could not make any sense of what they were saying.

"Coffins … Shug … Rab … crematorium … fuck … Magdalene … burn … red tag … alive … dead … fuckin' … burn … no time … stop … red tag … shut down … fuckin … conveyor … burn … now … die … help … please … now … dead … fucksake!"

"Can you please just slow down? What is your problem? Please take a deep breath and one of you talk slowly."

"Fuckin' coffin with fuckin' Rab, Shug, and Magdalene are fuckin' going to the crematorium and they are fuckin' going to fuckin' be fuckin' burned," Malky articulated as he managed to formulate his thoughts into an eloquently constructed enunciation.

Zeca thought these mad people were getting a bit emotional about a simple mistake. Okay, they are not getting their first choice of burial, but, *wasn't Malky supposed to be one of those to die? Where was the other girl? Had they changed their minds? Surely it was not such a big deal if they are dead anyway?* There was nothing Zeca had found that couldn't be resolved with the compensation of a hearty meal and a fine bottle of wine on the house.

"Let me apologise and please accept a free meal and a fine bottle of wine on the house as recompense for your dearly departed friends being unable to have their first choice of burial, but I can assure you the crematorium is very efficient."

"But they're fuckin' … are fuckin' alive." This did not compute with Zeca because, if they were alive, what were they doing in the coffins?

"I don't quite understand, my friends. Are you saying that they are still alive and waiting to die and have been advised that there are only incinerations today because the graveyard is too busy?"

"Fuckin' look here, pal. They are fuckin' alive. They are in fuckin' coffins on their fuckin' way … if not already fuckin' there … to the fuckin' crematorium and they are fuckin' going to be fuckin' burned fuckin' alive."

Zeca was still confused by all the swearing, but he had now understood enough from the phrases in between the profanities to lift the phone and instruct the on-call technician to quickly go to the control room and turn off the incinerator. "Fuck!" he said under his breath.

*

Rab heard the coffin in front of him being uncompromisingly consumed by the jets of flame from the incinerator. The smell of burning human flesh was overpowering. He could hear the loud screams of terror emanating from the coffin one behind his from the increasingly hysterical Magdalene and Shug. Up above

287

them, in the viewing gallery for the crematorium, there was an increasing buzz of conversation as the onlookers watched the spectacle unfolding below them and wondered why there were two coffins with the word 'CUNTS' written on each of the lids. One of the onlookers said he could hear screams and shouts coming from the coffins. A curious crowd was beginning to gather, like ants around a road kill.

Rab's life flashed in front of his eyes as he could hear the sound of the jets of flames stop and the crushing and grinding of the remains of the earlier coffin's incumbent taking place. It would only be a matter of minutes now till he experienced the same fate. The image that made its way to the front of his brain was of himself as a small boy, sitting in church and hearing the parish priest giving a sermon from the pulpit designed to put the fear of God in the parishioners. '*And you will roast in Hull, I tell you, Hull!*' ... pause for effect ... '*Your sins will find you out. I'm talking about impure thoughts. The devil himself will torture you with a burning pitchfork and you will burn in the darkest, darkest recesses of Hull! Hull! Hull!*'

Rab, despite his impending doom, was paradoxically being subjected to his delinquent mind recalling the insignificant thought that he had always had an aversion to going anywhere near East Yorkshire, never mind Hull. With a superhuman effort on his behalf to eject from his mind the possibility that his last thought on this earth would be about Hull, the grinding of the remains of the previous recipient of the incinerator stopped. There was a pause, a jerk, and the conveyor belt started to move inevitably towards its fiery destiny. *This is it*, Rab thought, *how perverse that I am going to experience the same fate as my stupid parents.*

Time seemed to stand still for Rab. He had read about this phenomenon of people undergoing a traumatic event such as being in a car crash or being shot and experiencing events playing themselves out in slow motion with time seeming to expand. All fear had departed, replaced by a stillness, calmness, and heightened awareness. His senses were enhanced as he heard clearly the various sounds around him of the incinerator and Magdalene's cries. His thoughts took on a clarity of perception that crystallised what was essential to him in these final moments of life. His past values, thoughts, and decisions arranged themselves in a matrix so that he could cross reference all of them both horizontally and vertically at the same time. In that moment, he felt more empowered than he had been in his whole life. *Although I am not here by choice, hundreds and thousands of other people have made the choice to use assisted dying and have passed this way. My own parents made the same choice, albeit coerced by the Communist Party, but it was their right. I was wrong to let my anger and wish for revenge override my reason. I did good work campaigning for people's right to choose to die. I am certain of that now. All the diversion into flawed 'man made' institutions of religion and Communism was ultimately a means of avoiding my coming to terms with adversity. If I ever get out of this, I am certain that I will fulfil myself and do what I do best and that is to campaign for people's rights to die.* Rab felt a quiet detachment now, accepting his fate, his parents' decision, and acknowledging his own qualities and self-worth. The moment enclosed itself like a flower bud in amber as the casket edged ever forward.

*

The crowds above in the viewing gallery had swelled as the news had spread that there were people alive in coffins rolling towards the incinerator. They gasped as they looked on with shock and alarm as one of the coffins started to move forward.

The technician now at the control room and in response to the instruction from Mr Silva put down the telephone, reached over, and pressed the red stop button just as Rab could hear an increasing grinding noise, as he felt the heat and saw in his mind's eye the devouring flames rush towards his coffin. And then – silence.

The jets of flames had stopped and Rab could hear the sound of running feet heading towards the coffins. The crowd at the viewing gallery looked down and cheered as the hotel staff unclamped the lids with 'CUNTS' written on them and out emerged a naked man from one of the coffins and from the other coffin, inexplicably, a naked woman accompanied by another naked man who was clearly, to the crowd, a bit stiff following his incarceration in the coffin.

"You don't see that every day," said one of the onlookers to her cheering friend as the three escapees gave a weak wave of embarrassed acknowledgement to the viewing crowd while trying to cover their nakedness. Just then there was the sound of a loud explosion!

Chapter 25 Resolutions

The dance of life in fates condensing to join the dancers in
their step

The Song of Villadedino, Saint Dino 240AD

Jiki and Tyson parted company at the central control room, where Jiki had entered enthusiastically into his favourite pastime of operating all the 'microwave ovens' in the room. He had, of course, succeeded in switching the destination of the green cemetery tagged coffins to arrive at the crematorium and the red crematorium tagged coffins to arrive at the burial holding chamber to await transportation to the cemetery.

Nothing here, thought Tyson as he ran off, glad to be rid of the monkey.

*

Jiki continued for some minutes to 'play' with the switches, buttons, and nobs, but became bored when there was no 'ding' to indicate that the microwave meal had been cooked. So, with his appetite for adventure whetted, he exited the control room to explore the corridors further. He opened a door to what was Angela Deff's office. Angela looked up as the small primate made a series of little chirping noises. Recognising a familiar contraption, Jiki leapt over the furniture to press the buttons on the coffee maker and, inexplicably in Angela's eyes, brought her over a cup of coffee and placed it on her desk. Angela weighed up the arguments as to whether the monkey should be categorised as a customer or not, as Jiki looked adoringly into her eyes. *Better safe than sorry*, she concluded. "Would you like a raisin?" she found herself asking her little customer.

*

Angela Deff was not sure what to make of the capuchin monkey that sat on her shoulder as she made her way to the eXi-theme Departure Suite being used by Hugh Mann. She could feel his little feet on her shoulder and occasionally he would part and groom her hair. She was aware that the monkey gripped on tightly to her and she could sense his tiny heart start to flutter as they entered the room to see Hugh. Jiki was careful to cross to the shoulder of Angela that was furthest away from the tray with the needle still displayed on it. Angela heard him chirp in her ear as if informing her of something important.

"Ah, there he is," Hugh said, "I wondered where he had run off to."

Angela was aware that Jiki was to end his life with Hugh. As she felt his eager little fingers part and stroke her hair again, she had a thought, "Mr Mann, it seems a waste of a perfectly good monkey if you carry on with your plan to kill him along with yourself. I would be happy to take him off your hands. He came into my office and made me a coffee. He could be useful to me around here."

"That would be wonderful," the relieved Hugh Mann

responded. This was the answer to his prayers. He could see that there was a relationship forming between Jiki and Angela. He was combing her hair with his fingers the way he had with Hannah when she was alive and he seemed to be comfortable with her. "I could now die happy," he said.

The deal was done and all three parties were pleased. Hugh could end his life knowing that Jiki would be cared for, Jiki had a new friend (with a coffee machine and a supply of raisins), and Angela had what was for her a very different experience, a relationship with another creature. With a final affectionate embrace, Hugh gave Jiki his little monkey companion's favourite stuffed toy panda and lifted him across into Angela's arms. Angela left the eXi-theme Departure Suite with Jiki and headed back to the Customer Care Manager's office, leaving Hugh now content to be completing his assisted dying procedure. A new chapter in Angela's life was starting. She was quite clear in her own mind now that Jiki was no longer a customer. '*Assistant*,' she thought to herself as Jiki allowed himself to be carried and worked out his training strategy for his new 'mistress'.

*

As for Mrs Merger, she did wait for Tyson; well, for a whole ten bad tempered minutes that is. She walked back and forth impatiently in the eXi-theme Departure Suite while the ghastly ghouls of her seven dead husbands formed a line behind her, imitating her perambulations interspersed with lewd comments and complaints about her dress, her hair, and her make up. In fact, they complained about anything they considered would irritate the far from happy widow.

"Tyson is so disobedient. Just let him get on with it. Running away like that is just such bad behaviour."

'We don't blame the poor little blighter. Only wish we could have run away from you, you old bat, when we were alive', commented one of the ghosts accompanied by loud affirmations and calls of, '*woof woof*' from the others as they bounded round the room barking and simulating the actions of a dog urinating against the table legs.

"You lot are absolutely disgusting. Worse than animals," Mrs Merger shrieked in exasperation at the seven spirit stooges.

She had run out of patience with the ghosts and the little dog. Mrs Merger was not conscious of the fact that the technician and the physician were both standing by waiting and had become increasingly wary of the strange behaviour and screamed phrases from the old woman. So, they were glad to get the process initiated when she instructed them to progress with her planned demise. "Let's get the show on the road. It's costing me enough. What's keeping you?" The seven apparitions broke into a rendition of '*Knockin' on Heaven's Door*'.

The show actually requested by Mrs Merger was a chronological pageant of all the videos from her seven weddings with, as requested, the insertion of a little entertainment she had devised for her own delectation. This was edited in by the technician at the end of each of her weddings and consisted of Tyson walking onto a stage with the amount of inheritance that

Mrs Merger had received following the death of each husband in the preceding wedding, displayed on his little tartan doggy coat. She laughed out loud to the great disgust of the seven dead husbands who had to watch as each time Tyson paraded on with the amounts $1,500,303; $1,007,060; $2,850,020; $900,050; $850,000; $790,000 shown on his coat. But when the final husband's inheritance of a disappointing $32 was displayed on Tyson's little tartan doggy coat, Mrs Merger lifted the potion that would end her life.

"Thanks for nothing!" she toasted, as she swallowed the lethal dose and started the drift into unconsciousness. Her final image, just as she was about to go under the effects of the administered potion, was not as she had planned. The seven spectres of her seven dead husbands emerged out from the maXiviewalls, holding chains and howling in unison a collective wail, announcing, *'We've been waiting for you!'*

*

What's that smell? Tyson, having escaped the clutches of the monkey, was making his way along the corridors to track down the various aromas that were flooding his senses. *Must follow that smell.* He eventually arrived at the kitchen, where he provided the cook and kitchen staff with an entertaining diversion from their work as they provided him with a tasty meal. Tyson was most appreciative to the extent that the cook befriended this now most amenable little pooch. Later, after her enquiries had revealed his owner to have recently gone the way of most of the hotel guests, the cook was given permission to keep the grateful little dog, And, as providence would have it, no ghosts ever arrived to haunt Tyson again.

Chapter 26 The Cover Up

The judge concludes my lifelong crimes and leaves them as a marble debt

The Song of Villadedino, Saint Dino 240AD

Zeca Silva and Chief Inspector Gillou, the principal detective inspector of the Principality of Villadedino police force, entered the interview room and scrutinised the five handcuffed Scots sitting behind the table in front of them. They sat down, took out their pens, and opened their notebooks. Inspector Gillou took his time and unnervingly looked deep into the eyes of each of the Scots one by one.

"You are in very serious trouble," he said with a precise and exacting tone to his voice like a pair of pliers pulling a nail from a piece of wood. Chief Inspector Gillou was tall and thin with a little pencil moustache. He wore a grey double-breasted suit, a black shirt, and a red tie. He had made his name investigating the body snatching operation that had been uncovered during the early days of the Hotel Euthanasia. On that occasion, he had caught certain members of staff red-handed shipping corpses in a lorry out of Villadedino to Figas and onto a clinic involved in illegal research into penile erectile dysfunction. The culprits, unlike the corpses, ended up with five years' hard labour.

"We want to ask you some questions," Chief Inspector Gillou began the interrogation by systematically taking a note of all of their names, dates of birth, and addresses. Then, they moved on to the serious questions, "How can you explain the explosion in the graveyard? And I want the truth."

Rab answered defensively, "It wasn't us."

"How, then, do you explain the traces of explosives in your baggage and on your clothes, sir?"

"Coincidence? Planted by someone?" Rab suggested hopefully.

"So, why did you come to Villadedino and the Hotel Euthanasia?" Gillou was starting to raise his voice.

"Three of us were here to die and the other two to say their last farewells."

"Ah! But our records indicate that those listed to die were Rab Lennon, Malky Cole, and Shug McTavish. Is that correct?"

"But I didn't want to get cremated," blurted Malky, thinking to himself that he could probably 'take out' the Chief Inspector and the Hotel Manager and make a run for it.

"I've told you, ya bampot, you weren't goin' to get cremated anyway," interjected Rab in an effort to cover up Malky's stupidity.

Detective Inspector Gillou continued, exploiting the disunited front of conflicting stories being presented to him, "So, why did you end up in the coffin, Miss Magdalene?"

"When I saw him go off to die, I thought to myself I would miss him, so I decided to spend our last moments together, Your Honour." Magdalene had watched her fair share of detective programmes on television to feel inspired to use some of the 'lingo'.

"So, what happened to the other coffin and why was it filled with explosives?"

"Somebody else must have done that, because it wasn't us," Rab responded.

"Okay, let us try another line of enquiry, my friends. Why didn't you take your poison if you were here to die and why did you scream and shout to get out once you knew you were going to be cremated?"

"We thought the poison might not have been 100% fat-free," Rashona jumped in, providing what she considered to be a helpful argument.

"I see! You would rather die a horrible death than take the proper preparation. So, why did you scream to get out then? Why not just go to your death as you had decided? And why did Malky and Rashona come to Mister Silva begging to get you out?" Gillou was hammering home each of his points, much to the admiration of the watching and listening Zeca.

"We changed our minds about dyin' because we suddenly realised that the sanctity of life was more important than choosin' to die," offered Rab, clutching at straws.

"It's not easy to decide to go through with assisted dying. You always keep thinking, will I regret this?" added Shug, wondering whether he should have said anything or just kept quiet.

"Rashona and I just thought that they would change their minds," Malky joined in.

"And we couldn't find the others in the coffins and thought there was a mix up with the explosives," Rashona blabbed, starting to spill the sugar free beans. In her defence, she hadn't had anything to eat for an hour and all these questions, combined with her state of severe malnutrition, were making her light headed and finding it hard to concentrate.

"We didn't have a bomb," interjected Rab quickly.

"No, I just meant that there must have been somebody else who planted a bomb and we couldn't find their bomb that was supposed to be in the crematorium and we thought that the other three would change their minds anyway," Rashona disclosed, digging them deeper into a hole, the emptiness of her stomach now feeling like an underground cavern with water slowly dripping and echoing into the expansive space of her hunger.

"I put it to you that you came to Villadedino to blow up the Hotel Euthanasia for a malevolent and dastardly purpose. You smuggled in explosives and planted them in the coffin to the crematorium and planned your escape in the other two coffins. Two of you planned to extract Rab, Shug, and Magdalene from the coffins in the burial depository chamber. However, the system was unexpectedly changed in the control room and instead of being transported via the conveyor belt to the cemetery you headed to the crematorium. The explosives, contained in the other coffin, were sent to the burial depositary chamber, taken, and buried in a grave, and then exploded, blowing away half the hillside. The sentence for terrorism in Villadedino is life behind bars! I also have in my possession your handwritten plan discovered following a thorough search of your bedrooms." He triumphantly held up the plan on the letter headed paper:

Catholic United Network for the Transgression of Sins
> *1. Arrange three coffins*
>
> *2. Smuggle explosives into hotel*
>
> *3. Explosives in coffin to crematorium*
>
> *4. Shug and ~~Malky~~ Magdalene in coffin to get buried*
>
> *5. Self in coffin to get buried*
>
> *6. ~~Magdalene~~ Malky and Rashona to burial place to get us out*
>
> *7. Make escape*
>
> *8. Hotel explodes*
>
> *9. Ya dancer*

"I don't want to go to jail," Magdalene blubbered. "This is all a punishment for my sins," she started to wail, with a small voice repeating in her head, '*Don't worry, mummy, I will come and visit you in jail*'.

The others sat shocked, realising that the 'cat was out of the bag' and the evidence was now stacked, as heavily as a vanload of bailiffs, against them. There was no way out.

"You are also evil CUNTS," Chief Inspector Gillou added with a flourish.

"Don'tfuckin'calluscunts,yabastard.Wemightbeguilty, but I'm not lettin' you away with insultin' us like that," bellowed Malky as he felt himself move into fight mode.

Chief Inspector Gillou held the letter headed paper in front of them and spelled out the acronym of the Catholic United Network for the Transgression of Sins.

"Fucksake," expressed Rab as they all realised that

they truly were CUNTS.

Malky felt a wave of humiliation roll over him. He didn't like anyone calling him names. But here he was having voluntarily signed up for this embarrassment.

"We already have the headline for the media briefing," interjected Zeca Silva. He held out another sheet of paper with the deliberately embarrassing headline: 'GLASGOW CUNTS TRY TO BLOW UP HOTEL EUTHANASIA'; followed by a blurb about the failed operation; a picture taking centre place in the media briefing of the three naked terrorists, one with an enormous tribute to the power of medication, emerging from their coffins and waving to the crowd.

Gillou stared petulantly at Shug and pointing at his monolith in the photograph said, "And you, Mr McTavish, are 'obviously' a hardened criminal!"

Zeca, aware that the Glasgow five were on the ropes, smiled charmingly. Like a magician, revealing the purpose of his illusion, he continued, "However, we could do a deal that would result in your freedom!"

*

Zeca Silva outlined the offer he had prepared in advance, "Villadedino does not desire the adverse publicity of your trial, assured conviction and incarceration for life. You will not be aware, as you have been under house arrest here at the hotel since yesterday, but the coffin with the explosives was placed in an excavated grave by the side of the hill in the

302

cemetery. Luckily, the gravediggers had returned safely to the depository when it exploded. The explosives blew away half of the hillside, revealing a cave. In the cave, we found some bones and a number of sealed pottery jars. Our museum staff are examining the jars at the moment and it looks to be an exciting historical find of the lost writings of Saint Dino, the founder of Villadedino." The Glasgow five were having difficulty following this. Malky could not think of anything other than the vision he had of the newspaper article framed and displayed disturbingly above the bar of his local pub. Rab was wondering how a cave with pottery could get them out of this. Magdalene was listening to her dead baby saying, '*Don't cry, mummy*', Shug was regretting ever getting involved, and Rashona was wondering when they were going to get lunch. All of them, however, held onto the one phrase signalling light at the end of this very dark tunnel, '*result in your freedom*'.

"Before we go on," Zeca leaned forward, as if a memory had just come to his mind, "I want to relate to you a story from my home in Alentejo, Portugal." He continued, "Once, there was a young navigator by the name of Pero, who was born in Beja and later moved to the seafaring town of Lagos in the Algarve. Pero sailed out past the Cape of Saint Vincent as one of the fifteenth century descobrimentes, discoverers, to discover new territories for the King of Portugal. Pero was very successful and discovered a wonderful new land rich with fruits, exotic birds, and native Indians. He sailed back to Lisbon to the king, along with some of the natives of the new land and other wonders.

"My King, please accept these gifts from this wonderful

new land."

"Thank you, Pero, these are truly great things, but more importantly, is there any gold in this new land?"

"We did not discover any gold, my King, but there are exotic wonders and skilful, cultured, and intelligent people there and I have brought some of them to meet with you."

"If there is no gold, then we will just sell these natives as slaves to the Spanish," reasoned the King.

Pero explained what was happening to the native Indians, who were both impressed by the spectacle of the Royal Palace and confused by the discourse taking place. "The King says that if you do not have any gold in your land, then we should just take you and sell you and all of the people from your land as slaves to the Spanish."

The Indians understood perfectly now what Pero was explaining and said to him, "But we have something more valuable than gold."

"What might that be?"

"Chocolate," answered the Indian, taking some chocolate from his leather pouch and offering it to Pero and the King. As they tasted the chocolate, the king's eyes lit up.

"This is the most wonderful taste." He embraced the Indian and asked through the interpreter Pero, for the recipe for the wonderful delicacy.

The Indian, with relief, provided all the ingredients of the recipe and explained how the chocolate was created.

"Does this mean that we will be free?" the Indian asked Pero, who relayed the question to the chocolate mouth-covered king.

"Why no," answered the king, "tell the native we still intend to sell them to the Spanish, but thank him most profusely for the chocolate recipe."

Zeca waited for the moral of his tale to sink in with the confused audience and proceeded to explain the conditions, which would have to be met for them to gain their freedom. Rashona, despite the seriousness of the situation, couldn't get the image of chocolate out of her mind.

Zeca continued, "So, in order to free you, we will say that you were a team of archaeologists from Glasgow who had come to Villadedino in search of the lost writings of Saint Dino. You discovered the location and excavated the cave with some explosives. We will explain what the people in the viewing gallery saw as a silly prank that went too far. You had a party to celebrate the discovery of the location of Saint Dino's cave – you got drunk, took off your clothes, fell asleep in the coffins, and two of you had a joke by screwing the others into the coffins writing 'CUNTS' on the lids as a warped insult. The two mischief-makers then went out to the burial site and set off the explosives to open up the cave." The explanation, apart from Rab, was mostly going over the intrepid terrorists' heads, but they got enough of a sense that this might get them out of a tricky situation.

"Okay, we'll do it," Rab said turning and receiving relieved nods of acknowledgements from his compatriots. He then went on, "But what about the natives in your story. Did the King really sell them to the Spanish?"

"And you don't happen to have any chocolate?"

queried Rashona.

"Yes, of course he sold them. The moral of the story is that you have to be pragmatic like the King and take all the opportunities that are available to you given the situation you find yourself in. Oh, and also that when you are offered chocolate, it is always good manners to accept this graciously."

"Thank you very much for comin' up with this solution to a difficult situation," a conciliatory Rab said, having understood the story.

"When do we get some chocolate, then?" said Rashona, getting the wrong end of the stick.

"Gentlemen and ladies, if you just sign your statements here." Chief Inspector Gillou handed each of them a statement about the true nature of events, ensuring their compliance to the fabricated story that would be presented to the outside world, which they duly signed.

"Finally," Zeca continued, "you will be pleased to know that, as the archaeological team who discovered the lost writings of Saint Dino, you will all be presented with the award of the Golden Bear and receive medals from King Eugene III himself. It is the highest honour in the Principality of Villadedino."

Zeca made a point of visiting every resident of the hotel and, with great charm and with offers of free champagne, explained the silly prank that had been played on the archaeological team.

*

Archbishop Romario was as surprised as anyone to see on the World News Programme the story about the archaeological team from the University of Govan who had uncovered the cave of Saint Dino in Villadedino. He thought the archaeologists looked very familiar. "No, it can't be!" he exclaimed.

*

Before a gathering of the finest citizens of Villadedino and the eager press, King Eugene presented the medals to each of the archaeologist impersonators in turn. The King made a public statement about the honoured status the five would always have in the annals of Villadedino as 'Companions of the Golden Bear' and asked Rab to say a few words.

Rab stood up and spoke into his microphone in as solemn and as dignified a tone as he could muster. "It is a great honour for my archaeological colleagues and I to be with you to receive the Golden Bear award on this auspicious day."

"Yes," Malky felt compelled to add into his microphone, "Thank you, Your Excellency, and we will wear this Golden Bear with a pride of lions on this 'arse-pish-us' day."

Rab, embarrassed by Malky's uninvited comments, continued, "It might seem strange to some people that we arrived undercover in Villadedino as guests seeking to take up the assisted dying service while all the time we have been working to bring back to life the founder of your wonderful Principality. However, the fact is that we did not so much want to get into the grave as get something out of the grave. And so,

307

it is that, after eighteen hundred years, we have resurrected the works of this great historical figure. Dino has sent us a message from beyond the grave that speaks to us today. I think of Dino in his cave, writing his thoughts down, packing them in the jars, and storing them for safekeeping. Time came to pass; Dino passed; the jars were forgotten at the back of the cave; rockfalls covered the mouth of the cave; and the thoughts of this great man lay dormant until we located and excavated them.

With the help of your museum staff we have translated one of his scrolls, which we are calling the 'Song of Villadedino'. If I can just quote to give you a flavour of his texts, '*The dance at the cusp of death is lighter than a feather dart'*. For me, this sums up the service you provide here in Villadedino. You help your guests leave this earth through the assistance you provide at the point of their death. You help them make their choice as sure, gentle, and as graceful as an arrow released towards its target goal. Let me just say that, because of personal experience, I have come to appreciate, more than ever before, that it is the right of all individuals to choose their moment of dying. We may not know how Dino died, but we appreciate the man through his thoughts that have been brought back to life. I hope that we can all learn from his words that have come down through the centuries to help us enhance our lives and our own deaths today. Thank you for your time."

Rapturous applause rang out around the room, as King Eugene III and Zeca Silva stood to applaud Rab. Zeca thought to himself, *Well, I never thought when we were coercing Rab into our cabal that he would be as good as this. What a find!*

Rab was about to sit down, satisfied that he had performed judiciously, when one of the journalists raised his hand and asked a question he thought would titillate and add some human interest to his article. "I heard that, as part of the celebrations after the discovery, you all got up to high jinks involving getting drunk and being stuck in a coffin. Is that true?"

"You know what it's like when you have achieved your life's work. You want to celebrate with a small alcoholic refreshment and we just got a wee bit carried away. No harm really and you could say that," Rab looking over at Magdalene and Shug, "havin' some fun really brought us closer together as a team."

"I have searched for the University of Govan and can't find any such institution. Can you explain this?" the journalist followed up.

"That's because it's a top-secret University funded by the government to ensure that no one steals our important work," Rab quickly responded, trying to deflect the question.

Malky, picking up on this theme, leaned forward, took hold of the microphone, and added, "As proof of how secret our 'archaeotecturologist' work is, I bet you never knew about our other great discoveries such as the diggin' up of William Wallace's motorbike or discoverin' Rabbie Burns' iPad in a pub in Ayr, never mind what we were doin' with this important 'archaeotecturological ejaculavation' to discover the writin's of Saint Dildo."

Rashona was warming to Malky's creative comments and her compatriot's 'in depth' historical knowledge.

With that, the now confused journalist gave up

and went back to preparing his copy for the next newsblog. *Headline?* he thought to himself, *how about with reference to the coffins and the cave of Saint Dino: 'Vampire Archaeologists Dig Themselves into a Hole.'*

*

Rab and his caucus of pseudo-archaeological buddies remained in Villadedino and were the exotic objects of much fascination amongst the local population. The discovery of the secret writings of Saint Dino was a major event for the Principality and Rab and his entourage were invited to a never-ending and glorious cycle of engagements and dinners. Rab was a much sought-after guest of the great and good of Villadedino for his interpretations of Dino's writings along with his rediscovered advocacy for assisted dying. He was a regular visitor to King Eugene III at the palace. The novelty of his and his partners in crime's Scottish accents and the obscure idiosyncratic terminology in their discourse made interpreting what they said a favourite pastime of the residents of Villadedino. Rab, as the leader, regularly read from the catalogue of transcriptions of Saint Dino's writings discovered in the cave. He offered his interpretation of these, which always seemed to revolve around his epiphany on his way to the crematorium. Rab's perspective and advocacy for choice of assisted dying was much appreciated by Zeca, who used this for publicising the hotel. Rab's reasoned position rubbed off on his four colleagues, who all cemented their commitment as followers of Rab's leadership.

On his outings, Rab received offers of crisply battered fare of the submerged persuasion (aka fish and chips) that the hosts and hostesses came to know as his favourite dishes. There grew an association between his commentaries about the writings and sources of saturated sustenance (aka fried food) to the point where the discourses and food courses became interchangeable and combined. People came to associate the writings of Saint Dino with meals of a deep-fried affiliation. This had a more profound and longer-term impact than any of them could have foreseen.

Throughout his stay, the local people grew very fond of him, found him intelligent, genuine, kind, and humble. A cult of the personality sprung up around Rab that gave him and his compatriots celebrity and fame. This fame preceded his subsequent return to New Scotland twelve months later, where the local citizenry and media could not wait to hear the wise words of the great returning Son of New Scotland, Rab Lennon.

Chapter 27 The Snowline

The dance at the cusp of life and death is lighter than a feather dart

The Song of Villadedino, Saint Dino 240AD

"You are quieter than usual, journalist," said Angela Deff as she passed Mark, walking slowly and aimlessly in the corridor with a hangdog expression on his face. Following all the commotion about rescuing people from coffins and explosives going off in the cemetery, Angela's programme had included the task of spending two minutes with as many guests as she could within the next thirty minutes. The journalist was a bit difficult, because you could never tell how much time would be required to spend with him. However, she was willing to give him the designated two minutes before moving on.

"Oh, Angela, sorry I didn't see you. I was just on my way to reception to leave your key and a note to say thanks for letting me see the video. It was very beautiful and so heartfelt. Estrela really captured the transition from life to death with the allegory of the snowline as a crossing point from this life to her death."

Angela was confused by the journalist's interpretation of the song, replying, "Journalist, I did not get the same understanding. To me, it is a fine song with lots of words, but not about death."

"I don't understand," a bewildered Mark replied.

"Journalist, clearly the subject of the song is the

312

hotel's remote cabin near the top of the mountain called the 'Snowline'."

"Snowline? What do you mean? I don't understand." Mark repeated, feeling surprised. *What if the 'Snowline' was a cabin, Estrela would still be dead. Wouldn't she?* he thought.

"Estrela was just singing about going there and for some reason she wanted to be near trees and snow instead of going through with her assisted suicide," Angela added and looked at her watch, noting that the journalist's two minutes were up and that she should move on to give another of the guests the pleasure of her two minutes' customer care. However, Mark restricted her movement and she was most annoyed by the journalist's strange behaviour. *Why is he sobbing, holding, and kissing me? What kind of behaviour is he displaying? I don't understand this. Does he not know that I have a work programme to get through?*

*

Mark, daring to hope in the possibility that Estrela may still be alive, wasted no time in hiking up the forest trail high up the hill behind the hotel and then up the stony track of the mountain. Following the directions given to him by the hotel staff, he had walked for an hour, when he sighted smoke further up the track. He rounded a bend in the thinning pines and there he saw a cabin, or rather something more resembling a cuckoo clock. It was all pine, with a dark overhanging, shingle roof and was raised on one side, to combat the incline of the hill. It had carved red shuttered windows and an open porch reached by a small set of wooden stairs. The name given to the cabin, 'Snowline', seemed very apt, as his feet crunched up the steep path, now bearing the crisp remains of the previous year's snowfall, with the trees beginning to thin out just beyond the cabin. He saw someone sitting on the porch on a rocking chair. *Could it be?* And as his eyes adjusted to the white glare of last year's snow, he could make out the familiar form of someone he knew. It was Estrela.

Mark's heart was overjoyed as he called out to her. Different feelings crowded around his head competing for space in his thoughts like carp in a decorative pond. Firstly came the overarching sensation of relief that his beloved was alive and sitting there in front of him. This was then countered by anxious thoughts, *Will she forgive me for investigating her background? Will she reject me?* In addition, he had some unanswered questions, *Why had she disappeared and not contacted him? Why had she left the impression that she was no longer alive?* With these conflicting thoughts in his mind and with his heart missing a beat, he walked forward, awaiting Estrela's reaction to seeing him here in this place after the passing of so much time and events.

At the sight of Mark, tears began to well up in Estrela's eyes. She rose from her chair, made her way down the stairs, and, as she got closer, began running towards him, extending her arms out, and throwing them round him in a loving embrace.

"Oh! I am so glad to see you," she sobbed, "I didn't know if you would come or even find me. I just needed to get away. I needed to be on my own to find myself once and for all."

"You have no idea how overjoyed I am to see you," replied Mark, delighted at her response to seeing him. "I thought I had lost you and I am so sorry for the hurt I caused you. I saw the news bulletin announcing your death and I had to come … "

"I've had a lot of time here to reflect on my life with all the adversity I have had to endure, but now my perspective on my life has changed. I have a positive view of the future. Reaching the lowest point and yet overcoming the desire to kill myself has, in the end, made me stronger. I had convinced myself that the assisted suicide would give me the relief I desperately needed, but the closer I got to it, the more I started to see things differently. I am happy with who I am now. I have reconciled my past history, my knowledge of where I came from and who my parents were, and I believe I can move on. I don't need to think of those people who, by chance, just happened to conceive me. I recognise I have my own part to play in the bigger scheme of things, despite the start I was given."

"Do you want me to stay with you, Estrela, or to go? I am just so happy you are here, alive and well. Whatever you want from now on, I will be just grateful to comply. The fact that I know you are alive is all I could ever have hoped for."

"Of course, I want you to stay. I was confused and upset, but having had time on my own in these beautiful surroundings singing and writing, this has helped me. I find it so peaceful here and the only thing I realised shortly after I came up to the cabin was that I was missing you dearly. I knew somehow you would come, that's why I left the clue. I just knew you would have been on my trail so that's why I wrote the song about the Snowline."

The words of the song came back to Mark and a tear, this time of happiness, rolled down his face as he gathered Estela in his arms and walked up the stairs to the cabin.

My love will find me on the snowline
Where the hardwoods grow along the outline
Traced slower than slow to redefine
The perfection of a harmony

Chapter 28 The Profit and Power

The father's core contracts and reaches currency harder than a slaver's heart

The Song of Villadedino, Saint Dino 240AD

In a secluded location in a small vineyard in the countryside of Alentejo, a secret meeting was taking place. In attendance were King Eugene III of Villadedino and Pope Leo Sixtus I.

"I am glad we could meet to discuss our little difficulty," Pope Leo Sixtus I said conspiratorially as he commenced the meeting, "Please, help yourself to another glass of wine."

"We are very grateful to the Holy Father for taking the time out of his tour of South America to hear our report," responded King Eugene III, "I assume you saw the news in the media announcing our solution concerning the archaeologists from New Scotland and the explosion that uncovered Saint Dino's cave with the discovery of his secret writings. The wine is very good, Your Holiness."

"Yes. I liked that touch with the medals, Eugene. You will be aware that I was completely unaware of the plans to attack our investment. I have also taken the necessary actions against the perpetrators. Archbishop Romario and Father Marionetta are now enjoying their calling to the Catholic mission in Chali, sub-sub-Sahara, so remote they subbed it twice as the saying goes. I am sure this will keep them gainfully employed for the next twenty years."

"I think that, with your help, Holy Father, we now have the situation under control. There has been no slackening in the numbers signing up for assisted dying or, as we like to call it, 'merciful moneymaking'. We are planning another two hotels to cope with the demand, so you can see that the Vatican's investment will continue to pay off."

"While it is a covert investment, it still fits in with my overall strategy. I see from your statistical report that there are very few Catholics who buy the service. It is mostly lily-livered liberals, atheists, decadent debauchers, and Communists. They are already on the road to hell, so helping them along the way gives me a sense of satisfaction. A world that has less of those types and more Catholics seems like a good idea to me. Okay, there are some who use the service for merciful relief from pain, but I will be stamping out any of that from Catholics. If God had not wanted them to be in pain and suffering, then He would not have ordained that this should be their fate. I am pleased that the earnings also bankroll my Retribution and Inquisition missions."

"I was pleased, Your Holiness, that you were able to give your imprimatur for the recovered writings of Saint Dino. That decision reinforces the Catholic Churches' teachings and goes further to cement our profitable relationship."

"The Vatican will, of course, ensure that there are no further hare-brained schemes to target Villadedino's industry and I have used the sanctity of Saint Dino as the means for ensuring this. All Retribution and Inquisition cells have received written instruction to steer clear of the sanctified home of Saint Dino, the land of Villadedino. So, you wanted to discuss some other business opportunities, Eugene?"

"Yes, Your Highness. We are proposing a reinforcement of a worldwide ban on euthanasia by the Vatican in order to maintain our monopoly on the assisted dying industry. This, combined with the plans for a further three hotels, will see our profits secured and extended."

"Yes! Excellent idea," replied Pope Leo Sixtus I, "We already have in place our powerful influential lobbies in governments around the globe ready to counter anyone who tries to muscle in on our investment. Is there anything else?"

"That is all, Your Holiness. We were pleased that we have been able to reconcile our little problem and set a clear path to further profit."

"Yes. Well thank you, Eugene, for meeting with me in this out of the way corner of Alentejo. Which reminds me, how is that son of mine doing?"

"Zeca is doing just fine, Holy Father. He is an excellent manager, very talented, and a real asset to the business. We will of course need to promote him with the expansion programme of hotels."

With this, Pope Leo Sixtus I rose from his chair and stepped out into the searing sunlight of Alentejo. He surveyed the rows of vines covering the hills and the olive trees reaching into the hazy distance, recalling his days as a young priest on placement in the local town. He recalled Maria, the vineyard owner's daughter and how her long, dark hair hung carelessly down her back. He remembered the times they spent together,

319

walking through the vines; the conversations, her smile, yes, her smile and that look in her eyes; the daring of her and his helplessness in her gaze. How he had debated with himself, each night committing himself to denying any advances and building spiritual and emotional battlements to impede the onslaught of those eyes, that smile. Yes, and the fortification was as weak as the man who built them. One afternoon, they came crumbling down about him, there in the heat of the Alentejo sun; the same heat he was feeling on his brow today. He had lain with the vineyard owner's daughter, Maria. The father of Zeca was of course kept secret, but, as the young priest made his way through the ranks of the Church, he was increasingly able to influence opportunities in aid of his son's advancements.

Chapter 29 The Article 'Checking Out of the Hotel Euthanasia'

When all revealed breaks down the meaning, thaws reason for the frozen lion

The Song of Villadedino, Saint Dino 240AD

Angela Deff held in her hand the 'viewprint' of the article written by the journalist Mark Goodwin. Jiki, the capuchin monkey and now Angela's constant companion, pressed the buttons on the machine, made her a coffee, and poured Zeca a glass of fine Alentejo vinho tinto. Angela was looking forward to reading this out to Zeca, having rehearsed the article a number of times with Jiki, particularly the part that commended her professional approach to the guests.

"Before you start, Angela," Zeca interjected, "you will be pleased to know that I have a little story for you from Alentejo."

Angela, used to Zeca's interruptions, reconciled herself to suspending the reading of the article, sipped on her coffee, handed Jiki a raisin, and adopted her usual disconnected listening mode.

"There was an olive tree that grew beside a dilapidated and abandoned farmhouse. There was something very important about this olive tree. Unknown to all but the oldest man in the nearby village, it was the oldest olive tree in the whole of Portugal. It had been providing olives since before

Christ walked this earth and was 2,535 years old. Well, a house builder came to buy the land the old farmhouse was on and instructed his architect to draw up plans for a suitably profitable development of 'apartamentos'. His one instruction to the architect was to get as much profit out of the land as possible and this meant leaving no space for trees or plants. This in turn meant that the olive tree had to be cut down.

The architect visited the site often as he prepared to draw up his plans and also took his lunch at the restaurant in the local town. The architect liked the olive tree and on one visit with his wife and children, the olive tree was in fruit and they gathered buckets of the beautiful olives it generously provided. Anyway, during one of his lunches, he was approached by the oldest man in the village who, in conversation with the architect, told him that when he had been a boy, he had worked on the farm and had been informed by the farmer that the olive tree was thousands of years old and may in fact be the oldest olive tree, not only in the village or Alentejo, but possibly also in the whole of Portugal. The architect, remembering the beautiful olives the tree had generously given him and his love for this oldest olive tree in Portugal, decided to ignore the developer's instructions and drew up plans for the housing to be built around a small courtyard, the centre of which was the ancient olive tree.

The time came for the building to be erected and work went well and the housing development completed in time. The housing developer returned for the opening and presentation of the property by the architect and was duly shown around.

'*Why is there a courtyard with a tree in it?*' he questioned when he looked out of the window in the first apartment, '*This was not how I instructed you to undertake this project. Can you please explain yourself?*'

The architect explained that this was in fact the oldest olive tree in Portugal and that it provided the most beautiful and delicious olives.

'*Well, you have cost me money,*' the developer shouted, '*and this was against my instructions. I will not pay you for the work you have done.*'

The architect was dejected by the judgement of the developer and thought for a while that he might sue him for his payment. However, he decided against this course of action, as the developer was well known to be a very influential and powerful man in the locality. So instead he decided to buy three of the 'apartamentos'.

And what became of them? Well, two of the 'apartamentos' he sold, but only after advertising them in Lisbon with a photograph of the ancient olive tree and accompanied by a narrative on olive trees in Portugal and the longevity of this particular one. Soon, the media were on to the story and the news spread about the oldest olive tree in the whole of Portugal. Two of the 'apartamentos' were sold for ten times what the architect would have been paid by the property developer and, as well as that, the architect lived happily with his wife and children in the remaining apartment. To this day, every year they receive the gracious gifts of a harvest of the finest olives you could ever have the pleasure to eat from the oldest olive tree in all of Portugal."

At this point, Zeca stopped talking and produced his

323

usual quizzical smile as he always did at the end of one of his tales. Angela, never able to fathom any of Zeca's stories and impatient for him to finish, took her chance to use her window of opportunity and proceeded to narrate the article. Jiki and Zeca sat back and listened.

Checking Out of the Hotel Euthanasia by Mark Goodwin

The grandeur of the Hotel Euthanasia only goes some way to tell the story of the enterprise taking place within its walls. Dying is alive and thriving here. Set in the tiny Principality of Villadedino is a multi-billion-dollar industry devoted to those who wish to choose assistance to die. How can they do this in Villadedino, when it is banned everywhere else in the world?

At the heart of this development has been the previously crumbling Hotel Villadedino. It has now been rebranded and unveiled as the Hotel Euthanasia, nestled in the foothills of Villadedino, with a view of the mountains and forests, this hotel has been renovated to its previous grand luxury through unlimited funds provided by wealthy investors. In addition to all the standard comforts of the hotel's outstanding accommodation, there are the eXi-theme Departure Suites, each adaptable, so that they provide the death experience guests desire. They, the geusts, literally 'check out' of the eXi-theme Departure Suite via what looks like a larger than usual elevator door. One can see on the other side a conveyor belt that brings vacant coffins. Once they have completed the assisted dying process, the deceased are placed by medical staff or their own personal party of mourners inside the coffins and then transported via

324

the conveyor belt to arrive at either the Crematorium or to the Burial Depository Chamber; the service is all very efficient. Currently, the hotel can cope with up to 200 assisted suicides per day. Yes, and you guessed it, people are lining up for the pleasure of dying.

There is a monopoly for Villadedino as the only country providing this service. As a result, money is flowing into the coffers of the Principality, which has become one of the richest places per capita on earth. Religious lobbying groups have continued to promote the 'sanctity of life' and argue against assisted dying. This lobbying by groups actively campaigning against euthanasia has held back the development of assisted dying enterprises in many other countries.

So, who are the customers in Villadedino and why are they choosing assisted dying there? There are those who could be described as people seeking a merciful solution to needless suffering. For example, those diagnosed as being at the end of life with six months or less to live or those with multiple long-term conditions and in constant pain seeking release from their agony. There are those that are tormented by the 'black dog' of depression and wish to end their misery. Then, there are those who are bored with life and just do not want to go on living. The Principality's 'Conduct of Assisted Dying' Act 2021 means, a simple 'Competent Adult Test' precludes people from accessing the service unless they have the capacity to make an informed decision.

This has gone some way to alleviating the major criticism of Villadedino's industry as a slippery slope towards *end of life coercion of vulnerable people by relatives and governments. However, there are growing rumours that some local authorities in Olde England have used compliant clinicians to sign the 'Competent Adult Test' as a means of exporting their older population to Villadedino to meet government targets within their demographic control plans.*

I asked Zeca Silva, the dapper and highly sophisticated Hotel Manager, how he justified providing a service that 'preyed' on people's weaknesses, 'How can you say you are providing a service to meet people's choice when there will be vulnerable people out there who will not be clear about what they are getting into? Are you not just exploiting them?'

'We believe in the sanctity of life just like any other nation, but we also believe that sanctity includes the right to choose. If you can think of it this way, there is also sanctity in death. What is a life if it is an extreme burden of pain and suffering to be tolerated and you are unable to choose what to do with it? Choice is the most fundamental right of any human being and Villadedino has always operated on that principle. So, we are not exploiting people, we are facilitating the reverence of their choice. There is no coercion whatsoever and individuals are always free to change their minds at any stage in the proceedings.'

I wanted to push Zeca a bit further and asked him, 'So, are you a murderer, then?'

'I have no guilt whatsoever. A murderer goes out and finds a victim and proceeds to take the victim's life from them against their will. In other words, the victim has no choice. I am

merely a facilitator.'

After interviewing Zeca, I met with Angela Deff, his Customer Care Manager. I found that I shared the view of many other guests I spoke to, who were personally grateful for her attention to detail and helpfulness. Angela's manner of speaking was very straightforward, 'I work to a programme here at the hotel. It is important that everything works like clockwork. It would disrupt my schedule if someone was late for their death.'

The person I especially wanted to interview was the son of the inspiration for the assisted dying industry of Villadedino, King Eugene III. The King invited me to the Garden Party in honour of the founder of the Principality, Saint Dino. This was where it started to become weird. When I interviewed the King, he was dressed in a bear suit, something to do with the traditions of Villadedino and Saint Dino having fought a wild bear to the death when he discovered the country. I put it to the bear, or rather the King dressed in his bear costume, 'What justifies the existence of a place like the Hotel Euthanasia in Villadedino? Should other countries set up their own assisted dying schemes?'

'It is correct that we are far sighted and radical in our thinking,' the King told me, 'Other countries are ambivalent about death. Here in Villadedino, we see it as the greatest example of things we hold true. Individual choice overrides all other principles. With choice comes happiness. How many sad and unhappy people do you know who cannot make a choice? We are changing the way the world thinks about death. I think

that death and dying have had a bad press for too long.' The bear looked at me and finished by saying, 'We are the acceptable face of death'.

While I was there, amongst the guests was the Scottish archaeologist, Rab Lennon. Mr Lennon had an interesting story to tell, working undercover as a guest seeking assisted dying but all the time being part of an archaeological team secretly searching for the lost writings of Saint Dino, the patron Saint of Villadedino and founder of the Principality.

I interviewed Rab on a number of occasions. In a certain light, under his naturalistic, colloquial dialect, lurks the deeper meaning of his beliefs. They form an unintended blueprint for dealing with the vagaries of life.

Another thing I learned about Rab was that he was locked in a coffin for a joke. His colleagues didn't know the coffin was going to go to the crematorium. It was a miracle he made it out alive. I asked Rab about his near-death experience and if it had affected him.

'I was pure meltin', so I was. I got out of that coffin faster than a Tory Prime Minister gettin' out of New Scotland!' In his inimitable Glasgow accent, Rab told me, 'I was so pleased to get out of the coffin that I could have floated in the air with the relief. It had a profound effect on me. Made me think about the purpose of life. After my near-death experience, I built up an appetite and ordered everything they had on the menu that was deep-fried. When I had eaten, man, I can tell you I was in heaven.'

On his return to New Scotland, Rab has become an

advocate of assisted dying and tours churches and town halls reading from the writings of Saint Dino and talking about his own near-death experience.

So, the Hotel Euthanasia ... Is it the answer to the over population of the world or is it just the ultimate choice for the disillusioned rich that can afford its services? Is it preying on the vulnerable or are people competent enough to make their own choice about life or death? Do you rely on the government of Olde England to make that choice on your behalf?

There was no-one partaking of the services at the hotel that I had spoken to who did not have the ability to make up their own minds. I suppose it comes down to choice. Who am I to deny someone the choice to do with their own life what they want to, as long it is not harming another person, particularly if they have a condition that is causing them suffering? But what about the people they leave behind? Surely, they are left to suffer bereavement. However, the same could be applied to people who divorce their partners. They surely cause suffering and loss through separation. But, we don't hold them accountable or restrict their ability to make that decision. Here, reader, I have a little confession. I undertook this article because I was interested in the Hotel Euthanasia and all that it has to offer. However, there was another personal reason I chose to go to the hotel. I am writing about this as I feel it important you hear my own experience of the assisted dying industry.

I had understood that my then girlfriend, now wife, had taken her own life at the hotel. Further, I felt guilty that my actions were the cause of her decision to end her life. I will not go into the detail except to say that I was definitely in the wrong. It turned out that my girlfriend did not go through with the assisted suicide. My feelings ran the whole gamut of emotion. At the point I thought she had died and had left me, I was in deep despair and when I discovered she was actually alive, I was elated beyond belief. So, you see, I am ambivalent about the feelings of those that are left behind by people who choose assisted suicide. My own personal experience, much like a child of a divorced couple, is that I would rather they didn't undertake such drastic action. Confession over.

A final thought, if Olde England were to pass a law allowing for the same type of facility as Villadedino, then the entire Health Care of the country could be supported on the proceeds.

Angela put down the article and looked over at Zeca, "The journalist thought very well of me and the customer care job, don't you think? I liked that he mentioned how good I was at keeping to an efficient programme of time."

"Yes, Angela, but what do you think of the story I told you about the oldest olive tree in all of Portugal?"

It was at that precise instant, as she looked into the dark eyes of Jiki the capuchin monkey, that Angela Deff suddenly, and probably for the first time ever, realised the true meaning of one of Zeca's stories. "I am starting to understand, Hotel Manager, why you tell me these stories. You are teaching me how to understand feelings and for an instant I sensed that the architect was connected to the olive tree through some bond of love. I too have felt connected for the first time to a feeling of love for my little friend Jiki. I think your story and the experiences of the journalist both connect to the feelings of joy he must have experienced when I told him about the Snowline cabin."

A tear formed in Angela's eye as she felt emotion for the first time. As Jiki fetched her a tissue, she said simply to Zeca, "It was because the journalist loved Estrela."

EPILOGUE

Chapter 30 Bless His Deep-Fried Name

*And the future holds codes of arriving and our destiny still
confounds the mind*

The Song of Villadedino, Saint Dino 240AD

In this, the year 2250 AD or, in the Rabite calendar, 210 AR, I
understand that everyone on the planet knows the facts concerning
Rabism. For this addition to Rabipedia however, I, Popess Dinolina
II, the supreme representative on earth of Rab, bless his deep-
fried name, will outline the most salient aspects of the religion
for the edification of seekers.

In the year 2235, for the first time, Rabism gained
prominence over the other great world religions to become
the single most practised religion on the planet. Rabism has
now grown exponentially to incorporate in excess of 3.3
billion followers and has been adopted in every corner of
the globe.

Since his symbolic and prophesised burning to death
in the sinful fire and then miraculous rising again from the
dead, Rab, bless his deep-fried name, has grown from being
an inspiration for a handful of disciples to progress to the focal
point of devotion and fulfilment for the majority of the world
population. What we know about Rab was that the reason he
was condemned to burn alive, sent to his death by the jealous
hands of the Archaeological Society of Scotland, who locked
him in a coffin because he would rightly receive all the credit

for the discovery of Saint Dino's cave. Rab, bless his deep-fried name, had burned to death but had risen immediately from the dead and emerged from the coffin floating into the air, enveloped in an aura of light. He had returned to Holy New Scotland the year after his experience in the hotel and had preached for three years, along with his biographer, Saint Mark Goodwin, and his closest disciples, Saint Malky, Saint Rashona, and Pope Shug, who married Popess Magdalene. After his initial return, Rab, bless his deep-fried name, was excommunicated by the Catholic Pope due to the heretical nature of his teachings, in particular, his newfound advocacy for assisted dying.

Some happier times followed for Rab when he opened a fish and chip shop in the Govan area of Glasgow with a friend he had met in Villadedino, appropriately named Suzie Sunfloweroil. Following the early writings contained in the gospels of Saint Mark in Olde England, pilgrims made their way to the fish and chip shop to worship at his feet and partake of the sacrament of deep-fried pizza. The site of the fish and chip shop was eventually used to build the now named 100,000-seater, Church of the Deep-Fried Sacrament.

The religion of Rabism, some have argued, might be considered to have arisen out of a series of serendipitous circumstances, which, taken together, resulted in a momentum that did not dissipate for two centuries. Others point to divine intervention and the prophecy of Saint Dino two millenniums earlier. It is considered that what took place with Rab could not have been due to anything other than the product of a supreme and omniscient architect; or in Saint Malky's profound words, that combined the result of the excavation of the soul and the building of the spirit in the work of a supreme 'archaeotecturologist'. Academic theologians have analysed Saint Dino's Song of Villadedino, written in 240 AD, discovered by the Glasgow five, and found the Song to foretell the death by incineration and the reincarnation of Rab Lennon, bless his deep-fried name, and his disciples at the blessed Hotel Euthanasia. The words of the song are themselves now considered sacred:

The Song of Villadedino
Saint Dino 240AD

The answer that remains unquestioned
Strong gravity the singer hears
Between the poppy and the means
The dancers of the spheres

The parable reflects the feeling
That prepares the writer's sign
In best laid plans of mice confused
To measure meaning or define

Life flows from the mountain streams
While precious metal weighs the body deep
Towards another travelling onwards
Sliding down the steep incline

And the careless wind blows random thoughts

Through the mind of saints
The act plays out the role concludes
The dance of life as ever thus

The pious hand in the riddle's glove
Deviously prays for a brotherly love
As the dance of bears give birth to death
The vault of crowns superfluous

Contained within provides the clue
That reveals a deathly hue
So sing the snow's sweet pure life
As words drift down from endless skies

To confuse the poor pilgrim's path
Confounding where the journey lies
We will gather at the dance of death
Lives entwined in fate and time

The question will remain unanswered
The future bones are undermined
We meet again truths to impart
To dance and then to separate

Truth will heal the heavy heart
As dancing seals us to our fate
The mind directs the hand of action
Inhabiting the game now twice

And sing another song of life
That leads on in time's device
And finding we've discovered snow
Forming to a blizzard ice

To shield the splendid times and deeds
That joy entreats us to excite
But fear can take the once sweet song
And scatter in a paradigm

Until the harmony of snow once more
Finds perfection in a perfect form
Chaos still confuses and compels
The patterns of the child unborn

A carbon eager for the stars
When sun demands the child's return
The dance of life in fates condensing
To join the dancers in their step

The judge concludes my lifelong crimes
And leaves them as a marble debt
The dance at the cusp of life and death
Is lighter than a feather dart

The father's core contracts and reaches
Currency harder than a slaver's heart
When all revealed breaks down the meaning

Thaws reason for the frozen lion

And the future holds codes of arriving
Our destiny still confounds the mind

There are many prophesies in the song that have come to pass. The references that have been proven beyond doubt are: to the pilgrim burning, in verses seven and thirteen, related to Rab being incinerated; the writer in verse two is Saint Mark, who was at the hotel as a journalist; the singer, in verse six, was Estrela Goodwin, née Pure, who is also mentioned with respect to a number of references to snow; and the bear in a number of verses refers to King Eugene II of Villadedino being killed by a bear. Academics are still studying the verses considered to be the most important of the writings of Saint Dino's revelations.

During Rab's stay in Holy New Scotland, he continued to preach to the local population until the time of his much-publicised persecution at the hands of the Archaeological Society of Scotland. This persecution took the form of denouncing him at public meetings and trying to kill him by throwing trowels at him as he preached. He is then said to have taken flight from his tormentors and to have travelled to Paraguay. There, he eventually revealed his true holiness, with his subsequent death, for all of us, caused by coronary heart disease.

The Gospels, written by Mark Goodwin, came to form the central tenets of the new religion's teachings. In the gospel, according to Saint Mark, it became evident that an all-encompassing omnipresent 'archaeotecturologist' throughout the cosmos revealed the location of the writings of Saint Dino to Rab through a series of miraculous events.

What has happened to the other world religions since the rise of Rabism? Catholicism declined in Rome, only to reappear in the sub-sub-Saharan desert. Hinduism changed entirely, due to the teachings of the late Swami Riva and his writings contained in the Birmingham Gita. Buddhism declined in the East, but merged with wine bars to become the religion of choice of the middle classes in the West. Judaism remained unchanged, but synagogues and comedy theatres combined their premises.

African Americans converted in their millions, when the prophet Saint Rashona, whose right and left temporal lobes had finally converged to reveal the primitive-instinctive nature of deep-fried food along with the mathematical probability of increasing the portions through religious ritual. She travelled around the United States of America, preaching the creed of Rabism. On his return from his good work in Asia where he made his name by combining Rabism philosophy with Kung Fu fighting, Saint Malky was instrumental in evangelising all of the prison populations of Scotland, who welcomed him with open arms, converting on masse when he visited to preach with ample supplies of deep-fried pizzas.

After the final death of Rab, bless his deep-fried name, Shug and Magdalene were appointed Pope and Popess and came to be revered as the mother and father figures of the New Church. Pope Shug guided us through his acts of ambivalence, where the faithful are allowed to choose assisted dying but can change their minds at the last minute to consume oily submerged cuisine. His wife, the Popess Magdalene, would famously commune with an angel who would reveal mysteries to the Popess.

Numerous traditional hymns and chants were written by the minstrel of Rabism, Estrela the Pure, the consort of Saint Mark. Congregations of Rabites would alternately drift into deep levels of fried food consciousness and contemplate profound soulful renditions of Estrela's songs as pure as a snowflake caught in a beam of winter sunlight.

The Hotel Euthanasia is the ultimate pilgrimage destination for disciples of Rabism, where they visit the holy cave of Saint Dino, meditate in the Snowline Cabin made famous in the film of the same name, make a final confession in an eXi-theme Departure Suite and follow the same route to the crematorium as Rab took while singing 'The Sun Is Shining Brightly the Trees Are Full of May' towards their holy incineration and ascension to join their maker in Deep-Fried Food Heaven.

The two major aspects, the mystical and the material, sum up the main beliefs of the Rabism's teachings.

The mystical element outlines the religion's view of the cosmos as, in the words of Rab, bless his deep-fried name, 'great, big things that are difficult to understand'. Rab revealed that life was created on earth when God formed a green island with two types of humans at first: ones with red hair and others that were small, wore green clothes and hid their gold at the end of rainbows. These original humans then evolved through a series of upgrades and came in a range of colours. They were also able to send each other messages using hieroglyphics and images leading to the growth of their brain to the point that they were able to discover the sacrament of deep fat frying.

The practicalities of the religion mean that choice and self-determination are attributes that all members of the religion aspire to and that the ultimate choice is personal death, which usually occurs at an early age because of the emphasis on frittering life away on plunged and tempura food within the religion. However, where followers live a longer life, perhaps into their late forties, they are encouraged to make an individual choice to partake of assisted dying. Rab, bless his deep-fried name, had to experience a time in the wilderness, where we know that he was tempted by the evil of ignorance to remove individual choice for assisted dying. But he overcame wickedness and reasserted his holy advocacy that individual choice on this matter is the highest truth. The outcome of his convictions means that people are now free to take their own lives in the way and at the time they choose.

Materialism was another of the great pillars of Rabism, enabling the organisational structures that facilitated worship at the holy centres of nourishment and healing, where deep-fried foodstuffs were the sacraments of choice. Administering these sacraments were healers, who provided individual eating plans for each member of their flock. These healers studied gastrology (a mixture of astrology and gastronomy), developed by Saint Rashona, as well as religious subjects, so that they were able to divine people's food requirements by consulting the movement of the stars through the heavens.

The ultimate goal of each member of the religion was to reach 'heavy enlightenment'. This occurred following years of disciplined gastrology, reading and studying the life of Rab, bless his deep-fried name, through the gospels of Saint Mark and pilgrimages to Villadedino.

The first International Conference of Rabism, held in Villadedino, brought together the leading lights from Africa, Europe, America, and Asia. The Archaeological Society of Scotland and the Society of Architects of Scotland were there to protest about the use of the term 'archaeotecturology', which they felt was undermining the status of each of their professional disciplines. This first conference set out the fundamental values, principles, and advocacy of assisted dying and deep-fried sacraments in the new religion.

Rabism has made the world a better place for mankind to grow spiritually into its next stage of evolution. Rab advocated the responsibility of the individual having control of the means of production, but also taught that the individual should be part of a collective society of brothers and sisters.

The global acceptability of the religion grew through the use of social media, where information about different forms of deep-fried worship were posted onto the Internet and shared across borders and languages to form a common deep-fried batter across the world. The drawing power of deep fat frying provided a universally recognised medium, which all disparate cultures could appreciate. People identified immediately with the message and understood the deeper coagulation of the fat of their souls that gave them instantaneous gratification. Warring neighbouring countries and religious factions found common ground in coming together to indulge in the deep-fried sacraments. Age-old conflicts were put aside, while enemies sat around at tables of friendship, sharing their deep-fried delicacies and appreciating the multicultural benefits of common deep-fried values.

Overpopulation was solved in the twin pincer combination of the sacrament of deep-fried food and the choice of assisted dying for all. World peace inevitably saturated the planet. Once the oil of the sacrament of deep fat frying has anointed a person, there is no going back. For this, we are forever grateful to Rab Lennon, bless his deep-fried name.

CALL TO ACTION

Dear Reader,

thank you for reading ***Checking Out of the Hotel Euthanasia*** by Gerard Graham. We hope you enjoyed the book.

If you would like to explore additional background material, artwork and blogs regarding ***Checking Out of the Hotel Euthanasia***, you can visit a dedicated website at

checkingoutofthehoteleuthanasia.wordpress.com

We recognise that ***Checking Out of the Hotel Euthanasia*** is thought-provoking and we would like to give you the opportunity to contribute your views about the novel and its subject matter. You can email a review of the novel, provide feedback or contact the author at

gerardgrahamwriter@hotmail.com.

Ringwood Publishing

Some other books from Ringwood Publishing

All titles are available from the Ringwood website (including first edition signed copies) and from usual outlets.

Also available in Kindle, Kobo and Nook.

www.ringwoodpublishing.com

Ringwood Publishing, 24 Duncan Avenue, Glasgow, G14 9HN

mail@ringwoodpublishing.com

Millennial Munros – A Postman's Round

Charlie Campbell

ISBN: 9781901514339 (£9.99)

Millennial Munros is the inspirational story of an ordinary bloke doing an ordinary job, who did something extraordinary. With the help of his mum and some mates, he got motivated, got fit and completed an unprecedented endurance event, in breaking the world record for a continuous self-propelled round of all the Munros, Scotland's 284 mountains over 3000 feet in height, in 49 action-packed days.

He averaged nearly six Munros every day and cycled or swam between them. Anyone who has done just one Munro in a day will know how big a deal this was. Charlie's entertaining account of his adventures comes complete with maps, routes and other details to help inspire others to tackle these mountains, but perhaps in a more relaxed manner!

The Volunteer

Charles P Sharkey

ISBN: 9781901514360 (£9.99)

The Volunteer is a powerful and thought-provoking examination of the Troubles that plagued Northern Ireland for almost three decades. It follows the struggles of two Belfast families from opposite sides of the sectarian divide. This revealing novel will lead the reader to a greater understanding of the events that led from the Civil Rights marches in the late Sixties, through the years of unbridled violence that followed, until the Good Friday Agreement of the late Nineties.

In The Devil's Name

Dave Watson

ISBN: 9871901514377 (£9.99)

Some of the locals in the small Scottish village of Ballantrae still tell tales about haunted Bennane Head, the cliffs just up the coast where mythical mass murderer and cannibal Sawney Beane is said to have dwelt with his inbred family during the seventeenth century. Never walk past there at night, they say, or heaven help you. Just a ghost story to give the tourists a thrill.

Phil, Griff, Sam and Cairnsey are local boys who enjoy a smoke, a beer and the occasional tab of mind bending acid, and celebrating the end of high school with some trips and a night's camping at Bennane Head sounds like a high old time. But when their drug fuelled revelry descends into a nightmarish fight for their sanity and survival, those who make it through the night will know that true evil never forgets unpaid debts.

Jinxs Dogs Burns Now Flu

Alex Gordon

ISBN: 978-1-901514-28-5 (£9.99)

Alex Gordon spills the beans in a frank and candid manner. Much is revealed within the pages of this book that was previously kept out of the public domain. And you'll see why!

Jinx Dogs Burns Now Flu is a rollicking, often hilarious, trip through the crazy world of Scottish newspapers. It's a journey that takes the reader behind the headlines of the biggest, most sensational stories of our national press. It also introduces the fascinating if madcap characters whose job was to bring you your daily news. Prepare to be bewildered by their antics as they chase front and back page exclusives. You'll be amazed and amused by the tales that did NOT make it into print. Until now, as Jinx Dogs Burns Now Flu brings many sensational stories into print for the first time!

The Gori's Daughter

Shazia Hobbs

ISBN: 9781901514124 (£9.99)

The Gori's Daughter is the fictional story of Aisha, a young mixed race girl, daughter of a Kashmiri father and a Glaswegian mother moved into the household as mistress alongside the Muslim wife and the children from both relationships. Its uncompromising exploration of the realities rather that the myths of race relations within modern Scotland is likely to have an explosive impact, challenging as it does cosy assumptions on both sides. The tale is often harrowing, always exciting and revealing, but is ultimately about triumph; a victory for resilience and decency over bigotry and discrimination.

School Daze

Elaine McGeachy

ISBN: 978-1-901514-10-0 (£9.99)

"School Daze is a hugely enjoyable romp through the social, sexual and professional dilemmas facing three recently qualified young teachers as they try to cope with the increased stresses in the modern day education world."

With great sensitivity and a refreshing absence of sensationalism, School Daze tackles the vexed issue of why smart, attractive young teachers risk reputation and career by romantic involvement with pupils.

The Activist

Alec Connon

ISBN: 978-1-901514-25-4 (£9.99)

The Activist is Scottish author Alec Connon's debut novel. It is a novel of formation, describing not only a physical journey, but the spiritual journey of a young man in search of his calling in life. Connon's passion for the subject is apparent throughout, yet his writing is never preachy or didactic. His story of devotion to the conservation of our oceans and marine life leaves the reader with little doubt regarding the worth of this cause.

CPSIA information can be obtained
at www.ICGtesting.com
Printed in the USA
LVHW082341041218
599303LV00008B/147/P

9 780692 047354